CONSCIENCE
POINT

CONSCIENCE POINT

Erica Abeel

UNBRIDLED BOOKS

This is a work of fiction. The names, characters, places and incidents are either the product of the author's imagination or are used fictitiously, and any resemblance to actual persons living or dead, business establishments, events, or locales is entirely coincidental.

Unbridled Books
Denver, Colorado

Library of Congress Cataloging-in-Publication Data
Abeel, Erica.
Conscience point / by Erica Abeel.
p.   cm.
ISBN 978-1-932961-53-9 (hardcover)
I. Title.
PS3551.B333C66   2008
813'.54—dc22
2008018615

1   3   5   7   9   10   8   6   4   2

Book Design by SH • CV

First Printing

To Maud and Neilson

"He seems to have a penchant for my children."

—EVELYN WAUGH, *Brideshead Revisited*

CONSCIENCE
POINT

First

I suppose it was the accident that wild, wet night on Wildmoor that got me writing this story. This . . . call it Gothic modern tale, complete with family curses, unquiet spirits, forbidden love—a bizarre crime, even; seasoned, of course, with '90s grabbiness and irony. A story rather in keeping with the fantastical contours of Conscience Point. Like some back-lot castle for *Ivanhoe,* Violet used to joke. Held together with plaster 'n' spit.

I wrote because the accident felt . . . fated; like a crack on the head from the past, capstone to a course set in motion decades back. A course that began one glorious May afternoon when I breached the garden wall to an enchanted country. I needed to understand: How could people so blessed by fortune so bungle it, and end in a pileup of buckled metal? Even allowing for the contrarian imp that rides us all? And my own blindness: How did I not see what was there to see all along?

Deep into my draft, though, new revelations surfaced, shoving a counterversion in my face—and forcing me to scramble for a foothold as old certainties crumbled like shale. And then, an odd thing: I discovered I was writing a letter of sorts, across continents and years, to a child in whom all the players in this tale are mingled.

If my letter should ever reach him, he'll learn how we're all bound up together—he and I, Laila, Violet, Nick. More entwined than through the usual ties of blood. And though we've all spun apart now, he'll sense, my reader, how those ties persist, like phosphorescence lighting the night sea. And he'll know, too—in the end, real estate rules—that Conscience Point is his to claim any time he chooses.

How strangely mixed up together we all are. Isn't that what Nick said in the library that stormy night?

But wait, I'm getting ahead of myself; better not hop all over the lot. After all, I'm writing, too—such is human vanity—to put the world on notice that our little caravan passed this way. The trick is to put a bit of starch in the narrative. The trick is to lay it out the way it happened. Before I start missing them all too much . . .

CHAPTER I

The Vertical Ray

It began in France on a May morning of their lovely stolen holiday. They sat, she and Nick, on the terrace of an inn shoehorned into George Sand's country estate, reveling in the morning sun, the silvery warble of *merles*. Air that felt breathed for the first time. When Nick nosed their Avis Renault into the driveway the evening before, they might have crossed into an earlier century. . . .

"Do you get many visitors here off-season?" he asked the innkeeper. Scoping out the terrain. He'd just signed up a book on Sand's beloved Berry region, a quilt of dreaming farm fields and dark hedgerows, in 1997 still little known to tourists.

"Not as many as now," said the innkeeper, a woman with '40s-style marcelled hair. "Though we did have a writer here all winter, working on a screenplay about George Sand and Chopin—and Sand's daughter. There's a girl knew how to make trouble."

Nick frowned, Maddy uncertain why. The innkeeper continued to hover. Not the first time Maddy noticed how she and Nick acted as attractants; they must give off a musk. She watched the woman's gaze linger on Nick: the wolf-grey eyes, longish space between nose and lips, tawny weave of hair. The tastiness of him. Humbly, she demishrugged at the innkeeper. Never flaunt happiness. Hide.

"Just think, it's this time of year we first met," she said when they were finally alone.

He circled an arm around her chair. "Have I told you you're nicer now? Back then you were kind of . . . thistle-y."

"Damn right. You were ogling me naked on the beach."

"You're prettier now, too." Blind—Nick the hypercritical—to the faint seam imprinted by the pillow on her cheek and other stunts of her morning face. He shifted his chair closer and planted tickly kisses down her neck and she laughed giddily. "Mmm, wanna go back to the room?"

"Might kill us."

"Uh-huh."

Last night Nick vexed at himself, at odds with his own body. Then, this morning, he'd surprised them both. Early farm sounds beyond their window, pails clanking; gamey barnyard smells. She imagined them wartime lovers hiding out in the countryside. Her face twisted away, throat arched . . . *wait, wait* . . . fingers at the hard ridge of muscle on either side of his spine. Their cries mingling with a rooster's below. They'd arrived at breakfast overflowing with the goodwill born of coming from the pads of your toes to the roots of your hair.

Their waiter, carrot-haired and fey, laid out breakfast with balletic flourishes: fresh orange juice and a basket of *tartines,* glazed earthenware crocks of apricot preserves and sweet butter, two white pitchers of steaming coffee and milk. They dug in.

"I been thinking, if they want, I dunno . . . Video Kitten, to hell with *Chronicle,* Nick said, picking up an earlier debate. "I mean, you give concerts *and* do the show—you give good value." Grimacing at his own expression.

"Nicky, the suits don't dote on me quite like you."

"Well, who does?" He smiled and daubed a crusty *tartine* with chunky preserves. "Anyway, I been thinking, maybe you should pare down a little, do just the piano. Give us a little wiggle room. More of *this*." He nodded toward the terrace. "Though maybe you enjoy"—raising an eyebrow—"working like a galley slave?" Maybe; how well he knew her. "Multitasking, as a new editor in my office would say," Nick continued. "She also 'transitions,' when she isn't 'partying' . . . or 'impacting.' . . . Never met a noun that couldn't be a verb. The other day she *flipped* her hair in my face."

At some point they'd descend into old-fart-dom, Maddy thought contentedly. But not yet. A clock chimed the hour from an ochre Romanesque church across the square. They listened, transfixed, the metal clangor seeming to summons the faithful from down the years. Nick fished the Michelin guide from the frayed pocket of his chinos. "So. We'll check out Sand's château first, okay? Hmm, says here she scribbled her novels all night on a dropleaf shelf in a wall cupboard. . . . Then we'll drive to La Chatre for lunch. After that"—his finger traced a road—"Bourges! I've always wanted to show you the cathedral. The musician angels in the side chapel . . . the archangel Michael . . ." As guide to the world's treasures, Nick had no equal. She sat back, luxuriating in his voice, a baritone dashed with boarding-school drawl, and the newly minted air and warbling *merles,* rolling and rerolling notes as if telling a crystal rosary. What more could there be than this? Let nothing change. She wanted to stop here at the vertical ray of the sun.

"WHAT LUCK, WE'VE got the joint to ourselves!" They stood in the courtyard of Nohant, as the estate was called, surveying the manor house where Sand had hosted a running house party for geniuses.

"Place really makes you believe in spirits," Nick said, glancing around. In fact, something *animate* about the weathered rose facade and pale blue shutters, dreaming at attention. "Uh-oh, don't look now."

Two yellow buses came chuffing up the driveway, raising a cloud of chalky dust. They air-braked to a stop before the château and spit out a cargo of twittering adolescents in shorts and knee socks. Maddy wrinkled her nose. "And they're German."

"For godssake, during the war they weren't even born."

She and Nick cultivated friction, she suspected, to certify they were two separate people.

The kids pooled in the courtyard. A boy with a platinum crew cut abruptly flung himself on a dark, gangly girl and kissed her with puppyish abandon. The other kids aimed cameras at the château or thumbed guidebooks, ignoring the passion in their midst. It went on, the kiss, gnawing, slurpy, desperate. Both comic and arousing.

Maddy shifted her attention to Sand's château, the large atelier-style window projecting from the second story. "Nicky, look, that must be the studio Sand built for Delacroix." No response. She turned to see Nick staring at the junior lovers in horror, as if sighting a pair of revenants.

"Darling, don't gawk." She elbowed his arm. "Imagine, Delacroix and Chopin used to walk around here talking Art capital A. 'Serenaded by nightingales,'" she read from the guidebook. "'In the azure of the transparent night, a sublime melody arises.'"

If Nick heard, he gave no sign.

Maddy slipped her arm through his and smiled at his clench-jawed profile. "Doesn't that child have a touch of Laila?" The same starved-cat allure.

Nick unstuck his attention from the couple. "Oh, Laila's a lot prettier!"

Nick doted on her adopted daughter, endowing her with a beauty she didn't quite have. That they'd knitted into a family was among Maddy's greatest pleasures—though she winced when Laila playfully called him "Uncle Nick." "Reminds me, I want to get Laila a present in La Chatre.

Maybe a Cacharel blouse—to wean her from the homeboy look." She sighed. "If only we could wean her from Jed Oliver."

"Classic mistake to interfere, just make him seem more desirable," Nick said in a prissy voice.

The lovers surfaced from their kiss. They looked around with the glutted eyes of beasts after a kill. The guide had arrived, dangling a giant metal key. Everyone traipsed after her into the vestibule, its stone walls exhaling a chill harvested over centuries.

They shuffled tourist-style into a dining room dominated by a Venetian chandelier of blue and pink glass. Nick, slightly behind, kept his hand at the small of Maddy's back. The room and air felt untouched by time, alive with presences, ghostly chatter, deaths and entrances. Chopin could have walked in, coughing.

The guide pointed out a sinister-looking drawing by Sand's son. "These peasant women are killing their illegitimate babies," she explained, first in French, then in German. Maddy pressed in for a closer look. The little murders of love, okay—but *kill your child?*

They moved toward the dining room table, a long oval set as if for this evening's dinner. Maddy circled it, reading place cards: Flaubert . . . Turgenev . . . Delacroix . . . Franz Liszt. To think these titans had eaten and schmoozed around this table. An old dream floated up: Why not create their own version of Nohant at Conscience Point—even if titans, in 1997, were in short supply. They'd restore the main house, invite musicians, painters, writers. . . . Yeah, she was high on country coffee all right—and the spell of this place. Still, over the years they'd flirted, she and Nick, with the idea of an art colony on his estate. There might come a time when they'd be happy for such a refuge.

She leaned into him and he smiled without looking at her and slipped a hand beneath her linen jacket and then under the waistband of her pants. The press of his fingers at her hip dialed up a delicious moment from earlier. A bonus of sex with Nick was reliving it all day. A little afternoon siesta might be just the thing. . . . They all funneled into a narrow corridor leading to Sand's marionette theater. On some impulse, she looked around for Lolita. There she was, at the head of the line. Lolita turned and peered at her and Nick. By a trick of light over her brow and mustache, the girl resembled a jackal, and Maddy wondered how she could have seen in that face anything of Laila.

BEFORE DINNER THEY wandered the carriage roads around Nohant, she fitting her step to Nick's rolling sailor's gait. Cows observed them in silence from a darkening field like the evening's eyes. A chalky moon hung overhead and lightning bugs flashed green points in the air perfumed by turned earth and flowering hawthorn. The road circled back to Sand's family graveyard. A tall angel beamed down a blind smile; its wings, the feathers finely etched in stone, shone lavender in the lingering light. *On me croit mort, je vis ici,* read the legend. "I'm believed dead, but I live on here," Nick translated. With a shiver, Maddy saw herself gazing up at another stone angel on a May afternoon. . . .

Since the morning in Sand's château, Nick's mood had darkened, like a sudden squall. He wore his out-to-lunch face, a cartoon character with cross-hatched eyes.

He'd busted out of the château just before the marionette theater, pleading suffocation; pale, upper lip misted with sweat. She'd feared a heart attack or stroke—though it *had* been awfully close in that narrow corridor. A panic attack, she'd decided. A real pity he'd missed Chopin's room upstairs . . . In the afternoon they'd roamed La Chatre, looking in shop windows and enjoying being tourists. She bought Laila a flowered Cacharel blouse, and then a miniature squirrel couple with parasol for Laila's collection of figurines. They climbed to a main square that spilled down from a central axis, as if the earth had shrugged. They stopped at a café, and bellied up to the cool zinc of the bar, and sipped syrupy *limonades*. A street photographer took a snapshot. Caught Nick doomy and glamorous in the amber light, she with her broad cheeks and almond eyes he called her "Khirgiz eyes." Wearing her smile, the smile of a woman with all the luck. On the way to the car, they saw the German schoolkids troop across the square into a patisserie. Lolita, the champion kisser, was not among them.

Nick's moods were an old story (and pain in the ass), part of the package; maybe a mild form of the taint that he claimed marked his family, the whole tribe an argument against inbreeding. *I'm a moody bastard,* he'd say afterward and apologize extravagantly. Experience had taught her to lay back. The funk would work its way out of him like a splinter.

She could absorb a patch of funk, they had much to celebrate, she and Nick. Friends were getting downsized and put out to pasture, losing mates to a rogue cell or a ski instructor, getting plucked too early from the party. She and Nick were both at the top of their game; Nick's imprint a holdout against the dumbing-down of publishing, she with her dual act of pianist and arts reporter. And darling Laila: spooky wise, her angelic nature the envy of friends whose children were mall rats or slackers. She'd even skipped the storms of adolescence—except for a deep sulk when Nick came on board. Maddy had loved him in some fashion since her twenties, and found him again years later through a blessed alignment of stars in the shimmering isles off Virgin Gorda. If something happened with her and Nick, she would not be all right.

SATURDAY NIGHT HAD brought an influx of guests to the terrace. An elderly woman with a dachshund; a foursome of English tourists, nattering away in the patois of upper-class Brits. In a corner under the eaves, a young French couple fed each other bits of cheese in slow motion.

The carrot-haired waiter arrived to take their order. He recommended the *poulet en barbouille,* a regional specialty.

The evening glow lingered and beat at them and they sipped the local Pouilly Fumé in a luxury of silence. Only with Laila did she feel so easy. She pondered the best way to bring up the art colony. Nick's sister co-owned the estate, but lived abroad and showed zero interest in it. Any mention of his sister, though, and Nick went medieval. Violet was a topic they tacitly agreed never to touch. They each had their reasons. Transparency, she'd decided, was much overrated.

"I'm thinking, it's a sad thing I never had a child," Nick said abruptly.

She held her wine glass aloft, unsure she had heard what she had heard; tried for a composed expression above the ice in her heart.

"A baby? At our age?" Her mind raced. What madness, *impossible.* Not for Nick, it wasn't. "Is that your creative thought for the evening? Darling, I just don't see you pushing a stroller around Washington Square. Like the *altecockers* strong-armed by their trophy wives into having a kid. Did I tell you? Sophie's ex was featured in an article in *New York Magazine* on second-time dads. He seems to have forgotten his first-time daughter is living in the jungle with guerillas."

"It's not Lester's fault she's run amok."

She tilted back her Pouilly Fumé. The alcohol felt dangerous, combustible in her blood. *Babies?* What *was* he talking about.

The orange-haired waiter sashayed over with their *poulet en barbouille.* "Is this sauce special to the region?" Nick asked. His manners impeccable, polished by years of putting the help at ease.

"*Oui, Monsieur.* The chicken is cooked in its own blood."

Maddy looked at the chicken smothered in a rich chestnut sauce. Why was there so much violence? The waiter's teeth, she noticed, were sawed-off greyish stumps. She watched Nick wield fork and knife, boarding-school graceful.

"Mmm, delicious, the waiter was right," Nick said between mouthfuls.

She moved the tortured bird around the plate with her fork, like an insect palpating air with its antennae. From the next table the woman with the dachshund, its leash tangled in her chair, shot them a look of naked envy. The French couple had progressed to nibbling each other's fingers.

Don't get sucked in, "take a chill," Laila would say. She would humor him, a fussy child with a fever. Above all, don't dignify the thing with serious discussion. Because if she did, a small voice might cry, *But what about me?* and that she wouldn't permit.

Nick set down his fork across the plate. "You're not eating. Christ, look what I've done, I'm sorry. I'm so terribly confused. I needed to tell you what I'd been thinking."

"Oh, Nicky, I'm glad you did. I mean, you've always gone on about *not* wanting children." *Discussing it.* He'd cited his own family as the best deterrent. Though what could have kept her from Laila?

"At times I feel you can't live purely for your own pleasure," he said, sheepish.

"You sound like a character in a Russian novel." She always made him laugh. He didn't laugh. "And what about Laila?"

"What *about* her," Nick said testily.

"Well, you have been a sort of surrogate dad for eight years." *And where the fuck do I fit in?* Did he plan on knocking up a surrogate mother? No, don't touch that.

Nick put his hand to his forehead and rubbed his eyebrow. "Oh, it's absurd, I know—"

"When we want to travel," she put in a bit quickly. "Ireland in August." A bike trip—though she hoped to make liberal use of the sweep van—and a ticklish topic: they'd had to lever in the trip between her concert dates.

She remembered how that morning Nick had mocked, she now thought, her busyness. At some point, needing to do your work was bound to piss off someone. Gingerly, she forked a morsel of chicken.

"What do you think of *poulet en barbouille?*"

"Not exactly kosher—but tasty."

"How do you put up with me?"

"Beats me."

He brought her hand to his mouth and kissed her wrist. "Mmm, jasmine." A moment. "I wish we could stay longer. We never got to Bourges."

"I wish we could, too," she said. Yet her fingers itched for a keyboard; she'd caught herself scratching on surfaces. And she needed to fax the office—before leaving New York, she'd picked up ominous rumblings.

"Gotta chase down my writer and hope he makes George Sand country *hot* for the '90s. The rural heart of France as the next Provence. Christ, I hate what publishing's become." He sighed; settled lower in his chair in his loose-limbed way. "And then it's back to the shop to brainstorm with Nessa."

"Nessa?"

"Yeah, Nessa Trent-Jones, my new hire. Our new publicity director," he prompted. "Remember? I told you."

Why was no one named Marilyn or Arlene anymore.

"Alison was doing a perfectly fine job, but she made the mistake of getting involved with the CEO of Richterverlag," Nick said. "Then she insisted he leave his wife, and he fired her."

"Poor Alison."

"Poor? How about not smart."

If Nessa is any smarter, Maddy thought, *she won't let love cramp her career.* Nessa would also likely be of childbearing age and equipped with a slush fund—who else could afford to work in publishing?

What was she doing with such thoughts. Nick couldn't want to fuck around with the best thing that had happened to either of them. She inhaled the freshness rising off the earth and watched the swallows, shaped like tiny archers, carve up the dimming light. Love found later in life made you wolfish to get your arms around the last best time. Alert to any disturbance in the field. Including all the imagined ones.

CHAPTER 2

The Three Doors

B *ailas como gringa.* Ma, the merengue's just a two-step: drop the hip, drag your leg at the same time." Laila demonstrated, high, round ass switching, Latina cool. She wore ripped jeans and a dish-rag tee, the uniform favored by private-school kids and crack addicts. She turned the salsa to ghetto-blaster volume, and they hit it again, Maddy, a tad shorter than her daughter, melting into the moves. "*Eso es!* Way to go, Ma. . . ." As they rounded a standing lamp, Maddy's toe caught on the Persian carpet; carrying Laila with her, she flopped onto the sofa, both of them laughing.

Laila's body had all the heft of a finch. Along with the merengue, she'd acquired a parasite from her Latin travels; insisted she was cured, but why should a mother stop worrying?

Maddy lowered the music and ogled her newly redone living room. The parlor level below a monkish space with two Steinway grands—but here on the second floor, a paean to Olde English: window seat in a William Morris greenwillow chintz; the new "heirloom" Persians Nick teased her about. Her flame-stitch wing chair, acquired in the lean days from Goodwill and reglued—talismanic. When they weren't together at the Point, Nick shuttled between here and a studio near his office. They enjoyed days off; from long habit each needed solitude. Nick had clocked a twenty-five-year marriage; she'd lived with Marshall for six—yet till they found each other, essentially they'd both been alone.

"Lou, let's teach Nick the merengue next weekend," Maddy said.

Laila slid down on her tailbone, coarse reddish curls fanning around features set a tad close in her face. The greenish eyes and caramel skin turned heads (while Maddy, slightly famous, was edging toward invisible). Her enchanting smile, like aromatherapy, made people around her happier in their skin. "Uncle Nick *dance?*" Laila pursed her pillowy lips. "No *way.*"

"Honey, he's not *such* a stiff."

Laila loved Nick—now that her loyal heart had forgiven him for displacing Marshall. She was comically protective, coaching Nick, a WASP relic, in modern folkways. Last summer she'd gone to Nicaragua to help build a school—in a village menaced by cholera—and returned to the States with a calling: to photograph the Third World's poor in the manner of Sebastião Salgado. This summer she was headed for Juárez with a photojournalist to document the fallout from global capitalism. The child had been born with a social conscience the way she herself had with perfect pitch. . . .

Maddy sank into her wing chair; four A.M. Europe time, and she was caffeinated with fatigue. Her eye wandered over a weekly lying open on the coffee table. She made out the byline *Jed Oliver.* Tenants' lawyer, unlikely mix of social climber and wolfman—and her daughter's fortyish boyfriend. Laila had started late, clinging longer than quite normal to *Babar* the elephant king and a battered picture book of Greek myths, dreaming and playing solitary games among the gardens and crumbling statuary encrusted with lichen at Conscience Point.

"Lo, something I wanna talk to you about."

"Oh, brother." Laila slid down on her neck, legs akimbo, caramel knees poking through her jeans. How had this child gotten so thin?

"Of course we all admire Jed Oliver for the cases he takes on, but isn't he a little—"

"*Old* for me." Laila always a beat ahead. "Like who gives a shit?"

Maddy startled. Laila never took this pit-bull tack; she was more Ferdinand, dodging the picadors to sniff the flowers. Maddy heard her friend Sophie: *If a guy's white, employed, and dates psychiatric social workers, he thinks he's exempt from AIDS, so why spoil the moment fumbling for a Trojan.* "Uh, y'know, Jed's run through an awful lot of women," she said.

"Ma. No one does unprotected sex anymore." In case Maddy doubted the existence of telepathy. "Look, he's just a guy I hang with, I'm almost nineteen, I know what I'm doing. Give it a rest."

That un-Laila harshness again. "Lo-ey, it's just . . . I don't want you to associate love with unhappiness."

Laila's gaze turned inward like a child's beneath her straight black lashes. As when she'd first learned about body bags, when Maddy had taken her—mistakenly; unforgivably—to *All That Jazz*. Peeling off the couch, Laila loped to the mantel and scowled at the photos in ornate silver frames: herself smiling gap-toothed from a rowboat in Central Park; standing with Nick, suited up and beaming from the dazzled slopes of Bromley—scenes of ordinary family happiness. Though Laila's passage into Maddy's safekeeping had been anything but ordinary. The official story: Maddy had adopted her from a foundling home in Rabat, Morocco, a star child in a carton grasping a silver rattle—a story about as credible as *Babar*.

Laila toed the copper fire fan with her black hightop. "Mom, there's something I gotta tell *you*."

"Oh, brother." Echoing Laila as a joke, yet her throat tightened.

"The thing with Jed—it's just not where I'm at anymore." A little huff of exasperation, an Ashcroft tic. "I've decided to leave college for a while and go work in Guatemala."

Maddy pitched forward in her chair. "Drop out?"

"*Arghh*"—Laila favored comic-book expletives. "No, take *time out*. Anyway, your view of Brown is totally unreal. Kids are like, *Hello,* who's Beowulf? They fly the Concorde to Paris, they do lines in the dorm. And there's this new course, a workshop on sex toys—"

"Surely you can find some worthwhile courses. Tara Gerson took time out from Yale and ended up in Oregon in a lesbian commune."

"*So?* I cannot *stand* your homophobia."

Maddy felt she'd wandered into someone else's movie. Laila usually caressing and wise, with greater tact than the nominal grownups. She was nice even to telemarketers! *You two are like sisters,* people would say, not altogether approving. Yet recently, Maddy now recognized—her thinking slowed by fatigue—Laila had turned moody and irritable; she sometimes lashed out in anger at the least provocation. Since . . . before the vacation in France?

"Guatemala's a dangerous place," Maddy continued, skipping over eggshells. "Those coeds hijacked and raped. The nuns murdered in El Salvador." Thanks to her daughter, she'd become an expert on mayhem south of the border.

"Third World violence comes out of the policies of the companies you and Nick invest in—they bleed Latin America dry. And lookit what's going down right here. Building owners, like your buddy Amos Grubb, are fucking over the maintenance workers who've gone on strike, bringing in younger workers they can pay less. Someday they're gonna raze the mansions on Midas Lane."

Oh, brother. She shut her eyes and shook her head. Not at Laila's outburst, which rather impressed her—she sensed it was camouflage. But for what?

"You don't give me credit for being an adult," Laila went on in a nicer voice. "I'm gonna work in a construction project in Lagunas, a village in San Marcos. And I've applied for a USIA grant to photograph the indigenous peoples for a show."

Struggling for calm: "But why not finish college first—"

"*Arghh*, why must you boss everyone's life?"

Sighing, Maddy rose, catching her image, haggard but svelte, in the night bay window. Well, the mother-daughter thing was famously toxic; she'd heard her friends griping about the resident bitch on wheels; she'd just been lucky till now. Suddenly she wondered if Nick found her bossy, too. And was she obnoxiously overscheduled, like those women who, Sophie joked, penciled in orgasms?

"You gotta trust me, I know what I'm doing," Laila said enigmatically. Then her pale eyes glittered and she was close beside Maddy, hugging her, yet Maddy hung back, hands against Laila's scary ribs. "I love you," Laila said.

She felt this taut little body. Laila once smelled of unfinished wood from her bunk bed; now she smelled womanly and complicated. Okay, probably Laila had never forgiven her for Nick—that's what was going on; with Marshall, Laila knew who came first. No matter that she'd bought her the Nikon F5 and created the darkroom on the third floor—Laila felt bought off. You did your best, and it wasn't good enough. That seemed to be the deal.

She pulled Laila onto the window seat beside her. "Lou, let's go away for a week, just the two of us. In September, for your birthday." She'd shave some days off the trip to Ireland, even if Nick already groused it was too short. "We could go hiking in the Rockies. Remember that climb to Cathedral and coming down for lunch at the Pine Creek Cookhouse? I've never been so happy." A girl's happiness, gamboling and free, needing no tending like adult passion.

Laila flashed her lovely smile. "Remember those *dogues?*"—one of their invented words, which also included goofy love-names. "The ones wearing backpacks?"

"And the llamas? And the way the breeze flicks the silver underside of the aspens?"

Laila's eyes clouded; she shifted away. "At this resort in the Caribbean they give the guests a choice of nine friggin' pillows. And in Juárez the *pepenadores* forage for food in dumps and compete with dogs."

That she could follow Laila's logic didn't help. Their connection crackled like a wire ready to short out. "So you won't ever go anywhere nice?"

"I'll go where I'm needed. I can have my goddamn birthday at the Point." She jumped up, eyes darting around the room. "I'm outta here."

Almost midnight, and she was leaving to meet Jed at that dive off Hudson where they'd just shot a dealer. Maddy stood in the middle of her lovely room, hands hanging. Well, here it was, delayed adolescence kicking in, plus a shitload of anger, and somewhere in the mix—Maddy tried to stifle *that* thought—a hint of hereditary damage?

Her fine reasons failed to satisfy. Something in her world felt out of joint. That bomb Nick had dropped about a baby. She was suddenly convinced he'd never mentioned any Nessa Trent-Jones before that evening in Nohant.

At the door Laila hesitated; turned and looked at Maddy. "I'm sorry. For everything."

"What *everything*. What is going on here!"—but she'd vanished down the stairwell.

STRAIGHT OFF THE ELEVATOR, she saw the huddle like the folded wings of buzzards.

"Wait'll you hear what happened while you were tripping through the poppies," Sam said. White-lipped smile. "Charlie Unger's out."

Oh, shit, her dream of a boss. She'd caught the early rumblings of course, but in France managed to put all vexing thoughts on hold.

"Bern Conant's our new executive producer." Sam rolled his eyes at Maddy: *Tried to warn you . . .*

"Bern Conant, Lord help us." Remembering last night's cryptic message on her machine. Conant was the new breed of broadcast exec as high school dropout, postliterate, mesmerized by ratings. She leaned a shoulder against the cinder-block wall, feeling its texture of petrified cottage cheese through her blazer.

"Guess they're grooming the local yokel for bigger things," Sam said. "Welcome back, darlin'! Let's hope our boy's not dumb enough to monkey with your segment." He steered her down the hall. "While you were away, Video Kitten badgered the powers to let her narrate a story on Hootie and the Blowfish. And in the rough cut of your Domna Scotti, she went with the least flattering shots. Watch your back."

WELCOME BACK, INDEED. Maddy took refuge in her office, a bright, ordered place hung with photos: she and Byron Janis and other music luminaries; Laila and Nick on the beach; a treasured Laila painting from second grade of a mother and baby shark, "from your one and only daughter" . . . Jesus, Bern Conant. Station manager from local, dubbed by the industry "Conan the Barbarian." He'd been associate producer on the morning news, and now, it appeared, the powers had judged him ready for his own show. *Chronicle* would beef up his bona fides before they handed him the evening news. Conan was known for looking at a story and taking out the best part. And when Martha Graham died, he'd assigned a piece on Martha *Raye*, the dentures queen. If they wanted to boost ratings by going tabzine, they'd found their man.

Heart leaden, she backhanded pitches and press kits into the trash. From one flyer leapt the name Anton Bers. God, they'd practically grown up together at Juilliard, she and Tony Bers. He'd been a prodigy and goofball who scorned scales and "practiced" by ripping through his favorite composers. Tony went on to win the Leventritt and join the exclusive preserve of pianists touring the world's capitals—then, like many a gold medalist before him, tumbled from the heights. Injured his right hand, went the story; performed left-hand repertory for a while. Now the *wunderkind* had washed up in Monmouth, New Jersey, playing chamber music in the local Episcopal church. She sighed, engulfed by a world of regret.

Anton's covering letter pitched a story about the current explosion of chamber groups. "Let's talk soon." She pictured the caption in a recent cartoon in the *New Yorker: How's never. Would never work for you?*

Now, none of that . . . You needed a gauze mask to avoid catching the arrogance that was epidemic among New York's players. And self-importance: marketing chlorophyll toothpaste for Procter & Gamble held the gravitas of religion. What she ought to do was invite Anton, for old times, to Conscience Point for a session of four-hands. And then they'd brainstorm how to spin his story idea. Of course now, under the new regime, she might be less of a player.

She'd somehow felt immune to the seismic shocks rocking broadcasting; eleven years on the show, she'd become a fixture; everyone was expendable, of course, but she perhaps less than others? She gave good value, Nick was right: concert pianist with an inside track on the arts who could write—plus poster girl for graceful aging with a devoted female following. Charlie rarely vetoed her ideas. He offered her TV's most precious commodity: minutes. He'd become a lone holdout against the prevailing dumbing-down, going for think pieces and arts coverage for the literate. He'd made *Sunday Chronicle* the class act of network television, the cultural companion to *60 Minutes*. And now? In one moment the palace Charlie had built could blow off like a heap of silt.

The world around her was growing curiouser by the minute. Maybe this the true onset of middle age, this loss of control and encroaching chaos.

She heard her friend, a correspondent they'd just cut loose: *I figured I was going to spend my whole life in this business. This was home, Mother Network. But somewhere along the line I forgot that you're always dependent on whatever exec is in charge. You could always be out on your ass, any day, easy.*

You'll work someplace else, Maddy had said.

Yeah? Who's gonna hire a woman over fifty? You know, it's like we get a moment out there. And if we're lucky and smart, it's a good long run. But then you're out, the next generation moves in, and it's someone else's turn.

But suppose you were a rotten sport and declined to bow out. Supposed you wanted an open-ended run. An unlimited engagement. Pianists performed till they dropped; Shura Cherkassky played Carnegie Hall at eighty; the great Horszowski tottered onstage, half-blind. at ninety-eight. And what of prostate city over at *60 Minutes?*

She thought, *I'll be damned if they'll shove me offstage. I won't move over till I fall over.*

SCRIPT IN HAND, Maddy headed with her brisk step for Bern Conant's office, the only one on the sixth floor with windows. (Cinder-Block City, they called CNB's dreary quarters in a former Wonder Bread factory.) A blowup of Madeleine Shaye smiled from a bank of network notables on the wall. Almond eyes, alluring overbite—Israeli? Magyar? unbrandable; subtly subversive among the lemon-chiffon blonds. She passed the familiar sign on Sam's door: "When I grow up I want to sit in a dark room and have people look at the back of my neck." They would screen the rough cut of her piece—she, Sam, Juno, and the senior producer—and get Conant's comments. Lop and shift graphs, turn the wrap-up into the lead . . . She'd always enjoyed this sculpting.

She harbored a special fondness for her Domna Scotti piece. The famed diva rose too young, too fast; sang too often, dropped too much weight.

Then fell for a master of the universe, who dumped her for a Russian model. Now Scotti lived in relative obscurity, teaching and singing in regional opera. The story celebrated a life in music as its own reward and took a whack at the infatuation with a few superstars.

"Lessee, how long does she run now?" Bern mumbled.

"Four," said Juno.

"Four?" said Maddy. "Last I looked it was seven—"

"We *should* get down to three and a half," Bern said.

Old joke: one TV reporter to another: *What's your story about?* Answer: *About a minute thirty.* "No way, material's too good," Maddy said.

"I don't give a goddamn if it's Christ resurrected—" Recalling whom he was talking to, Bern lifted his upper lip in a smile. "It *is* good stuff," he said in a phlegmy burr, and popped in the tape.

Maddy shook her head in disbelief. It was just Domna scarfing pills, the failed suicide, kicking drugs in a London hospital, salvation *ta-da!* in the arms of a good man—and no music. "This looks like a *telenovela,* I'll lose my credibility in the music world."

The others stirred uneasily; imprudent to start life under the new regime by breaking an office commandment: Be a *team player.*

"I mean, for Pete's sake, give us more than two bars of *Traviata.* This"—she was distracted by Bern's cut-rate nose job, which tugged down his pale, watery eyes—"this would strain the attention span of a mayfly."

"We bring in the war at two and a half," he said. "That's all we gave Bosnia." Maddy detected a spasm of amusement in Sam's long, whey-colored face. "We need *something* to goose this. Juno, we got some shots of the Russian babe? Trouble is, classical music—I mean, if it's Pavarotti boinking his secretary, or the Three Tenors at Giant Stadium, great," Bern went on, trying for the make-nice voice. He rewound to Domna getting coached by the great Tedarescu in Milan. "But this 'floradora' stuff."

"*Fioritura.* Viewers like technical details, they feel they're learning something." She was distracted by a fresh menace: her standup displayed a jawline in want of whittling. She remembered Sam's warning about her field producer, Juno, who appeared to subsist on daikon.

Bern lifted a paper off his desk, gave it a light slap with the back of his hand. "Gotta problem with this memo you wrote my pree-decessor."

The others bailed.

"This whuddyacallit Ray—is he hot?"

"Arundhati *Roy*. *She*. An Indian novelist, very telegenic, tipped to win the Booker Prize in '97."

Bern's pale skin pinked around the scalp. "And this"—he brought Maddy's memo toward his face—"Martha Arg—?"

"Marta Argerich is arguably the world's greatest living pianist. A force of nature, cancels more concerts than she plays, but audiences are fanatically devoted—"

"Yeah, really. But couldn't you do something less exotic? Juno's working up a story on girl rappers."

So Sam had gotten that right, too. "How about a story on cabaret artists?"

Bern bobbed his head. "Good, good. Liza Minnelli?"

"Actually, I was thinking of the cabaret *genre*. Wonderful artists like Blossom Dearie, or Bobby Short; he's been at the Carlyle for ages. Or Michael Feinstein."

Bern colored deeper. "Listen, this is too exquisite, people in America don't know from cabaret. They go to the Holiday Inn, they go to the mall, they listen to rock. Why not do—"

"Hootie and the Blowfish!"

"There you go!" A moment. "Actually, that's already in the pipeline." He looked at her uncertainly. "And not your kind of story."

Okay, deep breaths. "Bern, this show has always been a class act, one of a kind. They brought me in to cover the arts without talking down. We have a loyal base—"

"And you've brought up the ratings and . . . you're an essential piece of this." He walked to the bank of windows and eyeballed her. "But we're losing audience to *Sunday Today*. We gotta play to younger demographics and go easy on the highbrow."

"Of course." A long moment. "Well, too bad about the *Times*."

"What's that?"

"Yeah, 'Arts and Leisure' was planning a companion piece on Scotti, which would have publicized ours. But the way our story's angled now . . ." She produced a regretful frown. Bern's scalp went rosier. She could hear his thoughts clacking like teletype: *Madeleine Shaye a T-rex, but she could get the "get."*

With masterly timing: "Perhaps we could find some middle ground with the Scotti," she offered silkily.

ARMSTEAD'S, THE LOCAL recovery room. At least in Chekhov, she mused over a Virgin Mary, the barbarians whacking the cherry trees had charm. Her half-truth about the *Times* might salvage the Scotti. But in a fit of housecleaning, Conant could toss her like a yellowing antimacassar. The thought gave her dry mouth, as before a concert. She'd labored and schemed to assemble this dual package, an entrepreneur of herself. . . . Followed a husband to Fort Bragg, North Carolina; aborted her career as an Outstanding Young American Pianist. Abort careers is what women did in 1966, Maddy had told herself, relieved, almost, to fold into the pack.

After the marriage imploded, she returned to New York; accompanied ballet classes, pounding out Chopin waltzes and mazurkas—stop/start/ stop/start—on brittle uprights; survived on Campbell's pepper pot soup and cheddar cubes from art gallery openings. And woke mornings with the acrid knowledge that she'd missed her moment as a soloist, could no longer compete in the international competitions that shot a young performer into orbit. At thirty-two she'd outlived herself.

Then came Laila. She needed money now, for her Lou, who slept in a closet bunk in their basement studio next to the boiler, with its mystery leaks and view of feet passing like a TV "crawl." It was the moment of *The Women's Room;* the new feminist voices were shaking gold from the trees. Why not join the chorus? Over four years Maddy rose at five to work on a biography of her idol Clara Schumann. The rejections fattened a folder till one clairvoyant editor saw they could pitch Clara as an early feminist prototype, in a juicy ménage à trois with husband Robert and Brahms to boot. After the TV movie, Maddy bought the three-story brick redstone on Jane Street, the skinniest house on the block and a steal.

She was profiled on *Chronicle* with a group of the new feminist biographers. Afterward, Maddy convinced Charlie Unger she could do a better interview. He liked her performer's poise and insider's empathy—they'd just need to bland her down, lose the raccoon eyeliner and sound of Queens. He weaned her from the old print habits and taught her to craft a TV story, quoting Kuralt at her: " 'Listen to the pictures. Then write to them as you would write to music.' " He handed her the culture beat; she marveled that they *paid* her (and how!) for such fun. The visibility from *Chronicle* jumpstarted a modest concert career, which in turn swelled her prestige on the show—she invented synergy before it became the rage.

She signaled the waiter for another, gnawed by a fresh worry: Could she afford to leave *Chronicle?* Nick dipped deeply into principal, and theirs was a luxury born of expense accounts, fancy footwork—and her paycheck. Yet perhaps Conant's arrival had opened a door. If she went ahead full-bore with the piano, hell, maybe she could rise to, say, the top rank of tier two. Nick felt buffeted by the same downmarket pressures as *Chronicle*—no more books, he fumed, just "publishing ops."

She thought of Conscience Point, its crumbling facade and silent, closed-off rooms, its grounds choked with bittersweet, its becalmed air. Waiting to be tapped for some grand enterprise, to explode magically into life. Would Nick leap with her?

CHAPTER 3

Shadblow

La vraie vie n'est pas absente, mais ailleurs.
Real life isn't absent, just elsewhere. . . .

—ARTHUR RIMBAUD

S he'd balked when Nick wanted to buy the status car of the moment.
But the Lexus, she would now happily concede, handled with a pliancy almost sexual. At the usual jam-up around LaGuardia, she launched on her inner clavier into the *Spring* Sonata, set for an August recital with Viktor Vadim; driving, walking, flossing, she always had a piece working itself out in her head. She ascended a scale *crescendo,* then dropped to *piano subito.* It was that *wisp* of a second just before the downbeat that gave Beethoven such verve.

As the cars inched along, she cut a look at the old neighborhood climbing the scraggly heights to the right. The Queens of semiattached stucco houses with Flowering Cherry, rose of Sharon, and plaster Virgins in front yards. And the rancid patch of discontent that was her parents' lives. Butler Street, where she'd walked clutching her red tin lunch box with its cargo of bologna sandwiches wrapped in wax paper, its smell of turned milk. The evenings spiked with her teacher-father's volcanic rages over "sloppy" playing. After losing a competition, she'd slept on the floor to punish herself; done exercises to strengthen her fourth and fifth fingers, all but wrecking the ligaments. She'd stood on the doorstep in her pajamas, bawling to the point of retching, the night Imre Horvath left for Regal deli to buy she couldn't remember what and forgot to come home. Bawling till the lights winked on in the Gustavsons' across the street. He'd left her only his rage for perfection: *Thanks, Dad.* Odd, she drove past here every weekend, oblivious to that cratered world.

Out on the highway the willows tossed a lime-yellow spume. She loved May, this excitable spurt in the year before summer's tyranny of green. Closer to Riverhead a sharp eye could make out starry white blossoms. Shadblow . . .

She slid backward down the years and sat beside Violet Ashcroft in her fawn Mercedes. A roadster out of *Gatsby,* the dashboard made of lacquered, burled wood the color of strong tea. A Winston dangled off the driver's lip, and she smelled of the car's buttery leather and jasmine and sweat. She nervily sideslipped cars, shot ahead, abruptly downshifted, deaf to the honking; yakking and gesturing, a highway menace. *See those starry white blossoms? They're called shadblow. . . .*

Thirty weekends a year, Maddy reflected, she drove to Conscience Point without revisiting that fateful trip. She'd turned unpredictable to herself. Since the holiday in France. Nick's nonsense about babies, Laila acting out, her imperiled job—it was like three doors slamming, jarring loose memories, shuffling the coordinates of her known world.

She slowed, cursing, for a stretch of road work. A sign marked "Detour" with a flashing arrow directed all cars off the Northern State. She followed a thinning stream of cars along an unfamiliar road. Where were they hiding the signs for the expressway? She made a U-turn into a street abutting a stretch of tract houses, semibuilt and uninhabited; the builder must have lost his financing. The road ended squarely, eerily, against a grass embankment. As if the world it led to had evaporated.

On her right a ramshackle farm stand. She could make out faded white letters: "F—sh Straw—ies." Her skin prickled. She had been here before, at this very spot. Over twenty-five, thirty years ago.

On that first drive out Violet had stopped at this stand—the farm itself long since plowed under. They bought a quart of the season's first strawberries and ate them from the wooden box, the berries' juice rouging their fingertips. Why did everything taste sweeter then? How foolish she and Vi would sound now, conjuring their lives as artists, disdaining marriage, frightened by their own bravado. For Laila and friends those battles would seem as ancient as the sacking of Troy.

Maddy sat with the motor idling, gazing at the ghost farmstand, and the past lay heavy upon her.

Come home with me this weekend. Violet's cracked voice, a smoker's voice, with odd catches.

Come with her just like that? The girl was nuts. "I'm preparing a concert." Embarrassed by her status of music grind.

"You can practice at my place. Just come for one night—it's only Long Island, for heaven's sake. I'll put you on the train Sunday. Or lend you a car."

A car?

"You'll play on the Bösendorfer! There's one in the music room."

In truth, she disliked the small sound of this pretentious Cadillac of pianos. But she was also drawn to this world where someone lent *a* car, to the danger surrounding Violet. . . . Could she break her routine this once? "I'd be a lousy guest, with my nose in the piano."

"I would *forbid* anyone to disturb you. I'll lock you in the music room, like Colette's husband. And I'll paint upstairs in my studio. We'll be ruthless! Work all night if we like, and meet for breakfast."

It astonished Maddy that this arrangement might appeal to anyone besides herself. She barely knew Violet Ashcroft, this only their second encounter. Of course everyone on campus knew Violet by reputation and sight. She was easily the most alluring girl of any class. She hadn't much competition from the coeds populating Barnard in 1966: psych majors with pale, meaty thighs above knee socks, white cotton Lollipop underpants, Breck-girl pageboys. Rack up the As, then, to everything its season, land a Columbia premed with horn-rims from the other side of Broadway.

Maddy first sighted Violet on a crisp September afternoon of junior year by the dry fountain in front of Atkins. A new girl, a transfer student. She was arguing with a boy wearing chinos and a pink Oxford shirt, a preppy with the cameo profile of F. Scott Fitzgerald.

Intrigued, Maddy stationed herself on the far side of the fountain. Sneaking looks at the chopped silver-blond hair, dark brows, scalded cheeks. She had a myopic stare that Maddy would later translate as unfettered self-absorption. She wore a yellow painter's smock, green skirt, lavender stockings—like the Brangwen sisters in *Women in Love*. Her fingernails daubed a mortuary blue.

"Oh, for godssake, Christian, maybe you did leave Oxford on my account," came her raspy voice. "Doesn't make me your indentured slave, does it? And who asked you to leave anyway?"

"*You* did. *You* asked me."

"What has *that* got to do with anything?"

Maddy's cautious soul thrilled to the arrogance. She must find a way to meet this girl. . . . And now here she sat, amazingly, admiring the shadblow from Violet's snazzy car. Watching Violet's hand, ringed in antique amethysts and sapphires, work the gear shift like a racer at Le Mans.

"I'm taking you to my favorite place in the world," Violet announced as they careened off the highway. "I've brought us a picnic," she added, shrugging toward a wicker basket on the back seat.

They drove into Islesford past a glassy pond patrolled by swans, past a white steeple and a row of elegant shops. A stop at Islesford Spirits for two chilled bottles of wine from Violet's "old buddy."

They turned down a road past a grey windmill. "Peniston Way's more direct, but we're taking the scenic route," Violet said. "What a glorious spring. Look at that palette of greens." She gestured around her, the car drifting out of its lane, terrorizing an oncoming pickup truck. Sunlight gilded pistachio-green leaves, boughs were festooned with parasols of celadon or pink. Along the road bloomed some kind of furze the color of dried blood. A roller-coaster rise—and there in the distance stretched Weymouth Bay, a dancing hive of light.

They dipped to a hollow and screeched to a stop. Violet's hand with its gnawed nails cupped the vibrating gearshift.

"Green Glen Cemetery," she announced moodily. Did the place actually radiate a moss-colored light? "Jackson Pollock's buried here. Cracked up his car driving around sloshed. These roads have no shoulder. Best drive them sober."

A moment. "My good brother is buried here." Violet got out and disappeared over a hill. Maddy found her gazing up at a stone angel with a sweet, sightless smile. "Linton Ashcroft died in a tragic accident," Violet said in a stagy monotone. "Went for an ocean swim and never returned. Till someone found a pelvic bone washed up on shore."

"How horrible for him, for your family."

"For some more than others," she said oddly.

THEY WOUND DOWN Beldover Drive, its sides banked high with white dogwood. Turned right at a sign half-smothered in poison ivy: "Conscience Point," and, in larger letters, "PRIVATE, TRESPASSERS WILL BE PROSECUTED." The scrub oak bordering Wildmoor Road melted into a pine forest, a melancholy woods from Grimm; amazing to see towering trees hard by the sea. The afternoon sun angled a shaft of amber dust through the tall black boughs. Maddy sucked the resiny scent into her lungs.

"Over there's the cabin where Mother keeps her true children—all thirty of them." Violet waved carelessly toward a carriage road in the scrub oak.

"Thirty?"

"Her bird-children. Cockatiels. When she's pissed she threatens to leave all her money to Audubon." She downshifted with a *vroom vroom.* "Father died of a heart attack ten years ago—in the act, the clever man. With the carpenter's son. After that Mother went to the birds. The rest of the infamous Ashcrofts you've probably heard about."

Maddy vaguely remembered some Gothic tale about an Ashcroft forebear murdering his bride for her money.

"What about your people."

Her people. After her father split, she'd come home from school to find her mother on the kitchen linoleum, foaming at the mouth from drinking shoe polish. Her mother's relatives in Astoria gave her bed, board, and the word *shanda* to describe the disaster area named Horvath. . . . The tale somehow lacked the panache of the Ashcroft clan. "I use my mother's name, Shaye," Maddy said, midthought. "But I hate all that *David Copperfield* crap."

Already, Violet respected her silences.

THEY CROSSED A low-slung bridge spanning a large channel: "Eggleston Bridge, death trap when it rains," Violet said. "Aquaplane right into the water." A covey of startled geese lifted, flapping and honking, into the air. Violet lurched onto a causeway bordered on both sides by blue-green bay and dotted with broken clamshells—"The clever gulls drop clams from the sky to crack them open." Maddy blinked in the white light that seemed to boil down from a cataract in the sky.

Violet parked the car at the Point and they carried the wicker basket and a blanket down rickety wooden stairs to the beach.

"Mind the splinters and poison ivy," Violet called over her shoulder. "Muthuh considers it vulgar to add modern improvements. Well! here we are, my favorite place in the world. I want my ashes scattered here."

Violet seemed much taken up with death, but Maddy was too wonder-struck to hang on to the thought. She'd never seen a lovelier place: part New England, part Greek island . . . a place she *recognized*. Over to the right, a sand spit extended out into the bay, curving a sheltering shoulder around the water to form a jade lagoon. A sandy islet rose in the water a short way out. On the shore beyond, a stand for an osprey nest tilted at a rakish angle. All around stretched flats of lime eelgrass threaded by chan-nels streaming molten silver in the sunlight. And farthest off lay a green is-land with dark stands of oak, receding in a lavender haze.

She'd been here before. The scene strangely called up a memory from childhood, of a painting on a biscuit tin of a watery, sun-struck Eden. She'd sit in the mean kitchen on Butler Street at the table covered in oilcloth and stare trancelike at the landscape on the tin, a golden land that seemed a signpost to a mysterious *elsewhere* that she longed to reach.

"This is all ours," came Violet's voice. She made a sweeping gesture at the land all around. Snapping her back. She herself owned nothing but tal-ent, and planned to ride it far. What could Violet know about it? What did rich kids know about anything? She'd noticed something about the mon-eyed sorts who hung about the music world: they could do civility, but at stray moments out popped arrogance and entitlement, like a trained jaguar reverting to its natural savagery.

Violet was anxiously trying to decipher Maddy's frown. "Here, let's spread the blanket in front of this dune and break out the wine." Violet opened the wicker basket and expertly applied corkscrew to bottle. "Gewürztraminer—bet you've never tasted any of this quality."

She'd never heard the name. Violet freed the bottle from the cork, breasts bobbling through her gauzy flowered Hungarian blouse. Her penny-colored nipples peeked from among the green, blue, and red embroidered flowers. She lofted her glass, a figure from a pagan frieze.

"Welcome to Conscience Point, the first of many visits!"

The taste of the wine ambrosial. Violet set out a baguette, wedge of cheese, bone-handled knife on the orange, black, and green wool blanket. "Foie gras from Fauchon," Violet announced, brandishing a jar. "You let it melt in your mouth."

Afterward they lit Winstons and Violet sat knees clasped, head back, cigarette jutting from her mouth. Maddy cut secret looks at her grey eyes slanting down at the corners; spiky lashes, flared nostrils, hectic flush— created, she noticed, by tiny broken veins; the down above her fleshy upper lip. Her chopped Dutch-girl hair was fastened with a blue plastic barrette with a floral design.

"Here, your weed's out." Violet shifted to give Maddy a light off her cigarette. She held Maddy's cigarette hand, then seized the other. "You must be very, very careful of these hands. I am in *awe* of talent. It's the only thing I envy."

Maddy was amazed to feel a tingling along her skin.

Violet released her hands, and sat cross-legged, staring out at the bay. "Oh, look, a cormorant." Touching Maddy's wrist, she pointed out the dark erectile head of a bird bobbing in the water before it dove for food.

The wine, the beauty of the Point, Violet's admiration had lifted Maddy to a near-ecstatic state. The wheeling sun drizzled gold across the lagoon, the surrounding channels took fire. She wanted to wade into the blaze and dissolve in light.

"I see a mah-velous future," Violet said. "You'll be a concert pianist and play in the world's capitals. And I'll paint my little pictures. Of course I don't have half your talent and don't even try to disagree—I *loathe* false modesty."

A moment. "You make it sound so simple," Maddy said. "I see obstacles and sacrifice."

"Oh, there's always someone ordering you about. But when you come right down to it, who can really stop us?"

"Men. Husbands. If I place in the Queen Elizabeth of Belgium—big 'if'—I'd play concert dates all over the world, I'd rarely be home. To make it as a pianist you need a 'smoother' to arrange tiresome details. How many men would do that for a woman?" She thought of her steady and, to date, only beau, an intern at Einstein. Leonard of Pelham Parkway. Kind, earnest, banal. His very name struck a dissonant chord in this place. "A husband wants dinner on the table at night—not an artist on the touring circuit. And once there are children—"

"Well, what are nannies for?" Violet said impatiently. "Those are just excuses." She refilled their glasses.

Maddy gulped her wine, she whose acquaintance with drink was limited to the odd postconcert sherry. "We would invent our own way," she said, catching Violet's elation. "I mean, think of Edward Hopper. Who before Hopper saw the world like that?" Slurring the words. "The world of people who missed their lives." Like her father, the onetime "keyboard lion" who ended up teaching "Für Elise" to grimy-kneed kids on Butler Street. Like her mother, who never forgave him, her sense of betrayal echoing off the walls.

"Missing your life—what could be worse?" Violet said. The wine had heightened her flush. "We do have precedents, pioneers in living—like Bloomsbury, a group of kindred souls living for art and love. Virginia Woolf, Vita Sackville-West. And Violet Trefusis—my distant cousin and namesake. The Happy Few have a way of f-f-finding each other." Violet squinted at Maddy. "We could start our community with us. Today. This very moment."

Maddy lofted her wine glass. "To art and love and the Happy Few."

"To us. We'll call it the Republic of Art. We'll build it here at the Point, my swinish family be damned. This place was meant for artists, musicians. Look"—she gestured toward a meadow beyond the eelgrass—"we'll build a little stage for outdoor concerts. I can hear the fiddles tuning up. . . ." Sudden grimace. "Y'know, I can't picture Christian there."

Maddy had forgotten all about Violet's suitor at the fountain in front of Atkins Hall.

"After we're married, Christian will want to live in Bedminster and do the unspeakable in pursuit of the uneatable—Oscar Wilde's definition of fox-hunting. He'll go to tailgate picnics at his Princeton reunions. With old classmates with straw boaters and red pants and redder noses. Summers among the stiffs at the Edgartown—*Ed-guhtown*—Yacht Club. And of course he considers my painting just a charming hobby. Sets me apart from the debs doing charity work for Islesford General . . . But the upside of marriage to the Generic Groom is the freedom. Christian would just go on selling bonds and hounding foxes and saying 'Good-o,' without noticing a thing."

So: despite her high-flying talk, Violet would marry Christian, keep one foot safely anchored in the life she claimed to scorn. Maddy felt herself deflate. Violet was a bit of a fraud. Violet scrambled to her feet and stretched her hands to the sky. "Oh, why think about the old booby today? Let's go for a swim before the green flies descend. It'll be *glacial* but mah-velous."

"I didn't bring a suit."

Violet flashed Maddy a scornful smirk. She pulled the gauzy blouse over her head and tossed it onto the sand and unbuttoned her skirt. It fell around her feet in folds of terra-cotta. She apparently did without underpants.

Maddy couldn't pull her eyes off Violet, her broadish shoulders, round

Indian breasts, horsewoman's legs. Her beauty clothed her, she seemed the human extension of this place. She turned, a cello flare of hips and ass, sun glinting off the gold down on her back, and stepped over the pebbly sand toward the water. The tide had risen high on the beach as if coveting the land.

"Well, what are you waiting for?" Violet called over her shoulder.

More than the prospect of icy water, Maddy shrank at the thought of getting naked. With a backward glance to check for voyeurs, she quickly shucked her plaid Ship'n Shore blouse and stern unnecessary bra; stepped, tripping, out of her pedal pushers. She was slim-chested and hairy and bony-kneed, she would die of mortification. Alongside Violet, a pink-and-gold nymph, she was the dark, ill-favored changeling left in a basket on the farmer's doorstep.

Violet was already striding, laughing excitedly, into the water. She splashed her arms and chest and face, gave a little yip, and plunged in.

Maddy mimicked her. The water delivered an icy smack. She dolphin-dove and stroked and kicked, and the sting subsided. Violet swam over. The water had slicked back her hair, turning it dark yellow, exposing her finely shaped ears. Their feet kneaded the khaki gloom below, water buoyed their breasts.

"Race you to the island!" Violet said.

She cut through the dazzled water in a racing crawl. Maddy paddled in her wake. The bay abruptly turned shallow where the dredged channel ended; her fingers struck bottom and she was knee-deep.

They sat on the putty-colored sand, legs drawn up, warming themselves in the sun. "Y'know, there's a little beach over there I've never been to"— Violet looked over her shoulder toward the far green island. "It's on the other side, you can't see it from here. We must go there one day. To the other side of the island."

She pointed out holes in the sand from which clams spit miniature geysers of water. Maddy was aware of Violet's small tortured hand, beringed and nicotine-stained, lying beside her haunch on the sand. The wine, the bracing water and sun kissing her skin; Violet so close, her twin, almost touching, though they wouldn't, of course—had tipped Maddy into a rapture roused only by music. She'd drunk too much Gewürzt—

"Oh, goddamn." Violet stared across the water. "Wouldn'cha know."

To Maddy's alarm, a red MG crawled along the causeway above the dunes.

"I was hoping the dumb regatta would keep him busy all day," Violet said.

A man in chinos and tennis shirt emerged from the MG and stood on the dunes looking across at them, hand shading his eyes from the sun. "Water nice and toasty?" he called, his voice staccato and mocking, uncannily close across the channel. Maddy tried to hunch her body out of existence.

"Come on in," Violet called back.

"Think I'm nuts like you?"

"Crazier," Violet shot back. She stood, raised her arms high in a pantherine stretch, looked around with studied indifference, and sloshed into the water.

Maddy watched in dismay, praying the interloper would drive off. He turned toward the squabbling in the osprey nest. The set of his head and ears like Violet's. Then he reached into a shirt pocket and put on sunglasses and continued to watch them from the dune. Aviator glasses, she saw; so he, too, could make out details. How would she navigate the space from sand to water? Slither belly-down, a sea turtle returning to its element?

From the bay rose a silvery peal of laughter. "You mustn't mind old Nicholas," Violet called. "He's used to a lot of nude prancing about. Oh, excuse me, how rude," she added, treading water. "Nick, I'd like you to meet Madeleine Shaye." She gestured at the islet. "Maddy, my brother, Nicholas Ashcroft." A salute toward the bluff. Then she kicked for the mainland in her slow, powerful crawl, feet churning up an aqueous chuckle.

Maddy had made a decision. Abruptly she stood. Nicholas Ashcroft remained stonily facing her. She braved the gaze behind the sunglasses a beat longer than was quite necessary. Then waded calmly into the water.

After the burn of nakedness, she welcomed the ice. What kind of crazy family was this? They certainly played by their own rules. Today a milestone, she thought, eyes open in the green water: she'd been *seen*. Then came a sense of injury. Had she been one of his fancy debutantes, Nicholas Ashcroft would have had the delicacy to turn away.

She tread water for a moment, arrested by a new idea. She'd been almost as troubled "prancing about" naked in front of Violet as in front of her brother.

WHAT COULD HAVE prepared her for the house? She sights it first as they curve down a road hugging a grand sweep of lawn; catches it next through the red-black leaves of a giant weeping hemlock. Now it comes into the clear, a greystone apparition rising on the bluffs above Weymouth Bay against the copper sun. Before it stands a single shell-pink dogwood.

"My God, it's a castle."

An assemblage of greystone peaks and towers, an actual crenellated tower with four upthrust parapets, ogival windows, mullioned bay windows—a Gothic fairy-tale vision, pure folly. "Great-Granddad Gus kept building onto the place to house his huge, I'm sure despicably behaved, brood. He needed to do *something* with his money. Please don't disappoint me by being *awed*."

"And please don't pull that snotty rich-kid number."

Violet stops the car and stares straight ahead, the diesel motor idling loudly. "Listen"—twisting her head this way and that—"how can I explain? I'm so used to—fending off. Christian and the others. I scarcely know how to do anything else. But I want"—she sighs mightily—"I so want you to like Conscience Point."

Like *me,* she means.

Violet looks through her for a long moment, beset by some idea, while Maddy takes in her dazzled gaze, her features of a young czar.

"Friends?" Violet sticks out a beringed hand.

Maddy squeezes the hand and closes her heart against Violet. She distrusts this instant unearned devotion. Distrusts the whole setup. The rich walk through the world collecting amusements, then toss them when they're bored.

"Isn't a neo-Gothic castle a little out of place by the sea?" Maddy says coolly. Eyes opaque. Yielding nothing.

"I'm afraid they got their geography rather m-m-muddled." In her eagerness to please, the stutter Violet affects sounds real. "The house was originally designed to overlook the Hudson River, but then old Gus decided to build it on Long Island 'cause the sailing's better out this way. Islesford's founding fathers wanted it razed. It's awfully Hollywood, don't you think? A back-lot heap from *Ivanhoe.*"

She parks carelessly under the porte cochere. In the vaulted ceiling adorned with blue fleurs-de-lis, four faces grimace down from each corner. The bronze door to the entrance is flanked by two Roman busts. Violet tosses her beige duster over one.

"No one's here, thank God. Probably tying one on at the Weymouth Yacht Club. Look, it's all fake," she says with a kind of disgusted admiration. She taps the door: "Bronze is really wood." Flicks the marble trim with her nail: "Faux *marbre.* Whole joint's really a wood-and-brick house faced in stone. There's a faux finish on almost everything. Just like our family," she adds with a joyless laugh. "But some materials are real, which really mixes things up good."

They enter a dim reception room with rose silk walls and a bear rug. "Let me show you around so you won't trip over some carcass on your way to the john." Violet places her hand in the small of Maddy's back in a manner distinctly masculine and steers her left. "Here's the music room, *your* room. Muthuh calls it the conservatory."

At the entrance looms a white marble winged Cupid sorrowfully taking leave of a reclining Psyche with raised arms. Maddy bends to read the inscription: "Love cannot dwell with suspicion." Her eyes sweep over a rose velvet couch with carved mahogany back. Ceilings vaulted in gold—wood posing as stone, she guesses. Leaded stained-glass windows running floor to ceiling, depicting scenes with a phoenix or peacock. And parked by the windows, the Bösendorfer, ebony splendor belying its anemic tone.

Linking her arm through Maddy's, Violet draws her into a library with green velvet chairs, a table covered in green felt, a bookcase with ogival moldings. The house silent but for the ticking of a giant floor clock in the hall, which makes the place seem all the more an unmoored stage set.

Violet bounds up a sweeping staircase with curved white marble banister—real marble, Maddy judges from its chill. "Come see my little pictures," Violet calls behind her. They enter a Uffizilike gallery with barrel-vault ceiling hung with family portraits. In a section by the windows, Maddy recognizes paintings by Violet similar to ones exhibited at Barnard: rectangular slabs applied with palette knife of marigold orange, cobalt blue, cadmium yellow. Maddy admires Violet's pastels of what she now recognizes as the idyllic beach they just left: greens in spring, russet in autumn. Violet is a gifted colorist, moving with ease from abstraction to landscape.

She stops before an oil painting lit by sun burning through the stained-glass window: a portrait of a young man of surpassing beauty, a Brahmin version of Pan. Fair hair, impudent nose, dreaming eyes, helplessly self-infatuated.

"That could be Lord Alfred Douglas, Oscar Wilde's lover," Maddy says.

"Linton? Yes, but Linny preferred women. *Me* at any rate. I painted him from a photo. He never would sit for me. Now he's with the angels in Green Glen," she says with sneering piety. "Left for a swim in the ocean one day and—"

Her eyes have a mad shine and Maddy wonders if all the Ashcrofts have a screw loose.

"Gotta watch the water in these parts," Violet says. She taps Maddy on the shoulder and nods solemnly. "Last year a flood tide washed out Egg-leston Bridge. A local contractor tried to cross it at night and drowned in his car. C'mon, let's find you a room."

She scoots up three small stairs to a pink-and-gold room. The bed's carved wood headboard rises to a peaked dome and mimics a Gothic church. Above it an enormous lozenge-shaped window of pink glass. The dark-blue ceiling is seeded with gold—or are they silver—stars.

"Decor's a bit *overwrought,* but I hope you'll be okay here. Bath." She nods toward a tub with claw feet. Maddy's eye falls on a section of bath-room wall that seems to be spilling out its guts: plaster, sand, what looks like horsehair. "Oh, well, never mind *thaht,*" Violet says. "When you're ready, come down for martoonies in the library. Unfortunately *they* might be here, though mother practically lives in the aviary. Maybe you'll play something for us before dinner? That sublime piece you were practicing at the college . . ."

"Chopin's *Harp* Étude."

"That one, yes. Oh, would you play it again?"

Maddy frowns. "I don't know. I'd feel I was earning my keep."

Violet pauses at the threshold, fair hair and one grey eye glinting in a ray of sun. "He hates me, you know," she says abruptly.

"Who?"

"Nicholas the Vain."

"Why?"

"Because he's as phony as the materials in this house. And I'm on to him. And he knows it." She draws closer and narrows her eyes. Maddy aware of her musk through the flowered blouse of jasmine cut with BO; the down above her retroussé upper lip like milkweed silk. For a second she's tempted to reach over and touch her finger to the downy place. Her arms hang leaden by her sides.

"Promise me something," Violet says, scratchy voice pleading. "That harebrained fiancée of Nick's should be a deterrent, but—promise you won't go and fall in love with my goddamn brother. Like everyone else."

WHAT HAD SHE SAID? And how would it have mattered?

CHAPTER 4

Jump

The French hall clock chimed twice; Sophie, predictably, late. Maddy lingered a moment longer over her new piano, a Model D concert grand with a German action made in Hamburg, chosen after weeks of testing different models in the basement of Steinway Hall. It had a resonant bass, rich middle register with a violalike quality, treble like a vibrant *ping!*

Upstairs in the starry bedroom, she stripped down for a spot of gardening. Considered herself in the closet mirror. The small breasts that had once mortified her had somehow, given gravity's tricks, become her friend. Now girlish was good. Without undue effort—and to the annoyance of other women—she remained slim, maybe from all those hours with the Chopin D Minor Prelude, rather like keyboard aerobics. Behind, she was pleasingly meaty and round, with two dimples above the cheeks on either side of her spine. From this angle the tell-all neck was invisible. . . .

She pulled on Nick's old tennis shirt and a pair of gardening gloves and went outside to trowel the perennial border hugging the music room's French doors. Tender green shoots of Jacob's ladder and phlox poked through the earth of the "autumn garden"—named by Laila for the valiant flowers of October blooming in this sunstruck bed against the long freeze.

On fine nights she and Nick ate dinner out here at the baronial table under the oaks, the hurricane lamps glowing orange and the quiet broken only by the groaner at Weymouth Bight warning sailors off shoals. Nick would whip up his lamb stew, schooled by years of doctoring cans of Dinty Moore in the galley of his treasured Herreshoff sloop, the *Cherubino*.

She'd never imagined you could love this hard yet keep yourself for your work. They swung through the hours, grooved as trapeze artists. Nick understood the musician's life, its ardor and implacable demands. At her concerts he sat beaming and proprietary in the third row, shooting dark looks at coughers. She in turn marveled at how he teased out the shapely book hiding in some windy manuscript; he had the storytelling equivalent of perfect pitch, one author had said. And she shielded Nick from his own devils. She was the steadier; the social enabler. For all his patrician poise—or because of it—Nick was skittish about engaging with sweaty reality. . . . Since France, she reflected, he'd been pissy as hell. No, something more troubling: *polite*. A thought ghosted through, uninvited: Why, after all these years, the still fresh rancor between Nick and Violet? Had Nick tried, as Violet had once claimed, to grab her share of the Point?

She brushed the dirt from her knees and went into the kitchen to check on lunch. In the fridge she found shrimp salad in avocado prepared by Olga, the niece of old Eugene from Serena days, who now helped him run the estate. Maddy carried a bottle of Islesford chardonnay and two cut-glass goblets out to the autumn garden and settled on a chaise.

Sophie. Writer, dog lover, world-class hypochondriac—and that rare New York soul not too conspicuously busy for friendship. In the envy capital of the world, they were squarely on each other's team. Sophie had left her husband, Lester, during the Great Wife Walkouts of the '70s, and cobbled together a living teaching remedial writing at community colleges, one of New York's marginalized boomers, as unanchored in her fashion as the homeless sleeping in doorways. She had more talent than luck: her last novel had sparked a buzz, but then her publisher had folded; her ship had come in only to sail right back out.

She was scarcely luckier in lovers. Alex, a bankruptcy specialist who called himself Repo Man, was loosely yet permanently married. The past winter in Vail his skull had encountered a tree, and he'd woken up resolved to "rethink his life"—as soon as he recovered from that ringing in his ear. To unsolicited advice Sophie would reply, "Better follow your bliss, because tomorrow"—rolling her eyes—"you could be *diagnosed*." Repo Man was only her latest emotional terrorist, an advance over the one who'd said, during sex, "Get the affect out of it." She'd become a fixture at New York singles bazaars, braving blizzards to attend hellish mixers and slumberous talks at the Explorers' Home for Men, whose members had never emerged from the great Icelandic Cave Dive. If her forebears from Odessa had dreamt of making their fortune in the new land, Sophie's fervent prayer was never again to attend a lecture on the blue-footed booby or the penis gourds of New Guinea. . . .

"*Sooo* sorry . . ." Sophie charged nose first around the verandah and collapsed on a chaise. Her hair was orange, after last month's sinister aubergine. "Naturally the old heap stalled in the Midtown Tunnel, with all these honking maniacs on my back—"

"What a nightmare. Otherwise you're good?"

"Anything this side of breast cancer is good." She sneezed; eyed the bayberry studded with white flowerets. "What, is this allergy season already?"

"Here, try some of the local grape. They say it prevents heart attacks." Maddy filled Sophie's wine glass.

"Madd, thanks for having me this weekend. City's so empty, could be a plague on."

"You know you're always welcome." In truth Nick was happiest with just the two of them rattling around Conscience Point—but Sophie's was a four-season loneliness, covering the Thanksgiving through New Year's trifecta, Super Bowl Sunday, Polish Easter, Bastille Day, the birthdays of dead presidents; and though three years off, there was the worry of a date for the millennium. Sophie envied anything, including the screaming pea-hawk, that "had a life."

"And in August you've got a share in that group house," Maddy added—though both knew that Islesford ranked "groupers" below the Mexican hedge clippers.

"Right. And now for the good news!" Sophie raised her glass. "Alex has finally left his wife!"

Maddy cleared her throat. "Well, that is . . . progress." She thought of Repo Man's fired missus, though the condo in Vail could dull the pain. Of course she herself had deprived a wife of a working husband. It was de-pressing, the violence women did each other. "You mean, Alex has recov-ered from the ringing in his ear?"

"Y'know, I never asked."

Maddy noticed the start of serious damage time was planning for So-phie's eyelids, and felt a surge of solidarity.

"But it's a done deal," Sophie went on. "He's as separated from his wife as . . . as Nick. Divorce is just too stressful for these guys. Remember what happened with George? Years of wrangling, papers finally signed—and he keels over at the clothesline art sale. Where are the assmen of yester-year? Writing memoirs about prostate cancer. Or paradise regained with that new Viagra stuff." A rapturous sigh. "Just think: the hunt is over. No more lectures on barnacle genitalia!"

"Well, to your new life." They touched glasses.

She went into the house to fetch the shrimp salad in avocado. It would not be possible to get through the day if everyone voiced her true thoughts.

. . .

"HEY, NICK MUST be a happy camper," Sophie said, licking low-fat crème fraîche from her spoon. "I just saw an item in *Publisher's Weekly* about his baby."

"Baby?"

"Yeah, Nick's hot author, Thom Stark, an avatar of . . . whatever."

Oh, the big book on Nick's winter list. She was getting as nutso as Sophie.

"You're a charmed couple. It's quite disgusting."

Maddy looked out over the bluffs at Weymouth Bay. A fleet of sailboats was starting a race from the yacht club. "Actually there's trouble in paradise."

"Oh, my God, Laila's another Tara," Sophie said on hearing the Guatemala plan. "But I doubt she'll split. Too attached to you." She twirled an orange curl. "When I think that at Yale Tara could have hooked up with a Lazard Frere . . . But no, she organizes the maintenance workers in a strike and then wants course credit for her run-in with the criminal justice system. I'm all for saving the world, but can't someone else's kid do it?"

Maddy laughed.

"This is what feminism has done for our daughters," Sophie went on. "They used to just want to fuck Che Guevara. Now they want to *be* Che. I tell you, one of these days they're going to run into a Third World goon squad."

Maddy related the shakeup at *Chronicle*.

"Oy, d'you think historians will name this age the Great Dumbing-Down? And my freelance stuff has dried up. Tara's classmates are running the shop, assigning stories only to those saucy types who get periods. And never heard of Plato's Retreat. You know, women weren't supposed to live this long. Uh, why do I feel you're not listening?"

"Sorry to lay all this on you," said Maddy, who had long held the view that her troubles might not be of consuming interest to others.

"What's goin' on?"

"On top of everything else"—she swung her feet to the ground and eyed Sophie—"over in France Nick said he wanted a baby."

"*What?* A grandchild would be more like it. And how cruel, considering your history." A moment. "And where does that leave you? I smell a rat."

"Please, I'm in no mood for paranoia." Maddy refilled their glasses and focused on the tiny curved sails like white parentheses in Weymouth Bay. "What kind of rat?"

Sophie honked into the Kleenex she kept on hand for the world's longest-running cold. "Well, Nick can't really want a baby. Got his hands full taking care of himself."

"This is why there's no female Galileo: we spend our time trying to decode men's motives."

"Anyway, Nick gets to play uncle or dadso with Laila."

"Well, sports buddy." Laila had crewed for Nick on the *Cherubino* in the Block Island races. This March they'd overlapped on a ski trip to Colorado.

Sophie narrowed her close-set eyes. "Sooo, it's just a decoy. We're looking at a classic midlife caper: guy wants to knock up dewy babe so he'll live forever. Men are terrified of death. Me, I'm afraid to die because I haven't *lived* yet. . . . You want my advice? I'd keep a sharp eye out. Maybe tomorrow night, at Amos Grubb's party."

"Damnit, Nick is peculiar: he wants what he already has. It's *familiarity* that turns him on. It's the way he's made. Besides, he's no Alex-type flake."

"So that's what you really think: Alex won't deliver."

They sat in tetchy silence. Clouds had vacuumed the sunlight. A crow the size of a dachshund emerged, cawing, from the bayberry. Keep an eye out? She'd lost her muscle for surveillance. It struck her that Nick had been looking peaky lately. Gnawed-at.

"Ever run into Nessa Trent-Jones?" Maddy said abruptly.

"Who? Yeah, actually. Publicist at Doubleday. They call her 'that Brit bitch.' Guess she wasn't real popular. Her dad's Lord Whozit. Sort of looks like . . . Merle Oberon crossed with Jennifer Aniston. Why d'you ask?"

"She's Nick's new publicity director."

"No shit."

A pair of white piping plovers with black markings cut jagged angles through the air, making for the bay. Sophie ground out an unlit cigarette in the grass with the heel of her sandal.

"Okay, wanna know what I think? I think Nick just got some bug up his ass and you'll never hear another word about it."

"You're trying to humor me."

"*Now* look who's being paranoid."

"It's the wine. Women shouldn't drink in the afternoon."

"Anyway, what's wrong with humoring? Humor me, *please.*"

SHE COULD BE in the Met's Egyptian Wing, ringed by multiples of King Tut's bride; the lasers and lifts had erased all variation in feature and age— an effect Maddy found oddly funereal. In fact, she stood at Amos Grubb's "affair" among A-listers from the New Money crowd—even in 1997, Islesford remained strictly segregated in things social and sporting, but she and Nick toggled between Old and New. Hand wrapped around a glass of Swedish water, Maddy made commiserative clucks at an arbitrageur who was flushing scrotal-dark as he ticked off the horrors committed by his contractor, glitches in the renovation you wouldn't believe. She couldn't remember precisely when it happened, but suddenly anyone who wanted to live had stopped drinking and grown boring.

A string quartet struck up over the babble. Maddy winced at hearing Dvořák as aural wallpaper; Musak, it was said, used to drive Bruno Walter from a restaurant. On a far terrace of Grubb's multilevel retreat she spotted Nick, sexy and tan in rumpled seersucker. He'd be searching for the new honcho at Literary Guild. Book of the Month had made an offer for the Stark, Nick's big winter book; now he needed the Guild's counteroffer to bid it up, and hoped this evening to sniff out their intentions. That Nick could charm a lintel post of course couldn't hurt. Maddy stretched her neck to follow his progress, but got distracted by their host, who was greeting guests, rationing out attention as strictly as a flight attendant in coach. Amos Grubb was a munchkin-sized developer who'd gotten his start in arson. He was also that tricky item, a mogul who aspired to write—a few of his sentences taken at bedtime, Sophie swore, was like Ambien without side effects. Maddy had a fondness for Grubb; his passion for Letters was keen and unrequited, and he revered all toilers in the arts. This evening, though, she wasn't eager for a conversation. Grubb might tap her to read the "generational novel" he was shopping around. In the current market, she'd heard Nick grouse, only novels by brand names got published; or "event" authors: metamysteries by convicted serial killers, etc.—but what was more sensitive than a mogul's artistic vanity?

Rowena Grubb, emaciated in crimson pajamas, swooped down on Maddy. "How *are* you my darling." She had the haunting gaze of prehuman intelligence. The light of dusk was pitiless. Rowena's face was smoothed so tightly upward and out, it left nowhere for her smile to go. "How's that *darling* Laila?" Maddy's mouth flapped open to answer, but Rowena had moved on.

Davidine Swann, entertainment reporter for the *Ledger*, came bustling toward them, hungering, no doubt, for CNB gossip. Maddy escaped into the frenzy surrounding a waiter in tux bearing a silver platter of plump pink prawns. Against the house stood a row of tables freighted with baby lamb chops, buttery filet mignon, sushi, crepes. "Cheez, ya need a U-Haul to eat all this," said a guest, forklifting a pile, thumb as a brace, onto his plate.

And *she* needed something besides Swedish water. Why do you hang with those people, Ma? Laila once asked. Well, let's see: because they were *there*, like the tonsured privet hedges. Enmeshed in her and Nick's assorted projects. And they relaxed her. You didn't need to be on your best behavior. Lousy reasons, of course, that satisfied neither Laila nor her . . .

Maddy headed for the bar, steering around an immense figure in a caftan chatting with two women thin as Biafran refugees. The bar was set up in a Bali Hai thatched hut. Beyond it stretched a pond stocked with swans and cygnets, overlooked by a mansion housing a Dominican order that required a tax-free earthly paradise from which to contemplate the heavenly one.

Her nerves still fried from the afternoon sail on the *Cherubino* . . . The wind dies, they break out the Bloody Marys. Bad karma all round. Nick baits Jed Oliver about defending "rapists and mental cases." Then Jed hammers Nick on his human-rights missions—"ego massage for limousine liberals." She tries to make things right for everyone, but the testosterone on board could sink the *Yankee Clipper*. Then Laila dives off the boat—and *disappears*. When she finally phones from Minty Theobald's yawl, Maddy wants to wring her neck!

Now she longed to pack it in; she'd feel better in the morning, the philosophy of middle age. And she needed to sound out Nick on some big changes. . . .

Over by the pool house Davidine Swann was busy corralling some writers for a group photo. The writers stood about and eyed each other suspiciously; each, after all, was *the competition*. Maddy recognized an author with ferretlike features who'd written a memoir about a four-year affair with her brother.

"They say she made the whole thing up, you know," said a swishy fellow nearby, a columnist for *Gotham.*

"Literature is all sleight of hand, so why not, it's legit," his friend answered. "Anyway, do I care? All I know is I have cancer and I can't get a doctor on the phone."

Maddy positioned herself to catch more of the columnist's rundown. "Call it the year of incest chic," he said. "Guy over there got it on with his mom. Now they've coauthored a memoir with alternating chapters. Oh, and the hot number in the pink pants? He plugs products in his novels in exchange for free advertising. And next to *him,* we have an author known as the junkie editor. Among other things, she tells how she got through customs with a condom's worth of heroin stashed in—"

A knot of guests pushed the columnist out of earshot.

Davidine finally snapped her picture, jubilant. So many envelope-pushers, immortalized in her photo. Maddy feared for Nick. How would Stark's novel make a dent among all this distinction?

WHERE THE HELL *was* Nick? They didn't do Siamese twins at parties, but normally by now would have checked in. Scanning the sea of bright dead hair and vulpine jaws, she spotted him a way off on the terrace above. Staring at Viqui Troutt-Matlin, a former model, who was cradling an infant. Her husband the PortoSan mogul, sporting an orange comb-over, looked like something decaying into the ground as it stood. Before her marriage, Viqui had achieved renown in Islesford by going down on her twin sister at pool parties thrown by the boss of her modeling agency. Now she chaired the Arts Society.

Nick still drooling over babies? Maddy felt a kick of anger. She stitched through the crowd toward the terrace, where Nick now sat, ear bent to a bronzed dude in Bermudas and sockless loafers. The guy was sopping up the attention. Nick's social skills, especially around Islesford, were a thing of beauty. He actively *listened,* asked interested questions, kept his gaze on *you*—instead of spouting the self-aggrandizing rant, eyeballs rolling on casters, that passed around here for conversation. But why was the dude about to fall into Nick's crotch? Nick's androgynous allure spoke to men, too. . . .

Don't go there, as Laila liked to say. On a sudden impulse, Maddy slipped out of Nick's sight line. She'd decided to track his moves around this party.

"You gotta check out the house." Sophie, orange mop frizzed by the salt air. "It's done in Instant Olde English. They say Rowena hired a 'bookcase decorator' to put leather first editions on the shelves. The collected works of Danielle Steele." She declined a crab puff offered on a silver chafing dish. "These parties are better than Weight Watchers. I mean, you see some geezer eating deviled eggs and laughing, it zaps the appetite."

A flurry near the entrance signaled the arrival of a hot young director. "Y'know what Gen X talks about?" Sophie said. "Lapping speed."

"In the pool?" said Maddy distractedly.

"No. Lapping as in 'going down on.' That's what Ben Affleck was discussing in this hip movie, *Chasing Amy*—"

Davidine emerged from nowhere and shouldered Sophie aside. "So how's Bern Conant going to revamp *Sunday Chronicle?*"

"Can we discuss it during business hours?" Maddy said, ever gracious. She wove toward the terrace where she'd last seen Nick. In his place sat a white black woman with freckles who was famous for something Maddy couldn't remember. Where had Nick gone? Her breathing too shallow. A man with Mark Antony bangs was complaining how hard it was to get through to Dr.—Maddy didn't catch the name—from Mount Sinai. "He's the lower-bowel specialist of the Western world."

She climbed another level to a sylvan glen, with a burbling waterfall and path of polished grey stones flanking the free-form pool. A New Age rhumba piped up behind designer grasses. "What's the deal on this new fountain of youth?" she heard. "Sheeps'-balls serum. I can get it f'ya wholesale." A sudden bolt of heat shot up her back, her cheeks and forehead went slick with sweat. Then, directly ahead, she saw Nick.

And a float of dark hair, a woman of surpassing loveliness. Her head angled toward Nick, lids lowered, lips parted in a smile. Maddy recognized that smile, but couldn't place it. Her heart fluttered somewhere near her collarbone like a trapped bird.

"Oh, Maddy, *there* you are, I want you to meet Nessa Trent-Jones, our new publicity director."

"So pleased to meet you." Plummy Brit accent, hand cool in her own clammy one. She gazed at Maddy with the peculiar doubled-back vision of beautiful women: *I see you seeing me.*

"We've been brainstorming about getting a buzz going for the Stark," Nick said.

"Strategizing about how to position the book," Nessa added, nothing between her and her silk tee.

"Position the book," Maddy said. She'd long ago failed the penny test.

"You know what a pain in the ass Stark is about marketing himself," Nick said, eye severe.

"I do, a real pain in the ass," she echoed.

A muscle ground in Nick's jaw. "Nessa's actually persuaded Stark to go out on the road to promote his book. Do some TV, a few readings. He's been balking for months. I couldn't get anywhere with him. But Nessa is very persuasive."

"Looks like you two will make a great team. Well! I'll leave you to it!"

Somehow she'd arrived at the house. A Sophie dictum popped into her head: *Never marry a guy who's cuter than you.* She walked down a long hall lined with potted palms, noting the fronds were partly painted onto the wall behind. The bedroom a floral explosion by Ralph Lauren. A set of monogrammed Vuitton luggage lay open on a stand, black lacy undergarments dripping out. "VTJ" embossed in gold letters on leather. Several white tampons lay scattered on the spread. Vanessa Trent-Jones? She must be a weekend guest of the Grubb's. Maddy looked at the tampons. The years of blood and desire and baby-making had been the center. Without the life of the body, what remained? A haggard image drew her toward the bathroom mirror—when had she become her mother? She remembered now where she'd seen Nessa's smile: on the woman with all the luck.

NICK PLANTED A KISS on the crown of her head. "Mmm . . . lilac." In fact, jasmine by Annick Goutal—and *he* smelled of Gauloises, which he must be sneaking behind the barn.

He sank, loose-limbed, into his customary chair, hair nudging his collar, dissolute-sexy in his weekend stubble. Sophie and Laila off at the Islesford Cinema to see *L.A. Confidential*. Maddy kicked off her shoes, struggling, with help from Glenfiddich, to lower the volume on unproductive thoughts. Her eyes wandered over their lair: lime velvet chairs; vaulted ceiling—the plaster mimicking stone—with cornices of gold fleurs-de-lis; French doors crowned with stained-glass Celtic crosses. In an alcove, a white marble bust of Voltaire pondered human folly. They lived here in the library, trundling their meals from the kitchen on a tray; and in the music room and their second-floor bedroom, its dark-blue ceiling seeded with silver stars. Maddy sometimes felt they were children camping out in a castle, its other rooms sealed and dark and under a spell, waiting for revelers in bright colors and a throw of the switch to jolt them awake.

"Sorry I've been a grouch lately."

"Guess we need more grouch pills," Maddy said lightly; wondering where on Bleecker Street Laila had bought that vial of jelly-bean "pills." Nick offered a thin smile. Whatever was troubling him, they would deal with it.

"By the way, Amos Grubb wants me to look at his 'roman à clef,'" Nick said. "If he knew how many people 'got a story to tell.'"

"Amos would give a fortune—and probably will—to get recognized as a writer. Why don't we help him out and find him a ghost?"

"Mmm, good idea. Oh, reminds me—Minty Theobald has done *us* a favor. He's come on board as a Benefactor—you know, for the Chamber Fest. I'd say the war chest's looking good."

She clapped her hands together; smiled at him over her steepled fingers. "You did it, Nicky, you're *brilliant!* We've got our summer season. . . ." She rose and planted a loud smooch atop his balding spot. For months now Nick had been lobbying his old-boy cronies to cough up, a ticklish business since (a) the fest was dominated by New Money, and (b) Nick was the least *hondeling* of men. . . . But for her he'd suppressed his good breeding.

"Wish I could do something brilliant for my*self*," he muttered into her chest. "Guild's gonna pass on the Stark."

Drawing back: "Ouch, *no* offer? Oh, damn, I'm so sorry. What are those idiots thinking." She'd thought at worst a lowballer from this book club.

"New kid in charge says the novel's not commercial enough and hasn't got the 'preexisting audience.' The Guild at least used to sneak in a few books with the schlock. Now it's pure schlock."

No wonder he was doing Gauloises. And to think she'd been throwing a tantrum in Nessa's bathroom at Grubb's while Nick was getting this news. "You do have the other club, Book of the Month."

"Without the Guild to bid them up, BOMC knows they can pay us next to nothing. I laid out big bucks for the Stark."

Too much, too much. She'd never cared for the Stark, a sprawling

World War I saga set in France that was being positioned—by Nessa, no doubt—as the gay *English Patient.*

"Without a big book-club sale, it's gonna be tough to recoup our money. Very tough."

"But there's still the paperback auction," she said.

"Don't expect much excitement there after the Guild pass." Nick unfolded from the chair and pushed open one of the French doors to the garden. It had sprinkled, and a scent wafted in of honeysuckle and humus and salt. It mingled with the museumlike must peculiar to Conscience Point, and another scent, echoing her own, that hung like a trapped ghost in the mansion's dark deserted rooms: jasmine.

"Nick, surely getting Book of the Month means *something.* You believed in this book—and should still."

"Nah, with the Guild pass, it's gonna sink right off the launch ramp. And when it doesn't earn out, we know whose head will be on the chopping block. Could you not humor me? Like someone on death row praising his last meal?"

She bridled, then let it roll off her. Nick was damaged in ways hard to fathom; she'd known that from the first—and had to concede he was in for it with this one.

"I hate what publishing's become, the whole yahoo mentality," Nick went on. He sank into his chair and crossed an ankle over his knee, displaying a once navy topsider rotted by brine. She teased him that his distressed wardrobe was a jibe at the local squires in Ralph Lauren.

"It's definite, by the way. Greenaway is giving an imprint to that goombah who packages bios of TV celebrities. Not healthy for *my* imprint. Blame the fucking international conglomerates, pressuring us to produce profits of 18 percent, what they expect from film or television."

Maddy swirled the ice in her glass. "I hate what my job has become, too.

You try to dumb-down, but there's no bottom to down. And why should I pretend to be something I'm not."

They sat in companionable silence as the works in the hall clock whirred up mightily for a strike.

A flutter-kick of nerves. "Nick, why don't we jump ship and change our lives."

He startled as if hearing a gunshot. Set his glass down with excessive care on the green felt table. "In the middle of everything? I can't think of—retiring."

"No, of course not. We'd . . . shift gears."

"Oh, that self-help jargon."

"Forget the *words*." She sat before him on the table, shoving aside books, eyes shining. "Maybe this is the moment to quit the old day job. We've got some money. No need to tie ourselves in knots to please the cheesemeisters. You've been saying you want more time for Americas Watch. And you'll write—the book about *Transatlantic* and Paris in the '60s. I'll spend all my time on music. We can do exactly what we want."

His eyes clouded—in panic?

She swallowed. "I thought we could create our own art colony, right here at the Point."

"Art colony?"

"Yeah, like we've talked about, you know, on and off. We'd invite writers, the new composers . . . pianists to give master classes," she rushed on, hearing her own voice. "We'd hold evening readings. Maybe bus out kids from the projects for a music immersion week . . . We'd restore the big house. Laila could keep the cabin, or we'd set up a musician out there, it's plenty quiet. We'll incorporate and apply to foundations for money to renovate. Hell, maybe Amos Grubb would pitch in. He once tried to start that artists' retreat, but the town board shot him down. I'd put up money, too." She paused, breathless. "*Talk* to me."

Nick stared at her as if she'd proposed holding up the local 7-Eleven. "It's a huge undertaking. This place is a ruin—"

"We can start small. Restore a few rooms in the main house."

"You seem to forget: I'm not the sole owner."

She removed her hands from his knees. Merely pronouncing the name "Violet" turned him into Mr. Hyde. "But a good estate lawyer could structure a deal. You could buy out the *co-owner*"—ironic emphasis—"who has shown zero interest in the place for thirty years. You could jointly sell off a chunk of land to raise cash."

"Look. Even if it were possible to structure a transfer of property— which is far from certain—Would you let me breathe?" (though she'd said nothing) "I've got to shepherd the Stark book through—"

"Of course. But after that—"

"But editor is what I *do*. Jesus, everyone over thirty getting canned, me hanging on by my nails and you're telling me to step aside?" *As though she were trying to unman him.*

She moved to the sideboard and turned to face him. "What is this really about, Nick. I feel you've been shutting me out—ever since France."

"It's not 'about' anything. That psychobabble again. Next we'll be 'owning our issues.'"

"C'mon, that's a cheap shot. Does your wanting to stay on the job"— *let it go* . . . "have to do with Nessa Trent-Baldwin?" she said.

"Jones. Trent-Jones." Nick shook his head. "I can't believe I'm hearing this."

"I can't believe I'm saying it. But I need to ask, Nick. Humor me."

"God, it's like Fernande—"

"In no way is it like Fernande." A moment. "Listen, I saw you and Nessa—"

"Yah, two desperate people trying to figure out how to bail water from a sinking ship."

"Isn't Nessa a bit . . . green?"

"I hired the best."

"And best-looking."

"It's the game, you know that—we need someone tuned in to the youth market." He stood; jammed his hands in his pockets. Not looking at her: "I want to go back to the city. I'm sorry."

"Wait a minute—"

"I'm *sorry*."

"We try to clear the air, and you clear out?"

"I don't want to stay here tonight. I'm sorry."

"Stop saying 'I'm sorry'!" She clasped her hands before her. "I hate to think of you driving in such a state." *And going where?*

"I'm not in a state and I'll phone when I get in."

"Don't take the short cut, the bridge could be flooded out this early in the summer."

They stood watching each other warily from opposite sides of the room. "Nicky, you're not sick or anything, are you? You'd tell me if you were sick, wouldn't you?"

"I would. I'm not sick. I'm fine."

"I don't know—how to fight with you," she said in a small voice.

A moment. "Actually, we had the Charles Lindbergh fight." He sounded relieved. She'd accused him of defending Lindbergh's anti-Semitism. "Maybe it's not so bad to fight sometimes. It's damn peculiar not to fight."

She pushed out some words. She heard the door to the porte cochere snap shut. She heard the French clock ticking in the hall. She heard the crackle of tires on gravel. He would not get to the end of the drive before he turned around, swiping the copper beech with the car's aerial— impossible to separate leaving things so ragged. Then they would drive into town to Sal's for some late-night pizza. She remained propped against the sideboard, each tick of the clock hammering her. He'd make it to the Mobil Station, then hook a left and circle back. They might go to Sparky's instead, down on the dock, for *moules mariniere*. The *moules* were never gritty at Sparky's and the chef went easy on the garlic. Sophie always said, *I know the affair's over when he keeps asking if I've eaten garlic.*

They hadn't even kissed good-bye!

Tires crunched gravel like a reprieve. A door slammed. Steps. Joy. A voice, Sophie's. Another *kerthunk,* now Laila. Voices plaintive and thin, mingling with a presence lighter than breath and never wholly absent, a banished spirit out in the blackness.

CHAPTER 5

Gothick

She biked the blind curves of Wildmoor toward the Point—fortunately few cars strayed onto the property at night; the locals considered it haunted by Linton and other ill-fated Ashcrofts from generations past. The dogwood, buffed by moonlight, cut white trefoils against the dark oaks. She swung onto Point Road; pedaled over Eggleston Bridge and onto the causeway, tires crunching the odd clamshell. Peepers thrummed full throttle, a giant pipe organ in the marshes. Straddling her bike on the bluff, she watched the moon's train of silver wobbling in the inky chop.

How to fit the workaday Nick of the past eight years with to-night's . . . chilly bastard? The two Nicks seemed mismatched head shots Scotch-taped together: the lovely Nick and his horrid twin. *We spoil each other,* she'd once told Sophie. This despite Nick's blue meanies—really, he was a candidate for a pharma fix, but of course dismissed shrinks as "charlatans." Had a subterranean fault opened even before France—as far back as March? Since that ski trip to Aspen? Shit, did Nessa ski?

Tipping her bike on its side, she perched, wary of splinters, at the top of the stairs. The bay's tinseled surface smoothed her like a mantra. . . .

After Virgin Gorda and all the high romance, Nick—an unforeseen bonus—had proven *menschy.* He did girlfriend things, like shop, waiting sheepishly outside Bloomie's dressing room. He came with her to the MRI.

He cooked—partly by necessity. She'd curdled the beef Stroganoff for a dinner party, but Nick just laughed it off; their unspoken compact was *never blame the other;* the word "Strogo" became their code for gastric alert. Sure, he was bossy as hell in the kitchen, and as for the cleanup . . . But *ta-da!* he'd set out steaming bowls of *zuppa di pesce,* exuding essence of sea. Or linguini and white clam sauce—after shucking the clams himself on the great table under the oak; he knew just how to lever the clam knife into the shell's resisting muscle hinge—even clams wanted to live! Sunday morning brought omelets from leftovers in the fridge. Before concerts, he'd fire her up a porterhouse for energy. She felt literally nourished by Nick.

And the way he'd made room for Laila—after Marshall, a finicky bachelor who *tolerated* her daughter as part of the package. Snapshot: Nick crotch-deep in the bay, droplets seeded like diamonds in his tawny chest hair. That medallion of rough she burrowed into nose first at night. The happy times. Nick the Commodore at the wheel of the *Cherubino,* smiling around a Winston dangling off his lip, one eye half-shut, wind whipping his hair . . . Nick teaching ten-year-old Laila the crawl, starting with the dead man's float. *Keep your head in the water and blow out. . . . Kick, kick . . . No, head in the water!* Laila fearful, a city kid; her idea of water the suspiciously tepid public pool on Leroy Street. She herself a conservatory rat to whom nature meant what you passed through to get to the next concert hall. Enter Nick, with his WASP cult of man against the elements; playing *Two Years Before the Mast* in a yellow sou'wester as gale-force winds made the *Cherubino* groan and keel, and sent her tottering into the hold . . .

To her and Laila he'd opened the green world. Ritual hunts along streams for shoots of skunk cabbage, the earliest sign of spring. Those "pub crawls" in the Shawangunk Mountains in upstate New York. Autumn rambles through Islesford's "walking dunes." *Pick up the pace, goils,* he'd call, sandy head vanishing over a dune. . . . Nick taught Laila to wind up and really throw a ball, no weak sister stuff; man the coffee-grinder winch and trim the jib aboard the *Cherubino*. Camp CP, they'd dubbed the Point. Snapshot: Nick sits on the beach, Laila standing behind him in her droopy tank suit, a schmear of jam on her mouth, skinny brown arms draped around his neck . . . *My peeps*. Her word for Mom and Nick. With Nick they're complete.

And something more: playing the Schubert "Wanderer" one evening, she glances up to see Nick leaning against the French doors, spellbound, like a dreaming troubadour from a Giorgione painting, straining to catch something beyond the frame—an eerie *double* . . . joined with her in the secret rapture . . . He guarded her practice time like a duenna the family virgin. Nick's patrician disregard for money was deeply irresponsible, but it amused her. Sure, they could have used the cash, yet he declined all offers from Amos Grubb and friends for a chunk of Conscience Point—to keep the real estate lawyers out of his brain, he explained.

A snapshot from her night table on Jane Street: Nick a blur of wood-chopping, bare-chested in chinos and LL Bean boots, at an Ashcroft "camp" in Maine. The hair might be going, his skin faintly slackening, but he'd stayed lean and muscular. How had she remained enamored after the years of familiarity, the shared bathrooms, the potential for disgust inspired by another's body? She loved the silkiness of him, his fairness, a particular new-mown scent around his scalp, just above the ear. Daylong her pores gave off his most intimate odors. She liked the taste of his semen. He stood between her and the vertigo of solitude, of falling off the edge of the known world. They were mates in every way that mattered.

And now tonight . . .

She conjured Nick's face of an hour ago: obstinate, obtuse, like a dope-sniffing dog she'd once seen working the baggage at Kennedy.

She struggled to her feet, creaky from sitting in the damp, and settled on the bottom step, where the dune's tall shoulder formed a shelter against the wind. Well, Nick hadn't been so princely at that first go-round, either. May '66 at the Point, the first visit with Violet. Talk about hostile attraction. Then again, when it came to each other, the whole family seemed engaged in a blood sport. *Nick hates me, you know,* Violet had said. *I'm on to him. And he knows it. . . .*

AFTER THE PICNIC with Violet, she'd lingered in her second-floor bedroom; in no hurry to descend and brave the appraisal by Violet's mother and brother; almost missing her loyal beau Leonard. A crunch of tires on gravel drew her to the window: a red MG pulled up under the porte cochere. From the driver's side emerged a head of mussed tawny hair, tennis shirt with popped collar, canvas shoes called topsiders. Nick Ashcroft, Violet's big brother. Maddy colored. Barely an hour earlier at the beach, this man had seen her naked. From the passenger side slid a pair of bony knees and molded calves—pedigreed legs; then a white sailcloth dress with an inverted green triangle. Maddy felt jealous, and the full absurdity of that.

She retreated to a mirror set on a marquetry dressing table inlaid with mother-of-pearl. Head too big for her small frame, pushed-out mouth, fierce brows—all she needed was a babushka, she thought in despair. She wore her fancy "concert" dress, a black organdy empire affair with tiny flowers; gathered beneath her unimpressive bosom, the effect literally fell flat.

You've grown into your face, Nick sometimes said. *Have I told you you're prettier now?*

Drinks passed in a blur. "Martoonies," Violet called them. Laughing, she "reintroduced" Maddy and Nick, and his eyes rested briefly on her and went dead, like a blown bulb, and she thought, *Don't these people have manners?* The library they sat in resembled a Gothic rectory. Fernande, Nick's date, had a lank pageboy like a spaniel's ears and skin that had never known the sooty breath of the BMT to Queens Plaza. Serena Ashcroft, the mother, was as remote as the oil-painted ancestors lining the stairwell, her rain-colored eyes so vacant as to appear blind. She talked about Poombah, who could whistle "God Bless America," and Dingo, who was very protective of his mother, and only much later would Maddy realize Serena had been talking about her cockatiels.

The rest of the time the three of them chatted about skiing in St. Anton, some scandal at Choate (which she vaguely remembered as a prep school), and eight-meter racing machines, whatever those were. She could find no entry into their chatter. Violet looked tipsy and seemed to have forgotten her. Eugene, a pale man dressed in black like a seminary student, seemed to be the only servant; he alternately rushed about with strange mechanized motions and stood posted behind Serena staring straight ahead, like one of the marble statues throughout the house. Maddy wondered if he were also the cook. Occasionally Serena would whisper instructions to Eugene. Maddy guessed they had to do with keeping the pewter shaker of martoonies away from Violet.

She was exquisitely aware of the sun-burnished hair on Nick's forearms. His grey eyes. The patrician tilt of his nose. A misaligned tooth when he deigned to smile. Maddy rationed the amount of time she could look at him. He was slim like a fencer and wore white ducks literally held up with a belt like a rope around a gunnysack. Nick a masculine version of Violet—on him the face might be a shade *pretty*. Maddy searched for more flaws, to armor herself. If he merely brushed against her out there in the hall, she would dissolve. Or tell him to go straight to hell.

She tried to conceal her astonishment at the dining room. Everyone huddled at one end of the enormous table, defeated by scale. An ornate credenza from the Inquisition hugged a side wall, and at the table's center stood an ebony statue of Diana the huntress. Maddy eyed her five glasses: What were they all for?

"But you were doing so well at *Time*," Serena said in her booze-and-smoke-cured voice. "Why would you throw over a mah-velous job to drift around Paris?"

Maddy eyed Nick across the table. Her dream was to live and study music in Paris.

"*Drift*, mother? I'll be managing editor of the *Transatlantic*," he said in his nasal staccato. "I'll be at the red-hot center, publishing the best writers in America and Europe. And the magazine's a kind of salon. Styron's there, James Baldwin . . ." He talked on, hurling himself against Serena's vacant gaze, unfolding plans that included living on a barge on the Quai Malaquais.

"I still can't see why you'd leave a peu-fectly nice job with Mr. Luce."

"*Time* is a soul-suck. And Mother, Hedley Donovan is in charge now."

Nick had yet to address Maddy. He directed his conversation at the others, she might be invisible. She noticed Eugene at her side extending a silver dish. Maneuvering some grey meat onto her plate, she lost a drop of gravy to the ivory lace place mat—a *gaucherie* that did not escape Fernande, who winked at her.

"Oh, isn't the 'expatriate in Paris' a bit passé?" put in Violet, who hadn't said much. Her eyes looked glazed and bellicose and seemed to roll sideways. "It's more 'in' to follow the maharishi to India. . . ."

Maddy saw Serena whisper to Eugene. He glided behind Violet and captured a cut-glass decanter.

Nick eyed Violet's gauzy Hungarian blouse. "And I guess it's 'in' to expose your tits."

"Children, please," said Serena absently.

"I plan to be in Paris in the fall, too," Maddy jumped in, her timing somehow wrong.

Eyes converged on her, a void suddenly become a person.

"I'm going to compete in the Queen Elizabeth of Belgium. And if I place, I'll study with Alfred Cortot at the Paris Conservatory."

Nick looked full at her across the table, where she sat to Violet's right, as if just discovering her presence. Heat blasted up her chest and neck.

"What are the chances of placing in a competition?" said Fernande with her odd demismirk.

"Oh, Maddy plays like an angel," said Violet, slurring words. "She won a scholarship to Juilliard." She turned to Maddy, releasing a musk of jasmine and sweat. "Would you play for us after dinner? Would you please?" She rose, seized the decanter off the credenza, and sat heavily down.

"Deah, don't you think you've had enough?"

"I'm gonna live in Paris, too," Violet announced.

"Better go easy on the sauce or you're gonna live at the drying-out farm," said Nick. "Anyway, I thought there was a wedding planned before Christmas."

"Just changed my mind."

"Louise, don't talk a lot of nonsense," Serena said.

Maddy's head whipped around. *Louise?* Had she heard right? No reaction from the others.

"I'll study drawing at the Atelier Hayter in Montparnasse," Violet went on. "They say Hayter gives the best classes in life drawing."

"Have you told Christian about your change of plans?" Nick asked.

"How could I? I only just decided this minute."

Serena cast her pale eyes heavenward like the martyred St. Agnes.

"You don't seem terribly pleased that we'll be together in Paris, Nicko."

"Maybe I don't want to mop up after a lush."

"Go fuck yourself, Nick."

"Louise, I must ask you to leave this table," Serena said.

Violet struggled up from her chair. "Why would I stay? And don't *you* get all righteous. All you care about are those filthy birds." She smiled witchily at Nick. "And *you* wanna grab all the goodies without having to pay the piper."

Nick's hand gripped the table, his knuckles white. "Oh, go clean up your own sty," he called after her.

THEY MOVED IN SILENCE to the music room for coffee.

"That girl . . . my nerves," Serena murmured. She pressed her blue-veined hands, heavy with amethysts, to her temples.

"Let 'er sleep it off," Nick said. He sat with Fernande on a rose velvet settee with a carved wood crest on the back. He whispered something into Fernande's spaniel hair and she gave a little shiver and laughed. Seated stiffly on her tufted chair, Maddy watched them the way you might tongue a throbbing tooth, and plotted her exit.

"Deah, do you think you might play the piano for us?" Serena said.

"She's not a trained monkey, Mother," Nick said from Fernande's neck.

She. No doubt he didn't know her name. Maddy murmured about the late hour and not being warmed up. She felt it beneath her dignity to entertain on command; and she'd be damned if she'd provide a backdrop for the lovers.

"Actually, I would *adore* to hear you play, after that buildup of Violet's," Fernande said, hand on Nick's thigh.

"Something soothing," said Serena, pale eyes bulging.

Abruptly, not speaking, Maddy walked to Violet's vaunted Bösendorfer and opened it. When everything around you was going to hell . . . She'd *show Nick*, the supercilious prick.

She hung over the keyboard like a hovercraft. Then, placing her fingertips on the keys, she launched into Chopin's *Aeolian Harp* Étude. Faces, objects, the room fell away. Pressing into the keys with the full force of her shoulders and arms, she coaxed out the gentlest of sounds, dissolved into the music, an undulation in A major, wind and moonglow playing strings, the melody dreaming toward distant shores, lapsing back . . . billowing forward, licking closer, closer. . . . She struck the last note like a feather touching earth, and sat, hands in lap, head bowed. Silence.

She heard clapping and looked up to see Nick's face hanging over her.

"Why didn't Vi tell us?" he said angrily, as if catching out an impostor.

"She did, darling, she did." Maddy heard the click of Fernande's cigarette lighter.

"But you're world class," Nick went on in a barely nicer tone. He gazed at her hands, small, but with a python's reach. "Could I ask—could you bear—? I'd give anything to hear that piece again."

"Maybe Madeleine would rather play something different."

Serena speaking.

"And then after the Chopin—" Nick leaned toward her; his grey eyes were ringed with dark irises like a rare flower. "There's a piece by Schubert I've been dying to hear. A kind of waltz that sounds like a farewell to the world."

" 'Les Soirées de Vienne.' "

"Yah, I think that's it!"

"I love those pieces." Actually a Liszt transcription of Schubert, but she didn't want to sound pedantic.

"Darling, we mustn't impose on Violet's guest."

Fernande again. Nick leaned in closer. "I hope you protect that talent. The world will conspire against you." She thrillingly aware that he spoke as if they were alone. "You'll throw it all away. Girls do."

"*I* don't."

"Good!"

His patronizing heartiness jolted her back. Even when they flattered, these people offended.

"I have an idea," Nick said. "Let's turn out the lights. I want to hear the Chopin with just the moonlight shining in."

"Heavens, how will Mad-e-line *see*," Fernande protested as Nick moved about the room, dousing lights.

Nick returned and stood at the piano, leaning his elbow against it, chin cupped in his palm. The room now sunk in shadow but for silvered light puddled on the keyboard.

Maddy played the *Harp* Étude again; and after that "Les Soirées de Vienne," Schubert's farewell to the fever of life; and then she played the great D-sharp Minor Étude by Scriabin, steeped in Russian melancholy and impossible longing, delivered its heart's cry straight to Nick—until Fernande observed they really couldn't impose on Violet's guest any longer, couldn't expect Mad-e-line to play a whole concert, now, could they?

CHAPTER 6

Blond Sweat and Dark Stars

A fter that they all disappeared. Maddy felt used and tossed.
Where had they gone? She guessed Serena was off with the Papagenos, or whatever she called her bird children. She roamed the halls upstairs, laid with faded Persian carpets. At the far end, she put her ear to Violet's closed door. *Let 'er sleep it off.* Besides, she wasn't sure what she wanted of Violet or Violet of her. In a way she couldn't define, brother and sister vied in her mind for her attention. For the moment she wanted only to sort through her images of Nick.

She shrugged on her corduroy jacket and slipped out the French doors in the library; rounded the verandah, heading she scarcely knew where. Below the bluff, the bay was hoarding moonlight. Everyplace else had the dimness of a negative. She drifted down an allée, drawn by a grove of blossoms glowing psychedelic white. Gardenias, she recognized the perfume. These People, as she now named them, struck a dissonant chord among all this beauty. She moved toward the stone wall of a garden. Froze.

At the far end rose a statue of a winged Cupid bent over a reclining Psyche, and at its base sat Nick, spectral in the moonlight, eyes shut, head back, a woman drooped before him. Her head dipped, rose, dipped. Somehow Maddy the convent girl knew exactly what Fernande was doing and exactly how what she was doing affected Nick. And that she ought to disappear. But couldn't find the will to move. Suddenly Nick's head snapped back, throat arched, shoulders convulsed—he cried *oh oh* several times in a voice she didn't recognize. Fernande drooped lower and Nick gathered her up in his arms, pressed her to him—and in the same moment saw Maddy. A smile curved his lips. Folding Fernande against him, he moved his mouth over her hair, murmuring, smiling, never taking his eyes off *her*.

SHE'D ESCAPED TO the gardenias when Violet materialized in a duster and trailing chiffon scarf, like some revenant from the Edwardian age. "I hope you won't go and side with *them*," she said without preamble.

No apology or explanation for her disappearance. "Side with whom?" Maddy whispered, the image of Nick and Fernande still burning her retina.

"Why you whispering? Mother and Nick of course." A huff of exasperation. "They're conspiring to send me away. And they'll try to suck you into the plot."

Violet headed for the walled garden. "Come along," she urged when Maddy hesitated. No sign of Nick and Fernande. The tulips bordering the pebbled paths had shut their waxy chalices as if on a secret.

"Where would they want to send you?" Maddy said. And why should Nick "pay the piper"? she wondered, remembering Violet's parting shot in the dining room.

"Doesn't matter—just out of their lives. Married to Christian, living in Bedminster, riding to the hounds—the life I was bred for, and death to an artist. If I don't play along, it's off to McLean for attitude adjustment. Their 'concern' is a charade. They only want not to have to bother. I subvert the natural order."

Whatever *that* meant, thought Maddy. The rich *are* different—they don't bother to make sense. "Y'know, you've been given so much—"

"We're land rich but cash po'," Violet cut in, misunderstanding. "Whatever Father left me is tied up in trusts, and anyway he ran through scads of money, thin blood and too much sauce. When Mother shuffles her mortal coil, Nick and I will get this place, but would he sell it? Would I?"

"Violet, why does Nick have it in for you?"

She hesitated. "I'm on to him. His dirty little secrets. A family affair," she added brusquely. Glanced about, chased by a fresh thought. "Y'know, when we were on the beach this afternoon, this place seemed a paradise. If only one could live here with a soulmate." She fixed Maddy with dazzled eyes. "Maybe you *should* seduce Nick. Pinch him from that harebrained debutante. Then you'd become part of the family, and you and I could live here and create our republic of art."

Pinch him from Fernande? Fat chance. "What about Christian?" said Maddy, playing along.

"Oh, well, I'd marry the booby, but you and I could still . . . come here," she said vaguely. "In fact, why don't you."

"Why don't I what."

"Come spend the summer here. It would be mah-velous. What d'you say."

She sensed that for all her bravado, fiancé, trappings, Violet was at bottom a hurt girl. Alone. But she couldn't afford to be buffeted by Violet's whims. "I have to practice for the Queen Elizabeth," she murmured, pulling her jacket close.

"Practice here! What better place! You'll have your piano, the music room—and no interruptions. I'll paint in my studio upstairs—we'll be ruthless. Mother lives with those filthy birds or takes a villa in Todi. Eugene won't dare bother us. Say you'll do it!"

For a second, Violet's gaze merged disturbingly with Nick's, like some trick photo. "We'll see," Maddy muttered. Eugene *won't dare?* The highhanded phrase grated. Tracing the mazelike paths, they'd circled back to the winged Cupid. At the memory of Nick's groans, Maddy's knees went weak. "This is the same statue as in the music room. Remind me of the story."

"Cupid is telling Psyche bye-bye. He's splitting because Psyche didn't trust him—maybe she had her reasons." Violet crouched down, flax hair curtaining her face, and read the inscription. " 'Love cannot dwell with suspicion.' That's what Cupid's telling Psyche, the bastard."

THE NEXT MORNING Violet went riding and Maddy sequestered herself in the music room with Schubert's late, great B-flat Major Sonata, her concert opener. She was entranced with its Scherzo, the shifts through many keys that kept the listener on edge. And the sense of something ominous beneath its jaunty lightheartedness moved her to tears. At some point the hall clock chimed twice, snapping her back.

Violet had promised to return by two to drive her to the train. She packed away her scores and went out to the porte cochere with her battered plaid suitcase; scanned the sweep of lawn, its new grass fine as baby hair, for some sign of her hostess. A trill of laughter, and Fernande and Nick emerged from around the verandah, his arm about her waist. They wore tennis whites and looked burnished and perfect and forever immune to disappointment.

Nick quickly sized up the situation. "Don't tell me she's left you stranded."

"Violet went riding and said she'd be back by two—"

They both turned to look at the road curving beyond the dogwood tree. A cardinal alighted on a branch, crimson and black against the coral blossoms.

"Time's your train?"

"Two-forty."

"Typical." The little huff the Ashcrofts had patented. "Here, I'll run you over." Nick jerked his head toward the red MG parked beneath the porte cochere.

Maddy sat knees and lips pressed together in the low-slung seat. Clearly Nick considered it a *chore* to drive her to the station. Nothing to say now; finito last night's adulation; she'd gotten chucked with the morning's coffee grounds. She hugged her side of the MG jouncing along the pitted road and looked unseeing at the spring glories of Wildmoor Drive, the warm breeze delivering whiffs of the driver's blond sweat.

She saw Fernande's lowered head dipping and rising, and felt a spasm through her middle, a moistness in her crotch. Did he imagine she'd purposely spied on him? she thought, shamed and furious. And he'd stared at her naked at the beach. . . . She placed a hand over her eyes.

"Something the matter?"

"I'm not used to drinking much."

"Oh, the sauce. Don't take this wrong but—you're Jewish, aren't you?"

"On my father's side," she said, amused by his assumption that Jews didn't drink.

He drew a crushed pack of Luckys from the pocket of his tennis shorts. "Light one for me, please? And help yourself."

Her lips got the cigarette embarrassingly wet. As she passed it, they struck a pothole and she brushed Nick's fingers with her hand and felt a stab in her gut. His wiry legs worked the car's pedals, his hand cupped the shift as they vroomed into the curves, the wind blowing her hair across her face, along with the new-mown scent of Nick.

People stood peering down the tracks. "Looks like the train's late for a change," Nick grumbled.

"Please, you mustn't wait with me."

"I won't just abandon you here," he said irritably. He went to make inquiries in the station house, a gabled greystone structure with ogival windows that looked sired by Conscience Point. He got back in and killed the motor. "Track work."

The silence vibrated. Maddy watched a delicate green bug inch along the windshield.

"Vintage Violet," Nick muttered between his teeth. He lit another cigarette and offered Maddy one.

"No, thank you. Listen, I'm perfectly capable of waiting for the train alone. In fact, I prefer it." She pressed her door handle.

Nick placed his hand on her bare arm. "Don't."

Maddy huddled against her door. When the silence became intolerable, she blurted, "Why does your mother call Violet 'Louise'?"

Nick lifted his chin and gave a little snort. "Louise is her name. She calls herself Violet after a distant relative, though the precise relationship is murky: Violet Trefusis, bosom buddy of Vita Sackville-West."

And reputed lover, thought Maddy, fascinated.

"My sister sees Violet T. as a rebel to emulate, what do I know. It's appalling how we humor her. When mother gets pissed, she calls her Louise." Nick crushed out his Lucky in the car's overflowing ashtray. He relaxed back against his door. Maddy was aware of the lightly haired underside of his parted thighs in the tennis shorts. He glanced at her, then looked away.

"Hope we didn't alarm you too much this weekend. For an outsider the Ashcrofts must be a bit overwhelming."

Maddy wasn't sure whether to agree. "Original," she said, with a smile. "Glamorous."

He snickered. "If you have a taste for glamorous doom. " '*Je suis le ténébreux*, born under a dark star,' " he intoned in a mock-stagy voice. "What has Violet told you about Linton? Our older brother. The story varies according to her mood."

"She said Linton drowned."

Nick nodded knowingly. "The truth, if you care to know it, is Linton killed himself. Oh, technically he drowned. In late fall the roads around the Point get covered in sea slick, and his car went careening into Eggleston Pond. He was shitfaced." A moment. "Perhaps it was Linton's way of making amends, settling a score with himself," Nick muttered.

He offered her a cigarette again and this time she accepted.

"Linton was the firstborn, the golden boy," Nick went on—"brilliant student, captain of the ski team, everything ahead of him. But something happened when we lived in Mexico—Father worked for Dole—and Linton was around seven. We had a servant, Milagros. She couldn't have been more than twelve or thirteen. One day Linton and two friends—brothers named de Aguilar—somehow got hold of one of Father's guns. A .22-caliber rifle—Father liked to hunt. Linton and his pals were playing 'war' and they 'executed' Milagros. The gun was loaded and they shot her in the head. Not accidentally, mind you—according to the rules of their war it was intentional."

Maddy's eyes widened. "They couldn't have intended it."

"I suppose we'll never know. I was in the country at my aunt's when it happened. They were arrested, Linny and friends, but didn't seem to understand what they'd done. When the police questioned them, they repeated that they were playing war and Milagros was sentenced to death. It was never clear who pulled the trigger. Another servant found her lying in a pool of blood. No one ever notified Milagros's family. We'd never learned her last name. She'd been traveling alone from house to house working for food and lodging when Mother hired her." He added, "She was wearing the cheapest pair of black shoes."

Maddy put her face in her hands, sunk by the notion of this girl in the cheap shoes treated as so insignificant, her passage through the world went unrecorded. She felt flattered that Nick had chosen to confide this terrible story, then decided he'd chosen her because she was a person of lesser consequence. "Then what happened?"

"The judge recommended the children be taken on a long vacation. After that, moved to a different school and sent to a psychologist who would help erase their memory of the incident. Father must have bought off the judge and the press. One of the de Aguilar brothers is now the famous general." Nick stubbed out his Lucky in the ashtray. "Still like my glamorous family? Why don't you ask your friend Violet why she got booted out of Radcliffe—not that you'll get a straight answer."

Her splutter of laughter startled them both. She put her hand to her mouth. "I'm sorry. It's just that you make the Ashcrofts sound like the House of Usher or something. Chains clanking down halls, ghouls popping out of vaults . . . I mean, curses and dark stars belong in Gothic novels, don't you think? I see a man who's going to Paris to do amazing things."

Something relaxed around Nick's eyes. Then a dismissive smile curled his lips. She wanted to pummel him, and also slide her skin against his and drink him in and feast on him slowly. The mournful whistle of a train sounded in the distance.

"You're so new and fresh and fierce," Nick said. The train whistled louder. Neither moved, they kept studying each other's faces, gathering everything into memory against a long absence. "You know the smartest thing you could do?" Nick said, finger running over his lip. "Stay away from us. Just . . . stay away." He shook his head at her mock-sadly. "Why do I think you won't?"

LATER, OF COURSE, we'd all go crashing down separate paths into the brambles. Maddy marries Leonard. Nick marries Fernande. Violet doesn't marry Christian, disappearing instead among the druggos of Amsterdam . . .

I'm getting ahead of myself again. Without a semblance of order I'll lose the thread—as well as the dear reader, who will want to feel *someone's* in charge here. I'm reminded of "La Valse," the diabolical second half: the waltz begins to whirl unstoppably, rage building, a volume rising to pin you against the back wall . . . *self-destructing* in a shattering coda. But the audience must trust the pianist to keep control.

Hard *not* to lose the thread, though; for over a year now, I've been scribbling during downtime, on trains, planes—and today at the table beside the autumn garden blazing with wine-red and pink dahlias; beneath the oaks rustling through their topmost boughs. I write in a marbleized black-and-white notebook for "compositions," a holdout against the coming laptops. Often I'm struck by how storytelling mimics music: a slight flexion here, then *here,* and it spills forward, driven by its own momentum. A veer in the plot like modulating to a fresh key.

I've chosen to hide behind the third person. Mistake! Memoirs are all the rage, Nick would taunt—disingenuous; Mr. Contrarian, he shies away from anything trendy, not the ideal trait for a publisher! Where was I . . . Oh yeah, third person. Brings distance, as they say. Keeps shame at bay, or makes it easier to be shameless. Lay it all on Maddy and skedaddle off—hey, don't look at *me.* And let's not forget the tiresome egotism of "I," "me," et cetera. Oh, face it, maybe I'm just a goddamn coward. But what counts in this story, after all the subterfuge and lies—and the sly ones known as "withholding"—what counts is to lay out what Stendhal calls *"l'âpre vérité,"* the harsh truth. What counts is to map out in my faux memoir this strangest of family trees; trace the tortuous path that binds us all. . . .

So: THAT NIGHT of Nick's retreat to the city, she'd stood on the bluff at the Point, watching the moon scribble on the inky lagoon, and she heard

Violet's scratchy voice across a chasm of years, perfectly distinct, as if Vi stood in the darkness beside her. *Nick hates me because I'm on to him, the little fop.*

Suddenly she itched to know exactly what Violet had on Nick—or imagined she had. Did she blame him in some way for Linton's death? Even after eight years together, so much of Nick remained terra incognita. They'd tiptoed hand in hand around forbidden subjects—they were both rotten with secrets. Nick hated "psychologizing" about family history. She was his willing co-conspirator: Why trouble the noon's repose? But she recognized now that she'd never wanted to go quarrying in Nick's past to protect them both from what she might dredge up.

CHAPTER 7

Cheap Perfume

A tacky office affair was not Nick's style; there would be no questions asked about his midnight exit from the Point.

Monday she made an end run around Bern Conant, straight to Tom Leahy, prez of CNB—who bounced her back to Conant to "work it out." Checkmate: with Nick reluctant to jump ship with her, she needed to hang in at the job, if only to plot her next move. It galled her that the cachet of *Chronicle* upped her glamour for Nick. . . .

Later the same night, Sophie read in "Town Tattler" that Repo Man had indeed left his wife—for a trophy socialite partial to smart Jews. Despite the hour, Maddy cabbed it up to West 84th Street to find Sophie in fetal position on her convertible sofa, sucking down a pint of Rémy Martin. She was through with men and wanted only "fuck-you money," she ranted. So she could buy a fisherman's shack in Islesford and raise dogs. Of course she was also maxed out on her credit cards. Maddy brewed up some mocha java and produced an inspired solution. Why couldn't Soph ghostwrite Amos Grubb's lame novel and whip it into shape? Grubb would become a published author, Sophie could become a dog lady—she, Maddy, would play matchmaker. . . .

Now, gusting on a second wind, she stood on the lawn of Conscience Point with an old cohort from Juilliard days. Anton Bers, boy wonder, winner of the Leventritt—and midcareer flameout. It required some effort to bring this moist, chunky presence into focus. With all the recent *agita*, she'd clean forgotten inviting him out for a session of four-hands. He'd kept his child prodigy's pudge, and wore his thick hair brushed back like a Slav. The tan shoes might have been remaindered from GUM. His beautiful eyes—which she only now remembered—were smoky and dark with shadowed underlids, eyes you'd see in old photos of Russian students.

Anton was occupied with taking in the greystone mansion, the crenellated turrets and towers and ogival windows, the full-frontal folly of Conscience Point. " 'I dreamt I went to Manderley again,' " he intoned—"well, the Disney version. This place is more bizarro than I remembered."

Of course he'd been here before, she suddenly remembered. During the summer of Violet.

"You and your, ah, socialite boyfriend, you actually live in this pile?"

"Nick and I live here weekends and summer," she said, about to regret her invitation. "We camp out in a few rooms; the rest is closed off. My daughter uses a cabin in the woods as a photography studio."

They strolled around the verandah and Maddy showed him her prized autumn garden, in early summer a riot of color: blue and violet spires of delphinium, white nicotiana, freckled pink lilies, fragrant as an overperfumed courtesan. "This spot is southern and protected, so flowers bloom here even into the frost."

Anton cast his eyes around. "Doesn't it get kinda creepy here at night? The ghost of Rebecca prowling the halls? I'd be scared of running into Miss Danforth."

In truth, she occasionally sensed a presence inhabiting the dark. Watchful yet benign, like some sort of household god. "Actually, it's quite cozy. And everything that's shut off, it's like I don't know it exists." Rather like those nautilus chambers in Nick's past, she realized uneasily. "C'mon, let's have some fun," she said, eager to change the subject.

. . .

HAUNCH TO HAUNCH at the piano, they lit into "Midsummer Night's Dream," Mendelssohn's own arrangement for four hands. The piece gossamer-light, bursting with whimsy and fairy mischief and Mendelssohn's sunny spirit. She'd worried that Anton's bum right hand might not be up to the challenge—but his fingers skittered over hers into the treble register, dropping not a note, not even in the filigree *pianissimo* passages. They dashed to an *allegro* finale like an assembly of sprites evaporating. A pause before wrapping themselves in Brahms's *Liebeslieder Walzer,* its morbid sweetness and remembrance of loves past. Segue into Liszt's second "Hungarian Rhapsody." As a chaser, they knocked out Scott Joplin, "The Ragtime Dances"—and fell against each other, laughing.

Maddy moved to the rose velvet settee and slipped off her strappy sandals, a Harry's Shoes homage to Blahnik. The sunlight, filtered through stained glass, laid lozenges of red, green, and blue over the faded Persians.

"Tony, I once heard you play Bach's *Italian* Concerto at Young Artists, and it was one of the great experiences of my life. I know your right hand went out on you—but you're sounding pretty damn terrific. Play for me. I want to hear you."

He stretched his neck around in a nervous gesture that she remembered. Then long silence: he was counting to thirty, another tic from Juilliard days. His right hand struck four even Gs, a kind of tolling, as he entered Chopin's great F Minor Ballade. The piece more private rumination than meant for performance, its silences sighs blowing it through time. Maddy flexed her fingers, nerved by the minefields ahead.

Anton carved out the melody with exquisite *rubato.* A perfect melody, weightless and suspended . . . Now the fearsome convergence of all the melodies, where anger erupts in giant hand-splitting chords, the right hand carrying the original melody, but with a second, then third voice churning beneath. He levitated off the bench in the showy manner that had attracted both fans and foes. Her breath caught as he began the fiendish coda, an unhinged outburst—half the hand can't *know* what the other is doing—yet he made it sound seamless, his fingers a blur as he built a thundering climax to bring down the vaulted ceiling.

In one motion she was at the piano. "Bra-vo! *Goddamn*, Tony, that was *inhuman*." He nodded in agreement, to her amusement. "I can't believe it, you're better than before. How did you do it? I know for a while you were playing repertoire for left hand. . . ."

Pacing, he told her about the glory days after winning the Leventritt: top management, the CD, the date at Alice Tully—he'd kept the vaguely Continental accent of musicians recruited young for the international circuit. Then he started losing sensation and control in his right hand, the muscles like twisted ropes—"the gods know where to get ya!" Overpracticing made it worse. "Bet a whole bunch of us wrecked our fingers trying to sound like Horowitz," he cracked. Some sour reviews, and he could no longer command the same fees. *A far from note-perfect reading*, she remembered. "Then, with my career tanking, my lovely wife picks up with that hedge-fund guy." He scowled at the stained-glass windows. "Guy's got a spread out here."

Maddy recalled some wisenheimer joking that Anton Bers's right hand went bad to keep him from strangling his wife. She was sure that earlier she'd been condescending to him and regretted it.

"So fifteen years now I've been a pickup pianist with chamber groups desperate for someone willing to schlep to East Palookaville, towns not even in Rand's. Hey, beats playing the 42nd Street subway. God, all those stale cocktail lounges . . . If I ever hear 'Melancholy Baby' again!

"Finally I was diagnosed with focal dystonia, an 'incurable' condition. The hell it is. By chance, someone put me on to Rolfing, a deep-massage technique." He shrugged. "Whoever said American lives have no second acts was an asshole."

He turned a chair to face her on the settee, giving off a whiff of camphor— he must live out of suitcases, she thought, indignant at what he'd endured.

"But enough about you," Anton joked. A moment. "The thing is, nothing can give me back those lost years."

It would never be enough about Anton Bers. Self-involvement raised to an art form; the *me-me-me!* of the virtuoso—she knew it well from the concert circuit.

"I'm hoping to sign with CAMI," he said, fingers drumming the arm of his chair.

"Go for the best." But would top management take him? With the audience for classical shrinking, and managers wanting "crossover artists" fiddling in wet tee-shirts? Anton was heading down the same slippery slope as Sophie and Nick and herself. Superb—and irrelevant.

He crossed his arms, cheek nestled in his palm, and eyed her. He seemed of a different tribe than Nick, she couldn't help thinking, like someone who'd just galloped in from the Caucasus. *"Madeleine,"* he said French-style, "weren't you a brunette?"

She touched her hair, girlishly lifted at the crown with a black velvet clasp. "My handlers prefer peach." Pleased she'd put on a kicky retro dress with a ginkgo-leaf pattern this morning.

"Funny, I remember you *exactly* from back then. Down to your ferocious bangs." His crush on her had been a subject of some merriment at Juilliard. Did he have such hot eyes back then? Did he know how he was looking at her now? "You once turned pages for me at a concert," he said.

"You must have been ten, and I sixteen. What were you playing?"

"God only knows. Must have hit a lot of clinkers. All I remember is . . . you reaching across me to turn the page. And your ponytail pulled back tight—no, it must have come loose, because I remember your hair got in the way."

"Oh, great!"

"And your sort of buckteeth—"

"Thanks. We couldn't afford orthodontia."

"—wildly becoming, as you know. And some sort of lavender dress that tied in back with a bow, and little slippers."

"Those Capezios we used to wear. What an innocent age."

"Innocent? I dunno. You reached across me and I wanted to . . . reach up and grab."

"You always were precocious."

"I'm convinced that at ten I knew as much about love as I do now," he said. Didn't speak well for the learning curve, did it . . . "But you seemed a creature of a higher order. Way out of my orbit. You still are, with this castle and socialite boyfriend—"

"Uh, his name is Nick. And you're the one in the stratosphere. It's awesome, the level you've hit in your playing."

"Actually, I know one thing I didn't know at ten. 'Tis better to have loved and *not* fucking lost. End of story. Next time out, give me a low-maintenance woman who'll sit in the greenroom during concerts reading old copies of *Time*."

Yeah, right. But let the bluebird of happiness burst into song, and they'd pick themselves up, knees shot, half-blind, and go crashing through the underbrush after it. The room had turned sepia-colored like an old photo—clouds must have swallowed the sun. The lilies' cloying sweetness wafted in from the autumn garden.

"Mmm, I just remembered," Anton said. "That perfume you used to wear. I can still smell it." He was watching her, eyes smoky, a searching male perusal.

" 'Evening in Paris'—came in a blue flask, from Woolworth's." She flushed and surprised by where he was taking this. Old Anton, the kid who'd trailed her around the halls of Juilliard.

" 'Evening in Paris," Anton repeated. "To me it was the smell of paradise."

She laughed, from nerves and confusion. She had no business feeling this way. Never in the eight years she'd been with Nick, not for a moment—she and Nick were as mated as trumpeter swans, or so she'd always believed, and she'd do her part to keep it that way. "They don't make that perfume anymore," she said shortly.

I HAD a hard-on all the way out in the car, knowing you were there. Year one, Nick would say that. When he arrived, they'd fall on each other like bears. And today? A cheap perfume would smell—cheap. Still, the weekend carried a forbidden thrill, like eight years ago in St. Thomas. Punched up—no denying it—by the recent friction. As she nosed the car around the giant copper beech, the chimneys of Conscience Point loomed black in the steamy July night like a set for *Ivanhoe*. What Anton had kindled she'd take straight to Nick. He'd back her against the bookshelves or pull her onto the daybed, they'd not be able to wait. . . .

Then she saw his eyes.

He quickly set aside his magazine—furtively, she'd remember later. "New setback for the Stark," he said.

A grinding downshift to sympathy. "Oh, Nicky, what?"

"Softcover auction was a disaster. Just one bidder came in with a floor. And when they saw no one else at the party, they withdrew the floor."

"Oh, my God. Well, guess we saw that one coming after the Guild pass." Nick had been betting the farm on the Stark. First no book-club money, now this? A shellacking, yes. She sat on the arm of Nick's chair and leaned into him, inhaling his scent of gamey tennis shirt and clover—and whiff of Gauloise, after abstaining for eight years. But this no moment to scold. "Look, a great Sunday review and the softcover folks will mosey over for another look," she said.

"C'mon, marketing's already pulling the plug. They promised a budget of two hundred thou, now it's down to fifty. I complain to Rafe. He says, 'Can't throw good money after bad. As for the print run, let's get real here and put out twenty thousand.'

"I get pissed.

"Rafe says, 'Your bottom line wasn't so great anyway.'

" 'All *you*'ve published is weight-loss books.'

" 'And *you* can't run your own goddamn shop.'

" 'Fuck, at least I publish *books!* And my great-grandfather founded this company . . .' "

Nick twisted his head around and peered up at her. "Why won't you look at things as they really are?"

The words hung in the air like a smell of cabbage. She slid off the arm of his chair. Something here had turned horribly wrong. Her heart in overdrive: "And how are things really?"

He went to the sideboard for a hit of Dewar's. Looked up at the vaulted ceiling, down at the carpet, anywhere but at her. "Last week at a hotel pool, I saw a couple with their baby, they were lying on a chaise and he was climbing all over them." She went icy through her veins. "And it seemed the natural order of things, that I'd somehow missed—"

"And you'd wreck our life together?" A thought hijacked her: she could make a baby, with all the new techniques. There was that menopausal Italian woman.

"This is painful for me, too. And maybe—Christ, I hate this conversation. I swear I'd give anything not to have it, Maddy—"

"Then don't have it."

"—but maybe I'm not cut out to live round the clock, day in, year out with—*any* woman."

We could have more time together, he'd said in Nohant. She cast her eyes around in search of a loose object. The white marble Voltaire smiled inscrutably from his stand.

"It goes against my nature," Nick said. "I'm an aloof, alone son of a bitch."

"It hasn't gone against your nature for eight years! What's happened to you? Why are you saying these things—?" She faltered: How do you argue against being found undesirable?

"I've simply come up against the term of something, and can't move forward."

"I know you better than that, Nick. I know you've been happy."

"I was, I am. I just need—a hiatus."

"You're squandering our time together? This gift? Who knows how much good time we have left. Why are we wasting this evening. This hour. Why?"

"I—don't—know. All I know is I don't have answers anymore. It's nothing about you, it's me."

The oldest one in the book. "This is our *lives,* you bastard."

"Oh, God . . . Well, now we're down in the mud—it's *your* life. I'm yanked around by your schedule, Mr. Madeleine Shaye, water boy and consort."

He was leaving her, it bloomed like blood behind her eyes. This was where it was all heading, she'd tasted it for weeks. She sprang at him, taking them both by surprise, and pinned him against the sideboard. He captured her hands and held them off, trembling, held them wide by the wrist, as if they were flying together. She yanked her hands free. She walked to the door. She fought herself down like a rodeo rider on a bucking horse. She turned to face him.

"You're right, Nick." Her voice a luscious mezzo. "No insults, no recriminations—let's not get down in the mud. Let's not spoil all the happiness. I thought you were a serious person. I thought there was staying power here. I was wrong. I've caught your confusion. I feel sorry for you, so sorry—for both of us. Go sort it all out. But don't expect to find me here when you get back."

CHAPTER 8

Shimmer

I t's sometimes advisable to fly 30,000 miles above your own life, as over some unrelated savagery occurring on the ground.

Smile laminated on, she went to openings, benefits, screenings in sealed arctic spaces; kept moving through the July city, the sulfurous heat, yammering drills, tempers ricocheting off a sea of chrome. She watched a memorial on TV: last July on this day TWA flight 800 had cracked open like a lobster midair, its rear portion riding free and exploding seconds later into a fireball. How could her domestic dust-up register alongside that? The party was over was all, and now she had to clean up the mess. She'd had a good run, considering the shelf life of passion. Hard to imagine the legendary lovers in it for the duration. Tristan sweating his PSA test, Isolde on designer estrogen; Heathcliff doing Viagra.

She dove into work. There was work, after all! There was life after Nick—she hadn't pathetically staked it all on a man. She rehearsed the *Spring* Sonata with Viktor Vadim. Her legs ferried her to the office. In the ladies', she huddled in sweater and jacket, teeth clacking. *Anton Bers betrayed by his own body and now playing almost better.* Why fold up her tent here? Surely she could pull out a trick or two in the smoke-and-mirrors world of broadcasting.

She leafed through a swollen folder of story ideas, in search of popular appeal. "Sally Selkirk back for a three-week cameo in *Annie*." Selkirk a '60s movie star who'd vanished at the peak of her career . . . In record time, Maddy assembled a nosegay of Hallmark inspiration. Selkirk had lost fame, money, husband, in that order. *"Like fairy dust falling through my fingers."* Then fetched up in the kitchen of a Catholic residence in Peekskill. *"Been here twenty-seven years and I can truthfully say, I've found happiness."*

It hit a nerve, this life reborn from the ashes. And told the poor that true happiness is washing dishes, Laila would crack.

"We haven't had so much mail on a segment since Girl Rockers," said Bern Conant, scalp pink with joy. "Let's do your story on Wynton Marsalis, pegged to the Lincoln Center jazz festival."

Ba-da-boom: Madeleine Shaye was back in the mix.

A BENEFIT FOR Musical Theater. They were crammed into the Russian Tea Room's upstairs warren. Green, red, and tinseled, it was a land of perpetual Christmas—and a firetrap.

"Are you really, truly all right?" Sophie mouthed over the din. "I mean, you don't have to play cyberbabe with me—"

"I'm fine," Maddy cut her off. "It's simply a matter of discipline—second nature to a musician. And denial—a winning combo. How's it going with Grubb's novel?" She'd made the match, as promised, with a skeptical Grubb.

"I'm scoping out the best-seller formula. First, a concept so high only dogs can hear it. Second, frenzied romance followed by sacrifice in the name of family values, à la *Bridges of Madison County*. A pinch of down-home mysticism—the hunk as Jesus figure in a flannel shirt, think *Horse Whisperer*. The oversexed, wiseass girlfriend—that would be me. I'm so confident of this, I'm already writing my acknowledgments and my speech at the book party."

Maddy eyed Sophie's neck, which looked recently sandpapered. "Uh, speaking of frenzied romance . . ."

"Y'know, after Alex, I thought I was dead to carnal pleasure. But Howard has wakened the sleeping giant."

"I thought you'd given up on love."

"I have—this is hygiene. A way to remain part of the physical world. Love is just not in the cards with a guy who hauls out a laundry list of his 'needs' and says he's looking for his 'theme.' In bed, though—I've been sex-deprived so long I'd forgotten—"

"But Alex—"

"I loved him with all my heart. But truthfully, between his accident and guilt over the wife, the moving parts . . . With Howard it's nothing *but* sex. The flamelike purity of it! As if my entire body were reduced to one place. Like those baboons with magenta bottoms—"

"I loved your Sally Selkirk story."

Maddy turned to thank a woman with alarmingly even teeth and then she saw them. Shrapnel pierced beneath her breastbone and she sank to the floor. Her body double remained vertical. They were stuck in a narrow passage, sharing a look of mild exasperation, how we pay for our pleasures. Was that Nick's hand obscenely around her waist? His lips against her ear? So it wasn't about babies or needing space. It was about fucking Nessa. How many lies lay behind this one? Panic gripped her as if the room were filling with black smoke. She was socked in by flapping mouths, ripe perfume, brows glistening with sweat. *There is nothing here to fear. You are fine and you will continue to be fine.*

Sophie's hand steered her toward the bar and passed her a slender glass. "Stoli, drink up. Oh, Madd, I'm sorry. Fuckin' weird he'd come, this is kinda your turf."

Davidine Swann swam into view. She wore black lipstick and looked recently drowned. "*There* you are. They say Bern Conant is being groomed for *Nightly News.* How do you suppose yet another changing of the guard—"

Maddy watched Davidine's inkberry mouth shaping words, the noise bleating, an accordion swelling and fading. Her life a whirlwind of busyness, signifying nothing. Without Nick the center wouldn't hold.

SHE CANCELED AN INTERVIEW with Marsalis and drove out to Conscience Point—"Please, *you* use the place," Nick had said on the phone; "I've gotten to hate it."

Could it get more *banal?* A guy splitting for a younger woman? In the tristate area alone, this must happen roughly every six seconds. But so did death, and when it happened to you, it wasn't so fucking banal. The bitch was you had to live through the playbook you'd been handed because, cretinous though it might be, it was yours.

She longed to shut down for the season and sleep through the tortuous expulsion of Nick from her system. Let heart and mind do their work the way the gut pursues unsung its labors, and wake me when it's over. From the blue velvet divan in the guest room, she watched the revolving ceiling fan. They'd done the guest room in pink and blue, the colors of the Caribbean. The colors of the little hotel on Cowper's Island, its fan yawing, starved for juice from the island's one tiny generator . . .

TO CONVERGE WITH NICK in St. Thomas eight years ago was not the coincidence it might have seemed. Winter of '89, the Grand Palazzo, the island's newest luxury resort, had mounted a promotional blitz. When they offered unlimited use of a Yamaha C7 concert grand, she decided to stop there after an arts conference in San Juan and hook up with travel-writer friends doing a roundup of high-end St. Thomas resorts. Laila staying at

Sophie's, happy to hang out with Sophie's daughter, Tara. Marshall stuck in town for the closing on the weekend place in Pawling, New York, a rebuilt farmhouse just up the road from a riding stable.

She arrived in St. Thomas to find a Venetian palazzo painted tract-house yellow, flanked by villas forming a horseshoe—too new, too big, eerily deserted. Her four o'clock shadow loomed sharply against cream colonnades. The dining room was nearly empty, the tables shielded by giant fishtail palms so corporate captains could work up a froth in private for whatever they planned to bed after the Grand Marnier soufflé. A pianist in black tie gamely played classical lite for the ghost clientele. After dinner Maddy inspected the "infinity pool," its café empty. Lackeys raked sand with voluptuous slowness on the virgin beach. The sand had been trucked in.

She called American: she'd leave earlier than planned.

The second day, unnerved from having her least whim anticipated, she wandered over to the tennis "shack" to sign a sheet of players looking for a game. Then she saw his name. Recognized the handwriting first. The downslash of the "N," the spiky hump of the "A," a baronial flourish. She'd seen his writing only once before. On a postcard Fernande had carelessly left behind in her second-story bedroom that first evening at Conscience Point with Vi. *Why aren't you here. Ton petit Nicholas longs to be snuggly inside you.* What would have brought Nick Ashcroft to this Venetian mirage?

She added her name to the list.

Dinner with her writer friends at Bumba's in town, a "local" restaurant in a courtyard strung with colored lights, sanitized for tourists. They sat at a long table, guzzling tall pink daiquiris and telling bad jokes and laughing loudly. She and Marshall enjoyed the ease of longtime couples, but these friends offered a furlough from coupledom. Her life felt safe as a gated community. Hard to imagine needing something she didn't already have two of. She plucked a hibiscus blossom from the centerpiece and placed it behind her ear and leaned into someone very drunk.

It was then she spotted him. Seated at a table across the courtyard with a clone of Jack Kemp, arm flung over the chair. Nick in a faded green golf shirt much like the one she remembered from . . . good God, 1966? Hair thinning, less chin, the standard damage. He signaled for the waiter and then he saw her and their eyes locked. His wolf-grey eyes. A surprised smile, but Nick is not surprised. He has been to the tennis shack. The couple glances her way. They are surrounded, she and Nick, neutralized. A signal of the eyes, a slight nod, and they agree: *later.*

THE HEAT STUPEFIES, even at nine A.M.; they decide on the air-conditioned bubble. Her tennis in disrepair. He comes over to her side to show her the serve: "Do you mind?" Nick Ashcroft serving is a wonder to behold, a set of motions suggesting other possible motions. The slow setup, left hand reaching skyward, right shoulder cocked—then the powerful whip-release with the racket, the whoosh of the strings, the taut, muscled legs beneath baggy shorts rising on tippy toes.

"Here, you try some." He hands her a ball. Watches. "Better. But don't *push* the ball." He hands her another.

Suddenly, blackness. The hum cuts off.

"Damn, another power surge, happened yesterday, too." Nick's bodiless voice in the dark. They drift toward the courtside bench, creatures of the deep moving through perpetual night.

He has come here with a photographer for a book on Caribbean architecture, and this "palazzo place" seemed a good jumping-off point. "We're leaving in two days to shoot Great Houses in Jamaica."

They don't have much time. "Tell me everything," she says, "starting with Paris."

"You remember. Today's January 19, 1989, so it's been, what, almost twenty-five years?" That somehow feels like a long pause. "At *Transatlantic* I met many of the writers I now publish."

"And did you get to live on that barge on the Seine?"

"The Peter Duchin barge, Quai Malaquais, yes. You remember."

The voice, too; staccato, nasal, slightly prissy.

Nick is editorial director at Greenaway and agitating for his own imprint, a boutique within the larger house that will reflect his own taste. "I have a list of 'literary' authors, but the parent company is dragging its feet. I need one big breakout book to clinch the deal. . . . Fernande lives in the house in North Salem." He assumes, correctly, that she knows they married. "I often stay in a studio on Irving Place." *Where he sees his women.* They are basting in their own sweat in this black steambath. Through cracks in the bubble's seams she sees the sunlight of earth, as if from the caverns of Pluto. Her eyes have adjusted; she sees his whites, a curl of hair pasted to his neck; smells a blond musk remembered from a ride to the Islesford station. . . .

"And Conscience Point?" she says hoarsely.

"We've closed up the house. Serena packed up her cockatiels and moved to Antigua." He brushes his forehead with the back of his hand, a drop of sweat landing on her arm. She touches her finger to the spot, but her whole arm is slick. "Fernande refuses to go to the Point. The truth is, Fernande rarely goes anywhere. She's been unwell for a long time. We never had children."

And Violet? Violet cast off from the known world years ago, but she wonders if Nick has had word of her. Instinct warns her off inquiring. She remembers his violent antipathy and senses they must never, ever speak of Violet.

Never, ever? Whooaa . . . She must have sunstroke. "What are we doing here," she laughs. "We're about to liquefy."

Neither moves. Beyond the labyrinth of heavy curtains and revolving doors lie daylight and the throbbing world.

THAT EVENING THEY WALK the groomed beach. (After his phone call, she has canceled with her travel writers.) She hears, smells, sees as if she has flung open doors she never knew were shut. She registers the dry rattle of the palms, the flicker of lights across the harbor, the heartbreaking kiss of the trade winds that she has never found heartbreaking. Nick at forty-six reminds her of a stone angel licked by industrial fallout she once saw in Venice. She remembers the lightly haired undersides of his thighs.

"You mustn't take this wrong—but you somehow looked older at twenty-one. When I think of all the women who would kill for your job! *And* you're a pianist. You did it, Maddy, you got where you were going. I remember taunting you about giving up music. God, I was an arrogant son of a bitch."

"Mm hmm." A moment. "But nothing went as planned."

They climb steps to the pool, a landscaped islet at its center. "You married," he says.

"My first boyfriend—the doctor that girls of our generation were supposed to marry. I followed him to North Carolina, left my piano teacher and New York—exactly when I needed both to build a concert career."

"Why, Maddy? Why didn't you run with it?"

She notes something peculiar: Nick assumes she didn't quit the race for love of her husband.

"Maybe I didn't have the guts for the grind and pace of a solo career. Call it a failure of nerve." The answer closer to the truth than she likes to admit. "I wanted to be like the other girls, I wanted to be safe."

He turns to her. "And were you? Were you safe?"

"I lay on the floor hemorrhaging. My husband passed out in his

BarcaLounger, zonked on morphine—from the first he was doing Demerol. It was Rockford, Illinois, during a blizzard. I couldn't get to the hospital."

"Jesus Christ." With a convulsive gesture Nick moves toward her.

"The baby was a girl. I saw her face." She walks quickly on toward a floodlit terrace with white umbrellas and a bar curved like a gondola. "Now I have an adopted daughter, Laila. Means 'night' in Arabic."

"A lovely name," Nick says, voice cautiously impersonal. The air swarming with untold stories. They snake along a path hugging a pink pavilion perched above the sea. "Tell me about your significant other," he says. They both laugh at his assumption.

"Marshall produces specials on public television. We've been together a long while." She's suddenly shamed by her and Marshall. They have dinner four nights a week, confide work problems, cherish their "nights off" because they both sleep better, go to Anguilla in February, soon they'll have the weekend place in Pawling, Marshall knows the right moves, waits for her to come first, and now all this strikes her as shameful. She and Marshall are not looking, either of them, to change. And if she did move on? she thinks abruptly. Would Marshall suffer? Maybe a bad case of whiplash from getting wrenched from a comfy groove. She likes the groove, too, has chosen it over the demands of high romance.

"I believe I've met your Marshall. Producer at Channel 13? Does the Great Performances? He was up for membership at my club. Got black-balled, for some reason."

"What's a club for if not to keep people out," she says caustically. Marshall has never told her this. She suddenly wants to protect him.

They've circled back to the yellow palazzo. It floats above pretzeling flights of marble stairs, empty and blazing with light, as for a ball.

"I've made a curious discovery about myself," he says.

She smiles. What's curious is how men "discover" themselves like Captain Cook sighting New Guinea.

"I'm drawn to the people I've always known, or feel I've always known. It's like circling back to some root system. The excitement of newness—building something from the ground up—doesn't appeal to me in the least."

She laughs low in her throat. "That must limit your options."

His grey eyes are unamused. "Maybe I'm not looking for options."

NEXT DAY SHE practices on the Yamaha from nine to twelve. Hurries, instantly sweaty, back to the room: no messages. Before lunch she swims at the deserted beach and lies on the trucked-in sand; again checks her phone. Nothing. Over lunch she reads some pages from *American Pastoral*, the new Philip Roth about a lost daughter, and can extract no sense from the words. At the main desk: *A message for you,* the clerk says. Her heart races. It's from Marshall: *The closing went smoothly. Need your input on the music room.*

She walks herself down to the terrace with the white umbrellas. What has she been thinking, after all. They've both got lives. She remembers Fernande in the garden at Conscience Point, drooped between Nick's legs like a basket of white peonies. He'd be a drug she'd want more of.

She returns to her room to call Marshall and move up her flight on American, and then notices the light blinking on the phone. *Had to fly to St. Croix with my photographer early this morning and didn't want to wake you. Can we meet this evening?*

THEIR THIRD EVENING tour of the Grand Palazzo Nick says, "Can you get away for the day? I thought we might take a boat trip."

His voice neutral as a pilot's announcing the cruising altitude, but she hears the tremolo beneath.

He has booked them onto a day trip on the *Stormy Petrel,* a motor launch that takes small groups from Red Hook, St. Thomas, to the Baths in Virgin Gorda, snorkeling in Bitter End Bay, lunch at the Soggy Dollar on tiny Cowper's Island. Then back to St. Thomas down the Sir Francis Drake Channel.

Six or seven other people clamber aboard the little launch helmed by Cap'n Bob. Malaysians and Argentinians who speak only pidgin English. "Perfect, we won't need to make conversation," Nick murmurs in her ear. They sit thighs touching on the salt-kissed flotation cushions. The early sun glances off the water; a maritime bouquet of diesel fuel and tarred wood and seaweed. The sun burnishes the hair on Nick's forearms. Maddy has stopped asking herself where any of this is going, having lost her faculty for envisioning the future, along with guilt about Marshall. Usually she strains forward like a gymnast, reaching for the next handhold. Now she expands into the present, fills it to overflowing, she's engorged with the present. She sits in the early sun sensing her own body, the tips of her breasts, a Fingal's Cave of desire. Yes, she would love some fresh pineapple, she tells Cap'n Bob in the voice of civilization.

At Virgin Gorda they brave the traffic jam of tourists and swim in with flippers to the Baths. Then on to Bitter End Bay for snorkeling. Maddy and Nick swim along a reef of purple fan coral, their heads in masks close together underwater like two companion pike.

Cap'n Bob steers the *Petrel* through sapphire water rocked by swells to the Soggy Dollar on Cowper's Island for lunch. The group sits together on the terrace at a long wooden table and the waitress brings conch fritters and chicken roti and banana daiquiris. Maddy eats a thimbleful of something. Afterward, Cap'n Bob instructs everyone to get back to the boat by two-thirty. He'll sound the boat's horn as an alert.

Maddy and Nick follow a little path banked with bougainvillea behind the Soggy Dollar. She has changed from her bathing suit to gauzy white pants and a long-sleeved shirt against the sun. Nick wears khaki cut-offs, wallet making a bulge in his back pocket, and a once blue shirt faded to near-white, sleeves rolled up. There is salt on the sun-bleached hairs of his forearm. She's tweaked by an urge to lick the salt on his arm and legs, drop on all fours and lick. A small voice pleads, *Let's go back to the Soggy Dollar and the Malaysians.*

The tropical lushness draws them on. Elephant leaves, sea grape, orange and rose bougainvillea. Nick plucks a blossom and tucks it into the elastic band pulling back her damp hair. An electric thrumming crescendos from the foliage.

"The way I saw you in the restaurant," he says. He splays his fingers against her cheek.

She enraptured under his fingers. The thrumming wanes, then swells. *Don't, don't do this. Have pity on us.*

The sun past its zenith floods them in heat.

"We better go back."

Nick walks on as if she never spoke. *The same exasperating trait as Violet.* The path loops back out to the sea. A few feet from the beach stands a little pink hotel, Cowper Island Inn. They almost stumble on the small generator that must furnish the island's power. They stand knee-deep in sea grape, staring at Cowper Island Inn like Hansel and Gretel at the gingerbread house.

"I'm going to see if they have a room," he says, as if it's agreed.

Sweat has plastered a dark decal onto the back of his shirt. In the cool, dim entry a man is nodding off at a desk; an ancient yellow dog curled in a corner opens its eyes and raises one battered ear. Maddy sees an annex with blue shutters across a courtyard, an open-air bathroom.

The hunger is close to pain, they can't reach the end or find how to begin. The fan yawing through its cycle, their groans and cries, her eyes staring sightless, pleading, fluttering at the fan. He gathers her up, her ass, his hands, lips, her neck, his cock . . . Yes . . . oh, yes . . . She makes a tour of him, his hair in all its places, the snaggletooth, his smells . . . She draws him up into her mouth, lips swollen, a silken sheath milking him . . . Hearing him moan the way she heard him under the statue at Conscience Point . . . *Wait*, he mutters. Rolls her off. They grasp, grapple, hurt, too desperate. The fit, at last.

They wake and kissing she tastes herself, him, them. She thinks, *This is the best it will be.* They lie heart upon heart, his weight falling into her. A bleating sound. They've been hearing it for some time. The horn of the *Stormy Petrel.* Calling all passengers to board.

At some point Nick must have told the man in the hotel. She remembers Nick's voice across the courtyard, her joy at the sound of it, the lilting island patois of the hotel owner. The horn stops. Sudden rain drills the dry palms like grapeshot.

They sleep. When they wake, the light outside is the peach of a conch's inner whorls. Nick raises himself on his elbow. "I love the people I loved first. I feel as if I've always loved you." His lips move against her hair, sticky with salt and their fluids. "'Throughout all eternity, I forgive you and you forgive me,'" he intones in the poetry voice she remembers. William Blake? she wonders fuzzily. *"Say it."*

She nuzzles his shoulder, its dusting of childish freckles. A small green lizard scoots up the white stucco wall. "Better I shouldn't have to forgive," she laughs. He pulls her down over him; hardens beneath her pubic bone, skewing the discussion. They're nose to nose, she squatted over him, his grey eyes circled by the dark iris. . . . *Say it.*

That evening Nick phones his photographer with a fable about engine trouble on the *Stormy Petrel.*

They quit Cowper's Island two days later when the *Petrel* again swings by. It's priceless, the single imperious look with which Nick silences Cap'n Bob. Her crotch is sore and smells of low tide. They are both peeling from sunburn and abraded skin, covered with bites from insects and each other, wearing their same clothes stiff with salt and sweat, objects of fascination to the other passengers. Maddy and Nick wear the dazed, secretive look of divers who have ventured deep into the wreck and come up clutching rubies.

Years later she would sometimes marvel at how she never for a moment hesitated. It was never "whether or not," only "how." They moved forward with the ruthless economy of samurai. They knew they would pay, but they would pay later. Casting off from the harbor in Red Hook, they cast off from their old lives and never looked back.

NICK NEVER DIVORCED, *you know*, she wrote in the marbleized notebook. The tall oaks sway their top boughs; sun shot through leaves skates a lacey pattern across the back of her hand. Fernande was Catholic, she wrote. And mentally fragile at best. After Nick left, they said she ripped out chunks of her own hair. Fernande had round-the-clock help in North Salem, plus a permanent res at McLean, so they could tinker with her meds. Even after Nick and I went public, even after that Memorial Day in Islesford, Nick visited Fernande every second Sunday. Encouraged by me, hoping to work off a portion of my own guilt.

Back in New York I prodded Marshall to spread the word about a breakout book by Nick's hot new author, a John Grisham–meets–John Le Carré. Marshall gave his good buddy at NBC a heads-up. Nick's author got booked on the *Today Show*—yes, I flinch at writing this. The copycat mentality of the media triggered segments on other shows; the magazines and newspapers climbed on board—a best seller was born and Nick got his imprint, Arcas Books. Eventually Marshall connected the dots. He could take getting dumped—and quickly replaced me—but by a man whose club had red-lettered him? He invited the president of CNB to lunch at the Four Seasons and told him Madeleine Shaye had a habit of using professional affiliations to advance the career of her lover du jour. The boss surely suspected it was injured pride speaking, but fired me anyway, male solidarity and all that. Charlie Unger hired me back the next day. . . .

Today I'm struck by a detail from Virgin Gorda: Nick in his poetry mode, quoting William Blake: "'Throughout all eternity, I forgive you and you forgive me.'" Nick seldom that obvious—but was he actually seeking guarantees? In case I discovered a room at the end of the corridor full of slaughtered wives?

CHAPTER 9

Picnic

Fragments from a ruin:
I can't do this, I'm not managing at all.

It's Memorial Day after St. Thomas, and they're standing in the grass inner court of the Islesford Gallery at an opening. "I can't do this," Nick repeats. "Come away with me. Now."

"Now?" Without moisturizer and a change of underwear? They have agreed before that they can't go on like this. She has also wondered, having read her Proust, if such passion could survive without impediments.

"Wait one minute, then follow me, I've something to show you."

They meet up in a sculpture garden behind some wooden sheds. The sculptures turn out to be figures cowering on the ground, faces upturned toward Armageddon. Far down on Main Street, the Memorial Day parade strikes up, the tinny horns and drums of a Sousa march. She backed up against a shed, Nick standing, their impatient fingers, unbuckling, tugging down, straps, elastic, silk . . . The parade approaches, cornets blaring, drums pounding, jaunty and patriotic. He scoops her up, she braced against the shed, his head backtilted, and he lowers himself, levering them into position, to join her. The shed creaks and groans.

*   *   *

MADDY'S COMING WITH me. Nick takes her arm. They're back in the grassy court among the guests departing under a slow rain of ocean mist.

"Excuse me, sir, I'm afraid there's some mistake," Marshall says.

"No, Marshall, no mistake," she says wearily. Tasting Nick, crotch sticky. A splinter in her ass, she thinks.

Marshall pales beneath his olive skin. "Maddy, we're due at the Alderman's at six."

"I didn't plan it this way, Marshall, but there is no good way. Please give me some time so I can begin to explain. I'm so terribly sorry."

His eyes darken with knowledge. Then she and Nick walk toward the road in the watery dusk, formal as figures in a pavane, Nick's hand beneath her elbow, Marshall's eyes scorching her back; walk slowly through the emptying gallery and up the graveled driveway into their lives.

EIGHT YEARS LATER, in a city marinating in summer heat. The daughter of the woman with all the luck has decided against Guatemala. The daughter now wants to quit Brown and transfer to Hunter College. The daughter says that at Hunter minorities are the majority.

"Laila, that's a mistake. I was a romantic dreamer and I'd like to save you from that."

"Oh, Ma"—the old sweet voice—"you know it doesn't work that way. Why couldn't you have stayed with Marshall?"

"I didn't love Marshall. I couldn't arrange which man I loved for you."

Later, when she tries to call up what Laila said next, she gets only silence, as if someone had switched off the sound.

. . .

IT SCARES ME to think I might have missed you. Nick has more than once said some variation of this, genuinely aghast.

She flips on the light—two A.M. Floats in her nightgown down to a living room still in thrall to the day's heat, and settles in her flame-stitch chair. Has she jiggered up one bad patch to catastrophic? Suppose Nick really wants, as he said, just a furlough. The coupled life *is* too rich for daily consumption, like a diet of foie gras, though no one admits it. Doesn't she hunker down here on Jane Street before a concert, gorging on solitude? Maybe couples aren't built to turn stupid as turnips with happiness. If only he'd kept Nessa in the closet! So they could slog along together, she feigning ignorance, till Nick tired of his new toy. Like the look-away wives she'd observed at dinners, their husbands falling into a neighbor's cleavage. *Let the silly boy act out, he's bound to come slinking home.* They knew the odds, the wives. They knew that in New York, male ambition plus comforting habit trumps high-maintenance passion most every time. "In a woman's middle years," she'd once told an eager young journalist, "an extended family of friends and children becomes more important than a romantic partner." Now she'd sing a different song. Losing the last best time, she'd tell the journalist, is like getting stranded on the Khumbu Icefall.

Could she reboot her life, as she'd done her job? The Nessa thing might not survive the first frost—why not hasten its demise in a preemptive strike. And since Nick had baby lust . . . hell, there was that sixty-year-old Italian grandma who'd just produced triplets. The media was churning out stories about in vitro fertilization. Egg donated by younger woman meets husband's sperm in petri dish, and gets implanted in wife.

Hard to imagine, though, Nick jerking off into a jar. Especially after he learned about the hospital's "cupping room," where the prospective dad did his thing to porn 'zines and videos. Especially given the minor detail that she and Nick had broken up.

She would feign a need to talk, then seduce him. She would buy fresh eggs, claiming them as hers—like most men, Nick was ignorant of female plumbing. She would buy blue-chip sperm from gamete central, get the whole kit implanted—and voilà, Nick would have his baby. In some fashion. That seemed to be the terms these days. And in some fashion she would have hers, after the tiny smashed girl they'd pulled from her a lifetime ago, into a world of blood and snow.

She had leapt the track, she knew. She knew, yet could only sit here slick with sweat in her flame-stitch chair, gawking at a gruesome accident, like a rubber-necker—except that the accident was *her*. She pictured a train she'd once seen in some movie or nightmare that had plunged off a trestle into an icy canal. The details eluded her, though she'd retained an image of horses rearing, frozen solid in the ice.

"YOU ARE TRYING to do *what?*"

Sophie's double take from *The Honeymooners* drew glances from the Turnbull & Assers seated two tables away. They were lunching in the lugubrious splendor of Maddy's club—the one that had blackballed Marshall—now near-emptied by the August diaspora. "You actually started the workup?"

"Well, preliminary research, you know us journalists." Maddy sketched the scene at Mount Sinai's infertility bazaar: waiting room filled with greying yuppies, grimly determined to Have It All, menopausal boomers, second-wave feminists, even an old Movement star . . . *Oops, forgot about babies!* Everyone downsizing their age.

"But wait a mo." Sophie held up her palm. "How the hell can you get pregnant? Dr. Mitnick-Gazinsky is more into hormone replacement and bone density."

"With the new technology we can all play Sarah in the Bible. Our eggs have passed the sell-by date, but you can 'harvest' 'em from some grad student who's paying back tuition loans. A beauty queen with an IQ could make out like a bandit."

"When I think of those yuppies who popped Clomid and had triplets—they're creating gridlock on the streets of Manhattan with their strollers, I can't fit in my own elevator. And aren't older mothers more prone to heart attacks and diabetes? Maddy, why do this?"

"For my lost baby. To keep the last best time."

"Hold it, didn't you guys break up?"

Chasing frisée with her fork: "There's deep history between Nick and me. I mean, look at Mitterrand with his wife and mistress. They both came to the funeral—"

"Get outta here, only the French can pull that off. Besides, old Nicko doesn't strike me as superstud. In my summer share house those fiftyish guys can barely get it on with *one* woman. And that's only after a shot from Caverject. The house would be a sex-free zone if not for all the needle-play at night. God, remember when needles meant you were doing smack? Ah, the good old days." She tucked into the crab cakes, oblivious to the glares from Turnbull & Asser.

Maddy said, "A fifty-seven-year-old woman in Toronto just gave birth to twins."

"*Why.*"

"Why *not?* Men make babies till they drop. Look at Tony Randall—isn't he seventy-seven? And the Zorba the Greek guy. Look at Lester."

"Yeah, *look* at him. My ex-husband is like a granddad to his own kid. Can you see the octogenarian playing softball with his son in Central Park? Actually, poor Lester just had a hernia operation—I think he tried to lift his toddler. It happened right after that article in *New York Magazine* on him and these second-time dads who have 'rediscovered parenting.' And

now I hear Lester just had a, uh, whuddyacallit—microvascular event."
She sighed. "Next they'll do an article on 'The Second-Time Dad as Vegetable.' Lookit, there's only one good thing to do with male confusion: write a book and make money off it." She eyed Maddy pleadingly. "Please. I need you to stay sane."

SHE STEPPED INTO the arctic zone from the furnace outside. In an instant, she wore that congealed second skin affixed to the original peculiar to a New Yorker in August. Tin Aztecs cavorted on pink adobe walls. She'd chosen this Tex-Mex on 9th Avenue not for its decor but for its anonymity. Her hand gripping the sweating glass of Perrier jumped badly when she saw the float of dark hair in the glass vestibule. She realized she'd only half-expected Nessa to show.

They shook hands and sat in silent mutual appraisal, totting each other up at gigahertz speed, facing each other across no-man's-land during a lull in hostilities. She braved the full impact of Nessa's beauty, of a caliber to render sisterhood forever obsolete; her golden-brown eyes and forward-shot jaw, skin of a petal-y finish, like a distillation of light. Why *wouldn't* Nick want to possess this breathing artwork.

Before she started blessing their union, better trot out the prepared speech. "Nessa, I'll be brief. I'm asking you to let Nick go. You can afford to. You have a long future of love ahead—for which I envy you. And Nick can't mean to you in so short a time what he and I have built over eight years."

The oval of Nessa's face yielded all the emotion of a cucumber. "You've no right to ahsk such a thing." Accent to do the BBC proud.

"'Right' hasn't much to do with it. Besides, it's really not fair to you. You see, Nick's in the grip of some mortality panic, cheesy as that sounds, and he's not at all to be trusted. It would gall him to think this, because he imagines he's so original—but right now he's a walking cliché from pop psychology. You're a lovely woman, Nessa, you can do better. You *deserve* better." *Don't we all,* she added to herself.

Nessa's features yielded nothing. "Look, even if I agreed to your, uh, request, what makes you think I have any pah over Nick's feelings?"

"Oh, I think you do. Also, if you don't mind a bit of professional advice, bad idea to get too cozy with the boss."

Nessa's oxblood nails closed around her black alligator clutch. "Listen, this is all a bit . . . premature. Nick is still, as he says, trying to 'work things through'—whatever that means." Suddenly her mask fell away and she looked impossibly young. "Oh, bloody hell, I wish none of this had happened. I got this job because Daddy's, well . . . rather connected. Then Stark—you know, our lead author on the winter list—went and hired his own publicist. So I've bloody botched it—" Her eyes brimmed.

"But you haven't at all. Many big writers now hire their own PR people," Maddy said, wondering how Nessa had screwed up. She was chagrinned at seeing the adversary deflate so quickly, as though watching a tennis mismatch. "And you accomplished the near-impossible," she added. "You pulled Stark out of his lair. The guy's notoriously crotchety and difficult. You mustn't give up on yourself, really." She then proceeded to offer Nessa a five-step plan to rehabilitate her career, which would of course rule out all office nookie.

Nessa looked uncertain what had just transpired. She blurted, "How lucky Nick is to have a woman like you." She reached into her clutch for a hanky and tamped the corner of one eye. Then a vertical line appeared between her brows. "But what troubles me—I can't help wondering if I'm not a . . . you know, *pawn* in some little game you and Nick are playing."

Maddy leaned in. "Nessa, trust me," she said kindly, "on my side, it's no game. Though it's true I've been willing to share Nick with you because . . . well, he's bound to come back."

Nessa gazed into the middle distance. Then her raisin lips disclosed a gleam of pearl. "Oh, no need to shah."

INDIAN SUMMER GRASPED the Point in a golden trance. Each sound amplified: close to shore, the plash of tiny snappers lifting from the water as one; the drone of a yellow jacket working orange rose hips in the dunes. The black periscope of a cormorant broke the surface of the dazzled bay, the far island dreaming through the haze. The weakened sun, though, and the bay's deeper currents presaged the coming cold.

She and Sophie spread the blanket—always the Hudson Bay, green, orange, and black; laid out barbecued chicken, the season's good tomatoes, unhusked corn to roast on the fire. She'd called this picnic to mark Laila's nineteenth birthday (not knowing Laila's exact birth date, she'd long ago chosen September 10). But in truth, she'd called this picnic to invite Nick— invoking family tradition—so she could collar and grill him about his social life. Since the Tex-Mex, she'd been slip-sliding on a pane of greased glass.

Seated on her heels, she kept watch, a swiveling Cyclops eye; waiting for her moment. But he kept busy, Nick. She watched him go up for the champagne in the car parked on the bluff, and descend on strong skier's legs the rickety stairs. She watched him squat to craft the perfect fire from rocks laid in the sand. She watched him draw a crushed blue packet of Gauloises from his chino pocket, then hastily put it back. Laila, hair braided on her head, stood laughing with Eugene's niece Olga, a robust woman with florid cheeks, who sold seafood at Sparky's Marina. Laila moved on to chat with her mentor, the photographer Georgia Kidd. The woman wore a leather weskit and walked with a bully-boy swagger like a post-menopausal Hell's Angel.

"Publishers now actually deaccession books already in the catalog," Sophie said to Jed Oliver from their perch on a nearby log. He guffawed too loudly—must have forgotten his medication. Maddy watched Sophie kneel beside her daughter, Tara, in overalls and granny glasses, for a spot of nagging. Tara was traveling to Guatemala with a delegation studying human rights, and Sophie already had her "disappeared"—but at least Tara had stopped dating the mildly retarded convict she'd met assisting Jed in a death-row case.

A spat! They sounded, Laila and Nick, like squabbling gulls. He'd found *scuff marks* on the *Cherubino*'s teak deck, and Laila, carelessly wearing shoes instead of topsiders, was the culprit. "Well, ex-*cuse* me," Laila tossed back. "I hear they'd shoot you for less on the *Suzi Wong*, and bury you at sea." William Buckley's yacht, but Laila never ragged Nick about his annual ritual sail with the owner. And anyway, they were usually easy as locker-room buddies. Was Laila showing solidarity with Mom?

Scowling, Nick took his Swiss Army knife to a green bottle of Riesling. She saw the febrile motion of his hands peculiar to the Ashcrofts; the medallion of light-brown hair nesting below his collarbone.

Would she be staying the weekend for the American Way benefit? he asked Laila with icy politeness.

"Those jerks shell out ten thousand bucks for a table—and they don't even know what the friggin' charity *does*."

"At least the 'jerks' shell out for a worthwhile cause."

"Yeah, right, they're 'giving back' is how they see it. But they're mainly giving themselves a pat on their own skank asses—"

For a second, the sight of them, rigid with vexation, punished Maddy's eye like a grain of sand stuck in it. They seemed to be hamming it up like some touring company in colonial Singapore. Staging some sort of act—for her benefit? A preposterous notion took shape like a tarantula crawling up her arm.

She watched Laila stroll to the water and angle a flat stone out into the bay: it stitched the water three, four times—then boomeranged for a fifth. Jed joined her and skipped a stone that sank with a plunk. They laughed and he flung an arm over her shoulders. Both rangy as underfed cats.

Maddy pressed the heel of her hand to her eye. Whoaa, better cool down the brain. She wandered off unnoticed to the Point, where the sandbar jutted its sheltering arm around the inlet. She sat tucked into a tall dune, hugging her knees. Into the frame walked Laila, tracing the shoreline, breasts jiggling beneath the tee, absorbed in some song. On impulse, Maddy kept silent; watched her follow the shore's curve, her form incinerated by a riot of light; then disappear around the Point toward Weymouth Landing, where the *Cherubino* would be riding majestically at anchor. Eyes at half-mast, she grew hypnotized by the lagoon's pulsating glitter, as if by looking long enough she'd connect the molecules dancing in her brain in search of some elusive pattern. *No need to shah . . . Why couldn't you have stayed with Marshall . . .* Her chin jerked up: Had she heard murmurs from around the Point? Gulls shrieked overhead, fighting over a clam. Her head whipped sideways: *Nick missing from the group down the beach*—and then she got it, all hundred twenty-five neurons firing off in a giant *Aha!*

CHAPTER 10

Landing Lights

She'd given away her allowance to her "favorite bum." She'd stuck paper clips in the Winstons so Mom wouldn't smoke. The fridge was still pocked with Tintin cards to Mom affixed with magnets, *I know I don't tell you often enough how much I love you,* written on the back. . . . Could the same person have crossed that line? A daughter who put Tintin cards on the fridge with magnets and a daughter who fucked her mother's boyfriend couldn't coexist in the same dimension. It was a scientific impossibility, like the Heisenberg theory of waves and particles. Only Jukes and Kallikaks did such things. Only the odd celebrity. Her "evidence"? a ghost of Gauloises and whispers on the wind. *Who but her did Laila have?*

She walked two blocks to Miss Helene's Hairpieces to the Stars on 12th Street and charged a red wig to her Amex. Hopped a cab to Georgia Kidd's Soho loft, where, in theory, Laila now lived. The night's rain had rinsed the pavement, an autumn sun beamed in a cobalt sky. The knockout morning called up the ravening ambition of her youth. Fast-forward a few years, and through some cruel kink in the plot she'd become a stalker.

The upstairs neighbor peered down the steep stairwell at the woman in a red bob with bangs. Georgia was away, she said, and the loft unoccupied, although a "mule-otto girl" had stayed there over the summer. Now the place was used by a twelve-step bulimia group.

. . .

BARRELING ALONG THE expressway, she shuffled and reshuffled last week's scenes from an execution. . . .

She'd sat beneath the dunes unmoving, a smart bomb lodged in her gut. Next, she's sloshing through water. The perfect sense of it! She saw with a clarity that scalded her eyes what was there to see all along, signposts guiding her in like blue landing lights. *No need to shah* . . . Of course, Nessa nothing but a decoy. Laila turns bitchy—out of guilt? Or to drive a wedge between them, making it easier to do what she's about to do. Nick's *sudden phony* craving for solitude . . . His baby lust a ploy—to nudge her aside? put her off the scent? Surely Nick couldn't want Laila's child . . . The pieces all there, if she'd had eyes to see. . . .

"Hey, Maddy, whatcha doin' out there?"

Now she remembered what Laila had said: *And I couldn't arrange which man I loved for you;* echoing her own words. Of course! If she'd had ears to hear . . . The sun's red ball swooned down the horizon. Water greeted her thighs as the dredged harbor dropped away in a steep shelf. Laila always had the tact of a grownup, who had seen a child with such grace. Little gap-toothed Laila in the rowboat in Central Park. On the beach in her droopy tank suit, patting Nick's tanned back. "This is a smart uncle I've got. . . ." Little cinnamon hand going pat pat. . . Betrayed by her *own?* She didn't know how to *know* this. She went jelly-kneed, as if peering down a giant funnel. She placed her hands over her eyes and shuddered.

"Yo, Madd, need a little help?"

More stray pieces clicking in, the puzzling phrases . . . "I'm sorry—*for everything.*" Laila, way back in May in the living room on Jane. *May?* Fucking eureka, the tarantula right on her arm, if she'd had eyes to see. And the Guatemala plan: Laila trying to escape from Nick? Then she quits

Brown—of course! to be with him in New York. It was probably in August that they—No. Such things didn't happen.

"I better go out there."

Maybe they thought she'd had a stroke. Maybe she had. The words for the thing that didn't happen hung like poison apples just out of reach. Her legs had turned to stanchions in the cold water. Her feet sank beneath the sand. Fiddler crabs nipped her toes, snappers kissed her ankles. . . .

And then she zoomed in on the earliest piece: Nick freaking over the German nymphet in front of George Sand's château. Had the monstrous . . . *thing* hatched then?

Turning, she saw Jed Oliver, jeans rolled up, sloshing through olive-drab water. "Hey, Maddy, c'mon back to shore and have some champagne." He looked wary, maybe afraid she'd suffered something nasty to remind them all of mortality. He swatted at no-see-ums, tiny gnats that arrived with dusk. She reached across the water for Jed's hand. Jed a decoy, too, her fellow stooge. She squeezed his hand. Her eyes shot to the beach blanket. Nick and Laila stood gazing unconcernedly in opposite directions, like dogs when one of their fellows is taking a crap. Returned from their assignation around the Point.

Someone fetched her a towel and dry shorts. Someone handed her a blue plastic goblet. The champagne looked greenish in the blue goblet. The sun had smeared a jagged bruise across the sky, blood-orange and purple.

"What were you doing out there?" Laila said.

She searched Laila's eyes: *Where did you learn to do this?* Laila raised an arm to swat a no-see-um, and Maddy caught a pungent whiff of Gauloises in her hair. In that moment she decided. She'd play dumb. They thought they had the upper hand, but she'd play them every which way and take control of their game.

. . .

NOW, IN THE SOBERING mornings after, her eureka moment seemed a bout of brain fever. Yeah, she'd assembled all the pieces and notched them together—yet the picture they formed was not anything she could recognize.

At the turn past the Islesford windmill, a voice announced the date on the Saab's crackly radio—and she remembered the standup for her Marsalis piece. She called Bern Conant on the car phone. "Something urgent's come up and I can't make it in."

"Forget urgent, we gotta get you on camera for the standup—" Conant's spit hissed through the phone; she reflexively held it away from her ear. "Can't run Marsalis without it."

"Hang on there, Bern. I'll be in first thing tomorrow." She yelped in fright: a red-haired loony rode in the back seat—but it was *her* in the rearview mirror. "What's that?" came Conant's oleo voice. He affected deafness so he could mull over his moves.

"I'll be in tomorrow."

"On second thought, no need to rush. Another story's come in that we want to use as the lead. Juno wangled an interview with Phab Kat—got to him through his new manager. . . ."

Oh, the new *white* gangsta rapper, three hundred–plus pounds, who fucked minors and shot up nightclubs? "Wait a minute, Bern, the Lincoln Center series opens in two goddamn weeks—we'll overshoot the peg for Marsalis. Better hold Juno."

"Uh, Maddy, there's no easy way to say this. But we've decided to name Juno Kwan co–arts correspondent. Of course, we'll always want your work—"

"Of course. Till Juno eases me out. And why should I do the standup at all? So you can run little pieces of Marsalis as a West Coast only on a slow night? I don't think so, Bern."

She heard his outflow of breath. "Maddy, your contract's good for what, 'nother few months? You can come in . . . whenever."

WELL, SAYONARA, *CHRONICLE;* she'd conduct the wake for her late TV career mañana. Right now she wanted "closure," a term to delight Nick. She was in excellent spirits—fuckin' merry. She went careening around the curves of Beldover, a humped road with no shoulder; past Green Glen Cemetery, where she'd lingered one enchanted May with Violet. The leaves looked dusty and tired; summer slogged on, a guest outstaying its welcome. Eggleston must be flooded from last night's rain. She thought of Linton, descending through the murk in his steel capsule, and wondered, not for the first time, why he'd been driving to the Point, shit-faced, during a hurricane. Not just for kicks, she didn't think.

Before the bridge, she veered right onto a carriage road, its entrance almost buried in scarlet poison ivy. She jolted over the ruts deep into the woods to the cabin Laila used as a studio. She parked in a stand of pines; from here the Saab was invisible from the cabin's driveway. Glossy black crows flew briskly about like busy housewives. She never came here. On account of the aviary. Built onto the rear of the cabin, the aviary, now boarded up, had once housed Serena's thirty cockatiels, bird-pharaohs wearing a hieratic headdress stamped with an orange circle. The screened hexagon, with its crossbeams and droppings-splattered floor, still spooked her.

She slid open the barnlike wooden door, then the screen. A sweetish-rank smell, maybe mouse turds. Windows half-open. Unmade bed, rumpled sheets. Someone had recently slept here. On a table cluttered with empty film cylinders, Maddy saw an ashtray. She bent to sniff: Gauloises.

A lobster barrel served as a night table. On it a bottle. Mineral oil. She jumped backward as if it were radioactive. Her toe slid on a pair of underpants on the floor. White cotton "high-cuts," only sort Laila liked. The underpants twisted into a white bow shape. As if in a parallel universe, she picked them up. The crotch stuck together—a cocktail of Laila and Nick? She flung the underpants against a window and herself out the door.

SHE NEEDED PROOF, of the *in flagrante* sort.

She camped at Conscience Point and staked out the cabin, parking in the hidden cul de sac in the pines; kept vigil in the car in her red wig, immobile as a setter sighting a squirrel; an enterprising vine could have twined up her trunk. Patrolling Wildmoor one crisp afternoon, a Saturday, she guessed, she caught the scent of wood smoke. She cut onto the carriage road. Smoke from the cabin chimney drifted above the treetops. She spotted Laila's beat-up Buick wagon and swerved off behind the pines.

Ten, twenty minutes, then a car pulled into the cabin's driveway. Maddy strained to identify the car through the scrim of pines. A manic tread drew protest from the rotting deck stairs. She caught the flicker of Jed Oliver's beak and ponytail as he slid open the screen door.

She'd dreamt it all up—of course such things don't happen! A reprieve, as if she'd just passed the mammogram. How grand to be alive. So she was crazy. A fair trade. She'd take the cure at that Swiss sanatorium where they sent Zelda Fitzgerald. The alpine air, the snowy peaks. German shrinks to dismantle her delusions. And she could have Laila back.

The screen door of the studio slid open. Jed Oliver, ejected after barely ten minutes. Too quick even for a quickie. Jed's car engine coughed into action and was gone. Maddy shivered in her barn jacket. The long shadows on the yellowing pine needles edged the chill afternoon to dusk. Tires crunched the pitted road, and a car pulled into the driveway; a car she didn't need to see, she recognized the diesel purr of the engine idling before the driver cut the ignition, heard the door meet chassis with exacting workmanship.

A flash of brown tweed jacket before he ducked into the cabin.

A high trill of laughter burst from the cabin, delirium in the laughter. They'd find her here, a frozen howl. She heard fire snapping in the hearth; she felt the silken slide of skin on skin. . . . She started toward the cabin, a lumbering yeti. In the shed, croquet mallets. She would hammer and pound and smash. Douse the rotten decking with kerosene . . . but how would she pull Laila out first? She suddenly needed to pee. Squatting in the yellowing pine needles, she floated free of her body, and peered down from a bubble high above at a creature crouched in the brush, red wig askew.

I WAS PSYCHED to go to Snowmass because I can't ski Ajax and black diamond trails.

The entry dated Aspen, March 10. She's unearthed the diary, one of many Laila has kept over the years, from a pile of clothes in her bedroom. She's never violated Laila's diaries.

> *Uncle Nicks this* awesome *skier and he gave me pointers on planting the poles, how you let your skis float around your poles. Nice of Nicko to come with me to Snowmass, considering all his hotshot skier dudes were doing there thing over at Aspen Highlands.*

For a second Maddy heard Nick's lament about the illiterates turned out by New York private schools.

> *It's awesome how Nick can "inhale" a book, his word, and figure out how to fix it. Once this wacko writer camped out on the stoop*

at Jane Street all nite, *waiting to get his manuscript back. The thing is, when Nick's really into editing, he goes into this trance thing and holes up at the Point. "Going to the mountain," he calls it. I love old Nicko, even tho I kid him about being the "gloom-ster" on account of he's real moody. And I did give him a hard time in the beginning, because of Marshall. Marshall used to gaze at mom with this total devotion, like a dog tied up in front of the market waiting for its master.*

But I can't help wondering sometimes about Nick, with that Madwoman in the Attic in North Salem—I just know *she snoops around the grounds at the Point, it creeps me out to think of it. I'd be bummed if I were mom.*

March 11. *Majorly weird: after the last run me and Nick are in the Powder Shack putting away the Coors though I hate that faschist Coors. People throwing me the Look, the usual shit. Ain't America grand that we allow* them *on our white slopes?*

And there's this hootenanny band playing cheesy music and me and Nick both at the bar hitting the Coors, wearing these dorky bandannas around our necks and mellowing out. Nick says let's dance. I don't really want to, he's such a spaz. We clomp around in our boots and bib pants and hit the Coors, and dance again, naturally Nick clomping on my toes but luckily I'm wearing moon boots, and he's real thin Nick.

Then we get some slow retro, Johnny Ray I think, and all of a sudden he's like, staring *at me. In this* guy *way. Not uncle. What a perv. We're hardly moving and I realize I've never really* seen *Nick before, I mean, he's pretty clueless, but hot in this preppie way, people often stare at him when we go somewhere, trying to figure out is he a movie star. But to me he's kind of like mom's old*

*flamestitch chair, an "old dear," that's how he talks. And now—
am I fucked up, I can't look away even if I want to, but I don't
want to! his eyes are boring into me like he's pissed, or hates me,
it's weirding me out. I give him a punch in the arm and go back to
the bar. Ay caramba, no way.*

*Later at the lodge we eat dinner with his friends at this long
table only Im nauseous and don't eat. I'm sitting far away on the
other side, really bummed. On account of how close I am with
mom and how I can't tell her. Our eyes keep glomming on like
magnets. "The Great Pretender," that's what Johnny Ray was
singing in the Powder Shack.*

*I dreamt we got off the lift together at High Rustler. Nick bends
down to tighten my boot, which he kept doing that day at Snowmass
because I had crummy rented boots, and he stays kneeling, I can see
snow on his lashes and his silly blue and white snowflake cap, and
then he lays his hand on my calf above the boot.*

*March 12. Waiting for the connecting flight in Denver I couldn't
help looking at Nick's hair, the blond streaks, and couldn't help
thinking of his other hair, darker, I once got a crotch shot when he
was at the Point in his fratboy Hawaian surfer threads . . . I was
terrified he might like say something? but Phew, he didn't, and
me and him just sat in this orange booth eating fries.*

*On the plane home now, arghhh turbulence. This gross dude
with major hal falling into my lap.*

I've decided to sleep with Jed Oliver.

A glimpse of the real tale behind the last few months' shadow play. Seeing it in Laila's girlish hand hardened the gelatinous horror into fact. A
clump of pages appeared torn out. Then:

Cherubino becalmed. The heat and bad vibes bumming me out.
We raised our glasses to drink at the same moment. I was already
with him by then, in some out of body experience. I dove off the
boat and swam as far away as I could. Some secluded villa in
Lucca with statues and cypress trees where we could be alone . . .

Another clump of pages ripped out; then just a note to buy a fish-eye lens and polarizing filter.

A TUESDAY AFTERNOON in October; at Maddy's cryptic but urgent call, Sophie had met her for a walk-around in Central Park. It being a weekday, most of New York's viable citizens were vertically stacked in airtight office towers. Only the seniors, the downsized, and the homeless were about. Plus your odd lunatic in orange dreads, manning a shopping cart resembling a mobile yard sale. And your backlash stay-at-home moms, piloting Aprica Cadillacs—or the new all-terrain stroller, the Pliko Matic Sherpa—containing giant toddlers who could have been pushing *them.* "I was tempted to steal our Jack Russell's Valium," one mother said loudly. The mothers talked superloud to drown out their sense of inconsequence in a city where only those consumed by busyness could claim to exist.

Sophie, scarcely steadier than Maddy, was still reeling from a low blow following the picnic at the Point. At the auction for *The Island* all five publishers invited to bid had "passed"; despite Sophie's strict adherence to formula, the novel was judged "too literary." Grubb was furious; finito Sophie's dream of raiding Islesford's Rescue Home and raising a posse of dogs. Worse, Sophie tended to side with her rejectionists; her self-worth lay shredded on the asphalt—*But of course I'm a worthless piece of shit, what was I thinking . . .*

"No, don't do that," Maddy had protested. "You're damn good, don't give them that power."

"Look," Sophie said, "it takes the courage of Joan of Arc refusing to recant to still believe in yourself after these donkeys do their number. And I ain't no Joan of Arc." Sophie now left her apartment only to buy groceries and teach her courses. At Maddy's call, though, she'd heroically glued herself together, as women do when a good buddy sounds a Mayday.

"Our Laila?" she shrieked, cutting Maddy off midsentence. "I don't think so. Maddy, you better seek help."

"It came to me at the picnic."

"Right, St. Paul on the road to Damascus."

"I caught them at it in Laila's studio."

"Please." Sophie extended the palm of her hand. "It's yucky to imagine your kid doing it under *any* circumstances. Anyway, that stuff's for Woody and Soon—Oooh, the poor creature!" She pointed out a beagle trundling along, its bum hind leg in a wheeled contraption.

"Laila hasn't been living at Georgia Kidd's, either," Maddy ploughed on.

"So? Tara hasn't had her own place since Yale. She lives in group 'communes' or something. These activists all seem to equate integrity with skanky bathrooms. I saw this one shower curtain when I visited, did everything but tap dance and sing 'Guantanamera.' Hell, maybe Laila bunks at Jed Oliver's." She clucked at a passing Dixie dingo with deerlike ears. "At the picnic I couldn't help noticing Mr. Pro Bono has the smallest ass."

"In the cabin at Conscience Point I saw a bottle of mineral oil," Maddy said.

"Oh, dear, couldn't be for constipation. That's Alex's generation. He once said all he wanted from life now was to take a good dump."

Pulling Sophie to a bench: "Here, read."

Sophie scanned Laila's journal entries. "Could all be fantasy. Ski resorts are sexy—those dudes in the hot tub wearing Stetsons and nothing else. Though I will grant you the bit about 'already with him by then' is troubling. I dunno. . . ."

They rose and followed a path laid with stinky yellow gingko leaves. "I actually badgered Nick to let her crew for him on the Block Island race!" Maddy said. "To promote family togetherness!"

"Yeah, well, good deeds have a way of biting you in the ass, as they say. Why not just confront them?"

Maddy narrowed her eyes. "I'm not ready to confront Laila. I have my reasons."

"Oh, sorry, I forgot: your big dark secret history. Does *any*one believe that horseshit about the orphanage?"

"I'm going to crush them."

Sophie froze. "What, and play Medea? Watch out. She was a sorceress and her father a god, a player. When Medea got done whacking everyone, she rode her chariot and Dad's connections to Olympus; Jean Harris just got a heart attack in the slammer. I mean, okay, whack Nick. He's the grownup, he's responsible."

"I thought that, too, at first. Laila was seduced, ravished. . . . But Nick never pursues. The world comes to *him*. He must have been seriously provoked."

"Do I hear you making excuses for Nick? Me, I'd kill anyone who *wished* harm on my child. Even though my son the hotshot bond trader has fired his own goddamn mother and keeps me from my grandchildren—now, his wife I could kill. And Tara goes to Yale to major in guerrilla warfare when she could be CEO of a green corporation!"

"That's just the point: they're a pain in the ass—but they're *yours*. Laila's mine only by a choice, an act of will. She's not"—Maddy held both hands parallel before her, trying to grasp her own idea—"Laila's not of my flesh."

Sophie gazed at her, mouth ajar. "Oh, Maddy, you must really be pushed to the edge to say something so vile."

"I couldn't have produced a monster who could do this."

"Oh, please, blood relatives have been fucking each other over since the Old Testament, starting with Cain and Abel. Joseph and his coat—didn't his brothers hate his guts? Just watch the afternoon talk shows. Anyway, you've always been tighter with Laila than I am with my own . . . my blood daughter. You're soulmates. Even as a child, Laila had something you could call . . . grace." She cocked her head at Maddy, overtaken by a fresh thought. "I still think you've imagined the whole thing. Because what blooming young woman would choose a near-*altecocker* over a hot young dude? When I think of this guy before Alex—the wattles, the rattles, hairy ears, camel breath, leg spasms, toenail fungus, gas, gout—"

"Uh, Nick's a bit more appealing."

They crossed a bridle path and arrived at the reservoir. "Whatever happened with Nessa?" Sophie said, yanking a curl. "Didn't she satisfy Nick's craving for a hard-body?"

"And I should have been *grateful?*" *The excitement of newness doesn't appeal to me in the least,* he'd once said. "You know, Nick and Laila both consider me a control freak. So be it. I'll design the perfect payback."

"Wouldn't it be better just to give Laila a cuff on the ear, cut off her allowance, and send her to her room? And tell Nicholas Humbert you'll clap a restraining order on him? And then go about your business? That's what the professionals tell you: go about your business. You lose a lover, a kidney, a boob . . . 'Go about your business.'"

Maddy stopped and placed a hand on Sophie's forearm. "Revenge *is* my business. Hey, y'know what? You're looking at Revenge Inc. Open for business."

CHAPTER II

Safe Love

Ya got Vanessa-Mae, babe fiddler in a wet tee-shirt." With a switch of his reed, he beheaded some orange milkweed. "Ya got Michael Bolton singing Puccini—*and* it's number one on the Billboard classical charts." A backhand *thwack* at the goldenrod. "Now ya got *Newsweek* calling 'crossover' the future of classical music. *Future?* How about *death.*" Some purple asters floated free of their stems.

"Uh . . . Tony? That's still no reason to raze the countryside."

"What?" He glanced around, bewildered. "Oh, sorry, sorry . . ."

A silent groan. She revered Anton. But like a summons to jury duty, he arrived on her doorstep when her every molecule was focused elsewhere. And when they weren't astounding the world—she allowed the unkind thought—these genius types were barely civilized.

They continued along Wildmoor at a fast clip, she struggling a bit to keep up; remembering how Anton would bounce onstage, tunnel-visioned, and fall onto the piano. Turning onto Point Road, they arrived at a tree riven by lightning. One half was blasted dead; its living half sported scarlet leaves. That the live half was gamely soldiering on tipped her toward tears. *No, we will not blubber.* They crossed Eggleston Bridge over water churned by warring currents. Storm clouds boiled overhead, parting to release a beam of wan sunlight. Nick's catamaran lay tipped over on eelgrass. The wind rhythmically clinked its guylines, twanging her impatience to tend to business.

In her distraction, she must have missed a sentence, because here was Anton saying, "It's a goddamn fuckin' miracle."

"Wait, back up, what is?"

"I've signed with Columbia Artists." He shrugged and planted his fireplug shape to watch a giant V of geese stream honking through the sky. "E-flat major," he said, pointing upward. "It's sad how I know this, isn't it?"

She seized him by the shoulders. "My God, Anton, CA? Congratulations! And you didn't tell me first thing, you dope?" He endured her embrace like a sullen adolescent. Then he marched off with a tiptoey gait to the bluffs. She followed him down the stairs to the water. "Uh, is there something I'm missing?" she said.

He kicked at the sand with a prison-issue boot. "All my failure stemmed from her, hating her gave me a reason to get up in the morning," he said in a demigrowl.

A moment to identify *her.* "Oh, don't tell me—you mean you're still stuck with the ex-wife? Listen. You've come back from Palookaville, you got it, your second life—d'you realize? How many pianists get a second shot? Or anyone? It's a miracle, and you deserve it. And frankly, I'm envious as hell. Don't, please, go and wreck your own party."

He cut her a savage look. "Katrine's goddamn dying. Pancreatic cancer."

Maddy grasped his sleeve. "Oh, Tony, I'm sorry."

He roughly shook off her hand. "Do you know how many times I've wished her dead?"

"No, no, *no.*" She laughed harshly. "*You* cannot make her dead. Even *you* are not that powerful."

"She won't stay in that hospice place. She wants me to take her in. There's no one else."

"Do it, for godssake, take her in."

"What, in my roach motel?"

"Hire a housekeeper . . . a nurse."

"I'm nothing but her last resort."

"*So? Be* her last resort. It's a gift, don't you see? You should feel blessed." She looked down at the wet sand pocked with airholes. Clams and fiddler crabs, a whole universe of critters tunneled and grubbed away down there, oblivious to *them*. She thought of all those clams wanting a life; the riven tree still making leaves; and then she thought of the dancers in Radio City who'd come to New York with their American smiles and legs, now under the earth; her old tailor on Barrow Street with numbers on his forearm who saw no reason ever to smile—What ever made them imagine they could set the terms?

She sank to her knees. "I'm so fucking smart," she bawled, putting her face in her hands. Sensing him hovering, hand stretched toward her, clumsy, making her bawl louder, not bothering now to hide her face, mouth downturned in a rubbery grimace.

Finally he kneeled on the sand beside her and put his arms around her. She turned her nose into his neck, and he pulled her closer, his cheek smooth above the rough sweater, it was all she wanted for the moment, and she told him how it was with her and Nick, and there they remained for a while.

TO CELEBRATE ANTON'S new management—her vendetta could wait an hour—she broke out the Courvoisier and tin of pâté she'd bought duty-free in May at Charles de Gaulle. At least she'd had the presence of mind, back on the beach, to omit any mention of Laila. Anton, as in the old days, had a horror of drafts, and all heat had mysteriously deserted the downstairs. They carried the cognac, pâté, and two snifters upstairs, past Serena's gaze, and settled in the cozier guest room, with its mullioned alcove and blue velvet divan.

Anton knocked back his cognac, wrist elegant beneath his threadbare cuff. "Confession. When I was around ten and enamored of you, I used to spy on you. When we were in music camp. You must have been around fifteen and you had a pimply string-player boyfriend. One afternoon I followed you into the woods."

Maddy called up a dim image of a boy with white-blond hair, bursting groin, eager hands.

"I actually watched from behind a tree. You and him making out. Rolling about in a sand pit."

"Couldn't have been sand." Maddy laughed. "Merriwell was in the Adirondacks."

"Whatever. I found it terribly arousing. You sort of imprinted me. Became my erotic ideal."

If memory served, Katrine was fair and chesty, but it was all in the perception.

"God knows how you thought of me," Anton said.

She remembered, somehow, his armpits, pale tan like a cartoon bear's. "You were a scary prodigy. And a bit like my little brother."

"And now?"

A moment. "Hey, I'm really happy we found each other again. You're part of a time I love dearly. My God, the sense of possibility we had. You had only to walk through the door."

The cognac licked through her. He refilled their glasses. A silence gathered. They'd entered a zone where words lost their purchase; a different language roiled beneath. Outside, the wind drove rain into the windows, and the metallic patter and the Courvoisier fanned the warmth within. Anton had shifted into a corner of the divan and now looked at her, smoky-lidded, the full-frontal mating look. Dormant places inside her quivered alive. How long it had been . . . Not since Nohant . . . He felt less the little brother now, though maybe a bit, which upped the heat. She saw his wrists, a neglected male erotic feature, his thick comb-back of a Russian mobster, and wanted his weight to crush her, his roughness, the exciting strangeness, this body not Nick's. She closed her eyes. They would root around in each other and shut out Nick trawling down Laila's cinnamon body, fuck them out of existence. . . .

The divan's ancient springs released from under her. She opened her eyes. He sat watching her, arms crossed, from a fringed ottoman. "Guess the timing's off," he said glumly. "For both of us."

Had she entered the rejection sweepstakes? She was suddenly walloped by the *randomness:* she a fist of rage, yet snatching at pleasure; Katrine marked by a black X.

"Timing's off especially for *you,*" Anton added.

The booze slowing her reaction time. "Oh, I can take care of myself," she said shortly.

"Yeah, I know. But can I take care of *my*self."

She chewed that over. He'd read her and wanted more than a revenge fuck. Used to be, she reflected, a revenge fuck would do just fine, and you could always come back for more. Still, Anton's . . . *intentions,* you could call it, soothed her battered pride. They sat quietly, listening to the vast rustle of the rain, and she understood that he'd decided to take in Katrine. The thought yielded a melancholy twilight pleasure.

"The thing is, I could feel strongly about you, and I couldn't trust myself to deal with the consequences of that," he blurted.

She laughed. "Shouldn't it be simpler?"

"All I know is, why set yourself up for pain again? Why can't we have one of those grand friendships, a 'friend of the heart,' like in the nineteenth century? Or those BBC guys, you know—Charles in *Brideshead Revisited.* And the other, uh, teddy-bear guy—"

"Sebastian. But they were secretly in love, those two."

An uncomfortable silence; Anton stretched his neck around. "But you get my drift—I mean, not 'just friends,' in that ball-less way. I'm talking *passion*. Only minus the sex and torment," he added, as if he'd just discovered Velcro.

"But sex and torment is the fun part."

"Seriously. We'd be the one you always count on. I'll be your ear, you'll be mine. I'll sit at the back of the hall during your run-through for a concert. 'Sounds rushed in the end,' I'll say. You'll do the same. 'Not . . . *brazen* enough,' you'll say. 'Wrong tempo.' We'll be brutal. The one who never bullshits you. Us against them, each other's safe haven."

She nodded to herself, lips pursed. "Safe love," she said. "Why the hell not." And if it didn't exist, maybe they'd just invented it.

CHAPTER 12

425 Palenque

I*t's war between us now!* she declared to the empty house, like Rastignac throwing down the gauntlet to the city of Paris.

She knocked back two Nescafés made from hot tap water—vendettas were best undertaken sober. To get pumped for battle, she ran upstairs to Laila's room to pan for more scenes from the seraglio. A rogue draft squeaked the hinges of Laila's door. Her scalp prickled as she turned to peer at the dim hall. She pictured herself, a lone figure in the few lighted rooms of this hulking castle. The locals had it that a murdered bride dressed in white regularly appeared at the head of the stairs. Steady on . . .

Maddy's eye settled on Laila's books. On a shelf beneath *The War Against Children of Color,* a neatly stacked, battered set of Tintins and Babars they'd both cherished—through Laila she'd reclaimed her own lost childhood. She almost smiled at Laila's mental calculus: Tintin's author a possible collaborator; Babar racist and imperialist—yet for Laila nostalgia had eclipsed principle. And here was their green-covered *Myths and Enchantment Tales,* its pages taped with yellowing Scotch tape; in the frontispiece, in a pride of penmanship, LAILA SHAYE. She opened to "Admetus and Alcestis," a favorite; when Death comes to claim Admetus: "Oh, let *me* die for him," Alcestis says, clear-eyed and unhesitating. She paged to "Arcas and Calisto," who ended up the Big Bear and the Little Bear, the sky their playground. Here was "Jason and the Golden Fleece." "Because she loved him, Medea left her father's land and sailed away in the *Argo* with Jason and his comrades. But sad to relate, they did not live happily ever after." Spare the young reader. . . .

On the oak dresser top a neat display of Laila's treasures: shellacked stones from the Point; a photo that amused them both of Laila straddling Old Dobbin, its head down, heart longing for the stable; Laila's collection of figurines. Maddy picked up a tiny metal squirrel couple under a detachable parasol—the one she'd bought in La Chatre, near Nohant. Her palms ached. Why did a person's belongings make them defenseless? She saw herself in some parallel universe crouched in the pines, conjuring mayhem . . . How could you harm the owner of two squirrels under a parasol, the gent suited up under a red jacket, his lady in a striped skirt? Laila got a polio shot and the hateful prongs punctured her own skin.

It flooded back, the loveliness Laila had shown her . . . Day three without a phone and she's stroked out on the linoleum of their toadhole. Laila gets her to a chair. *Have some applesauce, Mom.* Briskly tidies the kitchen . . . Maddy wandered about Laila's room touching the frames of photos, the green glass shade of a kerosene lamp, awash in memories. Laila's dear face in the waiting room of St. Vincent's after yet another D and C. The white bowls with the blue stripe they'd bought one wintry Sunday in Conran's—to Laila they might have been the crown jewels. Her radar for the city's invisible, the smiling Paki baby who lived with his parents down in the subway newsstand. The tailor on Barrow Street with the numbered forearm—

This was a helluva way to launch Revenge Inc. She returned to command central in the library. She'd retaliate with silence. To keep Laila in the dark about her own past—at least for the moment—that would be plenty cruel and unusual.

Nick, though. If she could vaporize this body she still craved, desire living on like fingernails growing on the dead . . . But after one orgasmic spasm when the bullet lodges, she'd be caught in the coils of criminal justice. Violence was a bad idea for nervous persons like herself. If a bass tympanist played off-key, she heard nails drawn across slate. How did a murderer calmly eat a "BLT down" after feeding a body through a wood chipper? Why quibble over whether a killer was insane—weren't they *all,* or at least imaginatively neutered? If aspiring killers could envision what they unleashed: the convulsions, released sphincters, glassy eyeballs, bloody bubbles, green fluids, macabre rattles . . . She'd once seen a cremation in a Danish art film. The grisly efficiency, decor by Ikea! the charred skeleton appearing to rise up in the flames in final supplication—it was enough to send anyone screaming from the room.

She could outsource Nick's murder, so her finger need never touch the button. But her Rolodex was short on hired assassins. She'd go for a bloodless payback. Bring Nick down in a head game. And when the dust settled, Laila was welcome to whatever was left of him.

At the single chime of the hall clock, she rose, laser-focused, as when tackling a Liszt étude. Someplace in this house she scented blood. Whatever lay behind that evergreen hatred between Nick and Vi would furnish her best ammunition.

THE NIGHT THEY'D busted apart, Nick had been reading some rag on recycled paper that she thought he'd tried to conceal. She sorted through the pile of bound galleys on the green felt table, sudden heat blasting up her back—Nancy Drew with hot flashes. Paused at *Left Week,* addressed to Laila. Ads for a socially responsible index fund and a "compassionate listening tour of Israel." She skimmed a piece about protests at Harvard over the appointment of one Carlos de Aguilar as a fellow at the Kennedy School. The Mexican general had apparently long been in bed with the

CIA, and rumors still circulated of a bizarre crime in his youth, including a cover-up.

De Aguilar and a juvenile crime . . . it stirred a dormant memory. She was back in Nick's MG at the Islesford station, crickets thrumming in the afternoon heat. *Linton was playing "war" with two friends—or was it two brothers?—and they "executed" the maid.* When she'd since tried to draw him out about it, she'd gotten morose silence. She still remembered one poignant detail: The maid was wearing cheap black shoes.

New Left in hand, she ran upstairs to Nick's study and switched on a Tiffany lamp, uncertain what to look for. On the mantel, a stuffed owl's beady stare; wooden boat models and bronze sailing trophies, several awarded to Ashcroft père. She fell upon Nick's desk and rifled through a drawer, hands working like the paws of a terrier digging in sand. Bank statements, boat insurance, stock buys and sells slapped to the floor. She froze at a snapshot of Nick and Maddy in La Chatre, she wearing her smile of a woman with all the luck.

The right bottom drawer jammed; falling on her knees, she worked it open. An old *Daily News* clip dated 1965. She zoomed in on the headline: "Love-Crazed Heiress Stabs Self in Columbia Bar." A photo of a girl she dimly recognized, in Peter Pan collar and harlequin glasses. A fuzzier one of Violet in riding habit, her heedless, arrogant stare. The faces gazed out from the faded paper and the warp of years. The "heiress" had followed Violet into the West End Bar near Columbia. The heiress had reportedly said, "If you won't love me, then kill me"—then turned the knife on herself.

A rush of autumn wind rattled the casement windows. Why had Nick kept this clip?

She stood, and suddenly went light-headed. She'd been living on cognac and caffeine. Down in the kitchen she fixed a snack of sardines and water crackers and devoured them standing over the counter. Then she reread the story about the Harvard protests. A spidery footnote cited an article in *Excelsior,* a Mexican newspaper, dated December 16, 1952, for more on de Aguilar's "bizarre crime."

She headed back upstairs to her computer in their bedroom. *Www. Excelsior.com* brought Excelsior Cigar Company. She added "newspaper" and got the site. *Buscador* took her to *archivo,* then *documentas*— finally, December 16, 1952. "For more information check link to the original article." The account of de Aguilar's crime"?

The link returned 404: *page not found.*

Could someone have gotten the story deleted? She sat for several minutes, feeling the house lose heat, hearing wind worry the windows in their sashes. Her mind looped back to Nick's account of the shooting. Something jangled, a dissonant chord.

Violet had been a pack rat. Maybe a dig through her papers might yield more. She went to an alcove behind the stairs and opened a mahogany armoire that could stow a body. Violet's sketch pads, portfolios, cartons of old notebooks from Miss Porter's and Barnard. Long slog ahead, and no heat reached here. She pulled on an Irish sweater of Nick's, then attacked a carton. At some point she registered the downstairs clock had chimed three. From a moldy accordion file came scurrying something pale and larval—and there, in a fold, she saw a batch of newspaper clips tied with a shoelace—in Spanish. A leftover sob caught in her throat.

She lifted out yellowed papers fragile as dragonfly wings. One paper dated December 17, 1952. A bottom headline read, TRES NIÑITOS "FUSI-LARON" A UNA SIRVIENTA. A subhead read, *Nueve, Ocho, y Seis Años Tienen los Homicidas.*

Stiff with cold, she struggled to her feet and lurched downstairs to the warmth of the library. Then she read on, not getting every word, getting the gist, though. "Playing at War Three Little Boys 'Execute' a Servant," she translated.

Tres niñitos. Maddy moved the faded news clip directly under the lamp. A photo of dark-eyed Carlos de Aguilar. Another showed a grave-eyed boy of a beauty to entice Gustave Aschenbach: she recognized, from Violet's portrait, Linton Ashcroft. And beside him—her heart thudded— another enchanting face: bowl haircut, parted lips, round eyes staring into the camera.

Abruptly she got it, the piece that hadn't parsed: *the maid's black shoes.* She was back at the Islesford Station in Nick's MG. *I was away in the country at my aunt's,* Nick had said. *So how could he have known about the black shoes?*

A pause to savor her Sherlock moment. Then: "These three rascals executed their servant Milagros, who was twelve years old, when they were playing war yesterday," she managed to translate. "They were arrested by the police and . . . *No se dieron cuenta exacta de lo que habían hecho* . . ." Her Spanish faltered. The event had occurred the day before at noon at 425 Palenque, in the borough of Narvarte. The children had shot the maid in the left side of the face with a .22-caliber rifle. Then they had gone on playing. When another servant asked them what they had done, they answered, full of satisfaction: "Ya matamos a Milagros!" "We already killed Milagros!"

"At the police station the boys appeared disturbed because they couldn't play. Carlos, the oldest, seemed upset, but seeing his two friends, he laughed with them. They repeated over and over that they were playing war and Milagros was sentenced to death. . . . Most people felt the responsible party was Mr. Ashcroft, because he left the rifle within reach of the children. But Mrs. Ashcroft told the police the gun was in a locked closet, and only Milagros had the key. So it was the maid's fault.

" 'Milagros was a very hard worker and very clean,' Mrs. Ashcroft said. 'I'm really sorry about what happened.' "

Milagros's last name was never discovered. The girl had been traveling alone from house to house working for food and lodging when the Ashcrofts hired her.

She studied a final clip from a second paper, *El Universal,* its yellowed edges crumbling like ash. One quotation pulsed at her like an exposed heart: *"Yo la mate con un tiro."*

So here, finally, Bluebeard's throne of blood at the end of the corridor. Maddy sat unmoving, forehead in the icy palm of her hand. From downstairs, the French clock chimed five; she sensed the chill blackness outside start to come alive. She pitied him. To wake to this every morning. Though maybe he'd expelled it from memory like a fish shitting in the sea—like the psychologist prescribed, she remembered from Nick's account in the MG. Maybe he'd come to believe his own fiction.

Of course Violet had known—might even have been present—and never, in their mutual savagery, let him forget. While Nick counted on her sullen complicity because of what he had on her. Surely, though, he suspected Violet had these clips squirreled away. Why hadn't he destroyed them?

Maybe Nick had wanted *her* to know. Set up this moment. To share the burden? Receive her absolution? Or had Nick found a more creative use of his past. Something chilling came clear, dazzling in its logic, really. In Nick's tortuous reasoning, his guilt had freed him—*since he was already damned*—to take Laila.

She looked out at the dawn, in her mouth a taste of brass. They said you never really know another person. Like hell. You knew. She'd known. Just not specifics. She'd let the thing scuttle under the neo-Gothic woodwork. To protect their luck.

In the bathroom off the kitchen, she stared at the face of a woman who hadn't cared how many slaughtered brides Nick had stowed away, so long as they could go on together. That was then, this was now.

CHAPTER 13

The Argonaut File

Jed Oliver came rocketing through Panarella's beak first, endangering waiters, glassware, and other freestanding objects. Maddy watched in dismay as he vacuumed up bread, *caponata,* and Gavi di Gavi and rubbed his eye so the socket squeaked—practically in a single phrase.

She'd set up this lunch, she had to remind herself.

After Anton's wife had died, she'd driven in from command central to offer what comfort she could.

The next day she met Sophie for a drink. Sophie, it turned out, was newly energized by the ancient wisdom she'd internalized from her Zen body-sculpting class: the world will tell you NO in a thousand ways, but she would counter with chants: *I am power, I am light . . . What you reap is what you sow . . . I'm okay, you're not—er, you're okay.* DON'T LET 'EM FUCK YA! So Sophie was back revising Grubb's much-reviled novel. She'd consulted Jed on some legal hugger-mugger in the novel's plot, which had set Maddy thinking: Why not tap Jed's expertise for her *own* plot? She could hardly approach her tight-assed attorney at Debevoise & Plimpton; he'd consider her a traitor to his and Nick's class. . . .

Jed fixed her with blue avenger-angel eyes. "So why am I here? I know you've never much cared for me, and then after I got involved with

Laila . . ." *Dead meat,* said his shrug. "Though Nick seemed to dislike me even more, for his own inscrutable reasons—maybe oedipal." She choked on her Gavi di Gavi. "But the truth about the business with Laila is . . . complicated. Things no sooner started than she, uh . . . uh, signed off, yeah. Seemed almost panicked. Though the affair was . . . kinda *her* idea. I never did figure out what happened." He blew out. "Now you can add 'indiscreet and dishonorable' to your brief against me!"

"Jed, thank you for coming," Maddy said. She looked down at her napkin. Laila's try at diverting the flow of lust from Nick to Jed about as effective as diverting the Rio Grande. That Laila had attempted this doomed maneuver squeezed her heart strangely.

TIMELINE

March. *Laila and Nick connect in Aspen.*

April. *Laila throws herself at Jed.*

May. *At Nohant, Nick freaks over Lolita/Laila, desire flaring like an illness he thought in remission.*

July. *He sets up Nessa as the decoy.*

The wine went metallic on her tongue.

"After Laila, I'm convinced I'm the worst lay in New York," Jed said gloomily, giving the eye another squeaky rub. "I'm off love."

Like Sophie, like Anton—though Jed was a bit underage for this midlife refrain. Maybe they could all sign up for masturbation classes with Betty Dodson, the sex guru who conducted hands-on workshops in self-loving. At the next table four female rainmakers brayed in voices selectively bred to penetrate the infernal din de rigueur in happenin' New York restaurants.

"This is confidential," Maddy said.

"Say *what?*"

"IT'S CONFIDENTIAL," she shouted.

"JESUS, YOU CAN'T THINK THAT LITTLE OF ME," Jed hollered back.

Jed studied the Spanish newspaper clips and translation while her *vitello tonnato* aged on its plate. She'd never seen Jed as anything beyond Laila's *meshugga* boyfriend and a social climber. She'd been unfair, she now decided, with a rush of fellow feeling. The poor guy must indeed have been raised by wolves, he was a walking textbook of dysfunction. And those meds that maintained him must put the kibosh on his sex life. *Laila signed off*—Oh dear, some intro . . .

"Why does this not surprise me? I mean, about Nick," Jed said, barging into her thoughts. He handed her the clips. "And you want to know if we could reopen the case and put Nick's head on the chopping block. The short answer is no. Even if he was in fact as old as seven, as your notes indicate, the latest studies show that up to age eleven, kids can't really envision the consequences of actions. For them, dead hasn't the same finality. Plus there's a statute of limitations. And no one would testify against Nick. We don't even know the name of the girl's family. Uh, if you don't want your veal . . ." She passed him her plate. "But suppose this story appeared in some blab sheet," Jed went on, mouth full, a beat behind her own thought. "Nick could be tried in the court of public opinion."

She heard Laila's intake of breath as she ingested the story. A Third World domestic treated as subhuman. The same shot that snuffed Milagros would snuff Laila's—whatever it was.

Maddy tore off a bit of olive bread. Nick so finicky and private. A juicy tale of gunplay south of the border in the *Intelligencer*, and he might cast off in the *Cherubino* and never be heard from again. Suicide an Ashcroft family reflex. Violet, though of the living, had self-destructed years ago.

Jed formed his hands into a megaphone to be heard over their neighbors, now shrieking like howler monkeys. She pictured his words flashing across his forehead, like a libretto at the Metropolitan Opera. "You'll feed the story to the vivacious Davidine Swann, the new society flack at *Vanity Fair*. They salivate over tales of prominent families brought low by booze, priapism, homicidal itches. The Binghams of Kentucky, Stanford White the satyr, Skakel the patrician killer—and now the Ashcrofts! The tone set by the founding father—didn't he murder his heiress wife? Generations later, Nick Ashcroft, the last scion, strikes a blow for infamy. As revenges go, an article would have a certain elegance. Sure beats this talk show I saw about people stalking their exes and bugging the toilet seat . . . And doesn't Nick work for that Latin rights outfit? The irony is . . . *perfecto!*" He rubbed his eye. "Jeez, I dunno, I always thought you—" His words swallowed in a din to drown out the final blast of *Wozzeck*.

Had more class? She pressed the tines of her fork into her hand. "Listen, Jed, thanks for this—but please don't go all righteous on me. There's more to it. . . ."

Jed daintily applied his index finger to the remaining crumbs of almond pear tart. "I just think you've come to the wrong professional. Why not consult one of those couples therapists women are always trying to drag me to? I mean, Nessa's a fox, but a lightweight compared to you, Maddy; I give it another month. So Nick's CV is not exactly pristine—but we're talkin' forty years ago. There were two older boys present. Those kids had absorbed their family's caste sense of privilege." Jed looked at her, eyes swimming in blue. "Maybe you have to absolve people. If they've struggled to pay some sort of retribution. Help Nick get clear of this."

"Nick's way beyond my help. And while we're doing advice, why don't *you* put it together with a nice woman your age?"

Sheepish grin. "Oh, who would put up with me? I live on takeout, fart with abandon, scatter chips in bed, read all night. And where would I go to masturbate? Believe me, I've heard the brief: I'm 'withholding,' 'unevenly developed,' 'a borderline personality'—the guy they warn against in the women's magazines. I'm tired of hurting women!"

. . .

THE RAIN HAS made her late. She stands, umbrella dripping onto the Bokhara, in the Stanhope's lobby. The tireless Davidine is doing a "fly-by" at the Ileitis Foundation of America charity, chaired by Islesford's own Viqui Troutt-Matlin, and suggested this meet-up place.

Forget Rubens, Titian, *volupté*—here the feminine ideal is Starving Boy. Maddy bobs and weaves *catch you later!* in search of Davidine. She collides with Amos Grubb, exactly her height. He holds her at arm's length, eyeing her beneath shaggy brows. "Maddy, collect yourself." *How must she look?* "You are superb. He doesn't deserve you. Now, listen—come walk with me—I'm gonna want your input on the arts center I'm planning. Yep, I'm trying again! I just bought the land. . . ."

"Thank you, Amos, you're a pal. Always have been. I'd like to be a part of this, but give me some time. . . . We'll talk." She embraces him for a long moment.

Parked in a corner with his keeper, Viqui's spouse, emir of mobile toilets, nods off in a wheelchair, looking like an orange Yoda, recognizing no one. Earlier that fall he'd collapsed on the tennis court after a great get in the senior doubles championship; a tragedy, with him a new father, everyone agreed. A nose job from *Les Demoiselles d'Avignon* glides by. Up against the chipped gold wall, a jowly satyr nuzzles a doughy nymph, one of the new Viagra couples. Maddy spots the young editor labeled by Page Six "the hottest thing in publishing." The woman's accustomed to fending off importunate writers and agents, but since no one tonight is importuning, she appears to be batting away invisible gnats. And there's Jed, high on A-list vibes! Lunging at a woman with iron-colored hair who funded Artspace on the Pond.

Viqui Troutt-Matlin, a ripple of biceps and lats, swans toward the podium to introduce the speakers. "Pepperazzi," Viqui calls the folks whom Nick will attract like flies once she plants her ammo. "Viqui's come a ways since those pool parties," someone murmurs. "God, you look great!" (still alive). "But the rain forest *ruined* my hair." "Dictatorships are the safest places to travel." "Have you tried that dog psychiatrist? You can fly your pet to him in cabin, first class." "I'm *epically* busy!" Rowena Grubb hobbles by on a cane, disabled by workouts at Lotte Berk, one of many first wives who put themselves through the rack for fear of getting traded like the starter mansion. Hard on her heels come the brother-and-sister twins known as the "Holocaust hustlers."

And who is she to judge these people? They're spending down the hours like everyone else, albeit leaving behind a pavilion in a hospital bearing their name that in time will evoke zero memories. She's not so unlike them, she should have told Laila that time. She's always been as greedy, in her fashion, for *more,* as avid . . . *rapacious* as they. Just more graceful about camouflaging it. Oh, yeah, she's a member in good standing here.

She locates Davidine Swann, hair a knockoff of Louis Quatorze's, sitting in a cushioned alcove in the lobby bar. Maddy stands very still at the bar's entrance. She watches Davidine raise a compact mirror to the light and smile into it to check her teeth. A doorman darkens her peripheral vision, his schooled eye perceiving a threat to the silken hum of his universe. *Can I help you, madam?*

She shrugs on her raincoat and walks back out into the black wash on 5th, headlights flashing on gleaming pavement; opens *swock* her umbrella. Turns down 82nd Street. The maw of a trash can beckons. She could toss the packet of clips nesting in her bag, walk away from everything and start a new life in the Finger Lakes.

Toss your best ammo? Deny yourself deep satisfaction? You're owed. Payback restores the cosmic order. *I want to get him before God does,* said the Massad agent about an ancient, ailing Nazi. And didn't she just read somewhere that the need for revenge is built into the genes? That we're hardwired for it? Who is she to violate the natural order? Who is she to fuck with the cosmos? She circles the block in the pneumonia damp and fetches up under the heated entrance to the Stanhope. *Here goes, just sit back and enjoy the ride.* Davidine looks up, her eye the jolly black disk of a hammerhead.

"I'm sorry I brought you out on such a filthy night."

"Darling, I'm sure you'll make it worth my while. I think I'm about to hear something delicious. Sit, sit."

Perched on a barstool, a woman with spun-vanilla hair in high black boots shoots anxious glances at the entrance.

"*Sooo?* Talk to me. You're in good company: Mia Farrow, Claire Bloom—"

Maddy waves her silent.

"You're right," Davidine says, "by the time the book comes out, who cares? And when the miniseries rolls around—I mean, did anyone watch Mia's *Love and Betrayal* from Payback Productions? I don't think so. Actually, the timing for you, my dear, couldn't be nicer. You knew about Americas Watch, of course."

She didn't.

"The chief's stepping down—and they say Nick Ashcroft's on the short list to head it up."

Nice timing? no, *exquisite*. Nick's big book a dud . . . his imprint floundering . . . The job at Americas Watch would be no vanity post—it would throw him a lifeline. And she'll go snip-snip. She's on the side of the angels, could there be a more grotesque man for the job than Nick? So why does the side of the angels make her nauseous?

"Maddy, you look peaky. You could use a shot—Oh, waiter!"

Sweating like a demon under her Burberry. Such good company she's in: Davidine, queen of the bottom-feeders . . . the legions of wronged women . . . the buggers of toilet seats . . . the world's squealers and ratters and stoolies . . .

She's losing momentum, losing lift. Strike Nick down like this, and he'll take her down with him. This she hasn't foreseen. They'll be twinned in vileness, flailing in the sewer together. And the face she'll wake to in the mirror will not be anyone she wants to know. She's been so clever. Or not clever enough. Snookered. It's a giant fraud, this tooth for a tooth. You still end up minus a tooth. And some other intangible part as well. What happened to Medea, she wanted to know, the morning after the mayhem? Did she write in the Argonaut papers it had all been a dreadful mistake?

"You know, Davidine, I once saw this really cheesy B movie."

"Movie? What movie."

"Guy gets all his ducks lined up to destroy his enemy—and then he tosses his gun and walks away. The guy's a loser, a total asshole. Yet even *he* just . . . walks away."

"Could we talk cinema another time? Oh, waiter, there you are! A Dewar's! Maddy, how do you take it? Or do you prefer single malt."

"No, Davidine, thank you, no."

"You're right, booze is hell on the skin. Waiter, bring us two tonics with grenadine. Sooo, talk to me, hon."

"I'm truly sorry, Davidine, but it turns out I have nothing for you."

"Dearie, scum always rises."

"The truth is, I didn't think this through very well, I'm as surprised as you are. And disappointed. Call it a failure of imagination. At the last moment, I can't see myself doing what I came to do, literally can't see it."

"And you are literally getting me nuts."

"Look, I'm sorry I—I led you on. But I'm afraid you will have come for nothing. We do what we can do."

She gets herself up past Davidine, and past the puzzled waiter arriving with their drinks, out of the bar and past the doorman's Aztec mask, onto 5th Avenue brimming with wet, and steps smartly into the rain not bothering to open her umbrella.

CHAPTER 14

Schubert's Glasses

S he snapped upright on the daybed. Bach's Toccata and Fugue in D Minor powered on, notes striking like pistons—the very notes she'd been striking in her dream, only somehow she'd been playing it on the organ. What the devil—she was now, it appeared, *awake*. She gave herself a shake. Or *dreaming* awake?

Bring on the mayhem! The ghosts and hants and restless spirits that had always lurked in the woodwork, kept vigil in the silent, closed-off rooms, had finally taken over at Conscience Point. She went stumbling toward the music room, draped in the red afghan throw. Ready to join the *danse macabre*.

At the piano sat no ghost but a fleshly presence in a tan duffel, nose in air, eyes shut, indeed playing the Bach. She listened from the door, annoyance melting to awe at the springy touch, the rock-steady pulse. He cut off; acknowledged her with a curt nod before ripping into Beethoven's *Hammerklavier,* singing deep in his throat, abominably, as he played. Madame O had made her sight-sing . . . *Let the piano penetrate the air like a human voice* . . . Then he drifted to sections of Tchaikovsky's *Eugene Onegin*. Segued into "Eleanor Rigby"—and ended midphrase.

"You never answer the phone. Sophie's worried. What the hell are you doing here?" He pulled a muffler around his neck.

She adjusted the throw around her like a derelict preening, tasting the aftermath of an extended happy hour, wondering where she'd left the bottle. "What the hell are *you* doing here?"

Anton shuddered in his duffel. "Could we discuss it after you turn up the heat in this pile? I can't afford a cold."

She hiked the hall thermostat. Slipping into the bathroom for a spot of damage control, she brushed her teeth and drew her hair up at the crown into a barrette. She remembered Julien Sorel's crack about the worst feature of prison: you couldn't close your door to visitors.

"I OWE YOU," Anton said in his brusque manner. They'd settled in the library, hands wrapped around mugs of smoky tea. "Without your tongue-lashing, I wouldn't have had the time with Katrine."

Forgiveness: a country to which she lacked the passport.

"It was a gift, that time," he went on. "You helped me to see that. You've been a great friend to me, Maddy, and I have to say, after my career tanked . . . well, there went the 'friends,' too. So now I wanna . . . now it's *your* turn for a little tough love. I see you pulling the plug on yourself, squandering time, while Kat clung desperately to life—*sleep* exhausted her, Maddy, *sleep!* And I can't fathom the stupidity. Schubert wore his glasses to bed, so if he woke wanting to jot a musical inspiration, he wouldn't waste a minute—"

"Nick is fucking Laila."

"Whoaa!" He set down his mug with an explosive snort. Sat bobbing his head for a while. *"So?"*

Had she heard right?

"Bourgeois decadence," he growled. "Minor league compared to what happened to Kat. And famine, drought, boils, frogs—Schubert had syphilis, for godssake, great clumps of hair coming out in his hands . . . Listen, do whatever you goddamn need to do. And then do your work." She gazed at him, jaw slack. "You've got this gift, Maddy: when you play, you make the audience live through the music with you."

" 'Made'—past tense."

"You're saying that to *me?*" A raucous laugh. He rose on tiptoes. "Tell it to Byron Janis—he just recorded the *Ballades*. Tell Leon Fleischer, back playing two hands—after how many years?" Something groaned from deep in the belly of the house. "I know you, Maddy. We're made the same way, you and me. You get your teeth in, and you'd sooner die than let go—and you will if you sign off now. You'll be fucked. You'll be over. I can see you on those benches—y'know, on the divider on upper Broadway? And they'll say, *Hey, whatever happened to . . . ?* Be angry at the world's indifference as you sink from sight. Hate what happened to Katrine. Disappearing forever: that's worth hating. And self-pity."

She roused herself. "Who invited you to bust in here with your uplift and two-bit sermons?"

"Oh, you can dish it out, can't you. It's okay for *you* to play the . . . magnanimous card. But when *you* need to hear the truth? Oh, no, you're so goddamn . . . *competitive* or something, you can't stand—"

"Hold it, hang on there, Anton," she interrupted, presenting her palm. "You're presuming an intimacy. But you hardly register on me at all."

A long moment, and then he charged her, face a blur, lifted her by the elbows, fingers bruising, breathing hard. Then, not knowing what to do with his package, he roughly released her. "Sorry. Shit, why'd I do that . . . Shit. You're right, it's always been that way, hasn't it." He backed away, striking the glass-windowed bookcase; turned and delivered a kick to the oak base. "Where'd I leave my coat?"

"Wait."

"What the hell for?"

"Wait, I know you're about to, *ta-da,* stalk out of my life—"

"My coat, please."

"But don't. Okay?"

"Did I leave it in the hall?"

"Don't go." She approached him, trailing the afghan throw, a dethroned queen, and timidly placed her hand on his shoulder near the collarbone. "Anton, forgive me. For what I said. It was self-loathing speaking. Humiliation . . . To be *seen* like this. I can't even stick it to Nick. Please. Don't make me hate myself more. You must know"—her head drooped forward—"the truth is I care for you, I do."

His hand removed hers from his shoulder. "Listen, I gotta go."

"Forgive me, please."

"Manager's expecting me."

"I understand. We'll break out Nick's Glenfiddich."

"Gotta go over a contract."

"Yes, of course. Whaddya say we drink it English style. Splash of water, no ice?"

" 'A WINTER IN MALLORCA,' " Anton read aloud from a new book on George Sand and Chopin, sipping at his single malt.

" 'Because of Chopin's alarming cough, George Sand decided they should go south, with her children, to Mallorca. . . . She rented three cells for them in the monastery of Valdemosa, perched among rocky crags nearly fourteen hundred feet above the sea. On stormy nights, wind would go howling through a crumbling cloister in the all but deserted monastery. One ex-monk haunted the corridors, brandishing a knife and a rosary and drunkenly pounding on the cell doors. . . . Because of the site's stark beauty, Sand proclaimed the place a Romantic's vision.

" 'But with the onset of winter, Chopin's health worsened and he wasted away to less than a hundred pounds. The 'family' huddled around a single stove against the damp and cold, but the fumes exacerbated Chopin's cough. . . . By now he was coughing blood. Yet from these depths, by January 22, 1839, Chopin managed to send off the set of 24 Preludes for copying.' "

"Nick's Glenfiddich would have done Freddy good," Anton said, taking another nip. "Nine years Chopin spent with Sand. But after the first year she refused to sleep with him, and later wrote she'd sacrificed her vitality to a corpse. Sand drains him, then when she's got her 'material,' spits him out."

"Right, always demonize the woman," said Maddy, who'd stayed with smoky tea. "You could also argue that Sand conserved Chopin's strength by not making sexual demands. He was a consumptive, and sexually confused at best. In his youth he had a crush on a fellow Pole, was possibly a repressed homosexual. And of course, toward the end, Chopin was hot for Sand's cock-teaser of a daughter."

Hot for his lover's daughter. Maddy heard the innkeeper at Nohant: *She knew how to make trouble, that girl.* . . . She zoomed in on Nick's frown that had puzzled her. The whole story, if she'd had eyes to see, laid out in embryo from Scene One.

"But through it all," she went on, ragged by some hazy idea, "the seven summers of Nohant were the most productive of Chopin's life. Sorry, I'm lecturing you."

"Lecture me, I like it." Anton flipped through the book. "Sand was really into Chopin's music. Listen. 'She offered Chopin the fine example of her own steady working habits, an artist's understanding of a fellow artist's ways, organizing life at Nohant to accommodate them both—' "

He looked up at her, eyes shining. "Sounds like the ideal mate."

"That's what you're saying this week. Have you forgotten about your greenroom groupie?" *Lecture me, I like it.*

Anton read on—Maddy tuning in and out. The lovers went on excursions in the Nohant woods, Chopin astride a velvet-saddled donkey. . . . George walked alongside, prodding it with her parasol. . . . As he painted, Delacroix heard music from Chopin's open window, mingling with the sound of nightingales. . . .

She'd stopped listening, in the grip of something.

"What a marvelous incomparable time!" Anton said.

Maddy nodded, fixed on the vista unscrolling in her head. "The trick is to come up with a fresh mix," she murmured.

"Sorry?"

She brought him into focus. "Listen: we both love the Chopin-Sand stories. It's high-end soap opera. And wouldn't it, well, add a new dimension—open up the music, help people *hear* it—if you could frame it with these stories—"

"Yeah, go on."

"Make the composers come alive. Right there at the concert. Create an evening of stories and music both."

They grinned at each other like assassins.

"First, anecdotes about the composers' lives," Anton said.

"Then I'd play key passages, to help the audience hear what the composer was aiming for."

"C'mon, let's do it." He grasped her hand and all but yanked her through the hall to the music room. She sat at the keyboard; he stood facing her, arms folded.

"Okay, I've just described the horrendous conditions at Valdemosa, the freezing rain, the smoky fumes, Chopin coughing and shivering. Because of his TB, the Mallorcans wanted to burn every bed he slept in. Yet despite this misery, Chopin completed his set of preludes, among them the famous 'Raindrop Prelude,' with its drip-drip rhythm. The story goes he composed it while Sand and the kids were caught in a violent rainstorm, and he hallucinated, in a kind of waking nightmare, that they'd all died. Even if it's just legend, it's pretty to imagine."

"Daa da daaa," she sang, slipping into the famous D-flat Major Prelude. "The innocent, angelic melody sits atop a gently pulsating note in the left hand." Playfully exaggerating the bass: "Guess that's the raindrops, huh? Then"—shifting into the C minor section—"the music turns dark and lugubrious, swelling up to a pinnacle, Nature at its most menacing—can you hear thunder and crashing waves?"

"Sand was surely thinking of the D-Flat Major when she wrote"—she shut her eyes, searching for the quotation: "'The shades of dead monks seem to rise and pass before the listener in solemn and gloomy funereal pomp.'"

"Yeah, give 'em dead monks, mad monks, all the Romantic folderol!"

"The somber interlude seems almost like . . . a burning inhale—but then the key shifts, like an exhale, to the opening D-flat major—and voilà, relief, sunshine again. She struck the final hopeful chords. "Of course this prelude has been played to death."

Anton thrust his hands in his pockets and rocked on his heels. "But Madeleine Shaye will reframe it and make it fresh for a new audience! Uh, don't take this wrong, but—you wouldn't be starving, would you?"

THE FIRST SNOW, like a benediction.

Except for some local fishermen huddled in silence before Sparky's corner TV, they were alone in this wooden sea shanty immune to Islesford chic, perched high over the silent, whited-out harbor on rickety stilts. The blond-wood tables gleamed with shellac; their place mats, a map of Weymouth Bay, felt suspiciously slick. They ordered mussels, fries, Caesar salads.

"You'll need to invent a snappy title for your gig," Anton said.

"'Keyboard Commentary'?"

"Hmm, maybe." He swiped a fry through a puddle of ketchup. "You could rotate in guest artists, chamber groups."

"For each concert I'll wear a different designer gown to capture the spirit of the music—pick 'em up at Encore, that 'resale' boutique where royalty dumps its Guccis and Chanels. For Chopin, Romantic black lace. For Mendelssohn, bouffant green taffeta."

"Isn't that a little hokey?"

"Ton, maybe you're not the man to consult about wardrobe. And this has gotta be part show biz." She swooshed a chunk of bread in the mussels' garlicky broth, blessing safe love.

He snapped his fingers. "I've got a pal at Alice Tully who runs the Fridays at seven. We'll take her to lunch. But first, when you're ready, do a run-through for me."

"Only if you promise to be brutal."

"If you promise not to hate me."

"Hey, a deal's a deal. I'll pull together an evening on Brahms—but with a fresh angle: how the great Romantic was influenced by Handel and Bach."

"Mmm, I like that."

"Tchaikovsky and the melancholy Slavs!" Maddy went on.

"The fever of Vienna, complete with excerpts from *Fledermaus!*"

"I'll recycle my Clara–Robert Schumann–Brahms. Another upmarket soap."

"Oh, your life could outsoap any of 'em—" Anton caught himself. Their eyes connected, her lip trembled, she bit it, but there was no stopping, she erupted in laughter, Anton, too, they couldn't stop, only she was seriously losing it, eyes tearing, mouth stretched in a frightful sob-laugh— she hid her face.

Sparky's regulars cut them curious glances, thinking, *Weekenders*.

She tamped her eyes with a napkin. Sipped the local water spiked with runoff from the Islesford Links.

"We'll play the *Liebeslieder Walzer* for two pianos," Anton got out.

We. Anton didn't need her.

"Tony, thank you."

"For what? It was your idea."

"I meant for not letting me drive you away."

"Clever of me, wasn't it? My *mishegoss* didn't scare *you* off."

"We make each other better than we are."

"An advantage of safe love, which I know you think is a load. You *can* be a bee-atch, you know. Listen, I hope you understand what I'm about to say."

"Uh-oh, one of your pronouncements. Let's have it."

"Maddy, whatever else is going on—for either of us—we're in this together. You 'n' me. Do you understand?"

"Oh, yeah. Yeah, I do."

CHAPTER 15

A Pair of Squirrels

O utside the music room December mist shrouded the black boughs, a dream of trees from a Chinese landscape painting. She played every scale in every key, notes punching holes in the stillness of Conscience Point. *Paganini made people weep with the playing of a scale,* Madame O once said. Arpeggios, octaves, shakes—she played them *prestissimo* and without the slightest break, modulations flowing from key to key. All these weeks estranged from the piano, yet the music resided in her fingers like a neglected lover who'd remained perversely loyal.

Then, a favorite regimen, she warmed up with a batch of Chopin études and preludes, each a technical gauntlet. First the daunting C Major Étude, like calisthenics for the fingers; playing slowly at first, she watched the right hand for the most comfortable way to attack the stretches, then gave the right-hand part to her left—a strengthener, like using a Nautilus machine. The *Revolutionary* Étude pumped blood into her hands and arms. In the F Major Étude, she threw both hands in opposite directions, letting 'er rip. Then she played the D Minor Prelude, the big leaps in the left hand like jumping on a trampoline, and wound up with the B-flat Minor—a finger-buster she'd never play in public.

She was now ready for her day's work.

Her first of the "Piano Conversations"—"Chopin and the Sand Years"—consumed her like new love. For company she had Eugene; now semiblind and doddering, he might be the family retainer in *The Cherry Orchard*. His niece Olga, a robust presence, cheeks florid from handling fish, would arrive around dusk, and rustle up chowders or pan roasts, or broil the catch of the day. After dinner together, Maddy would run through portions of her program for Olga in the music room. She'd wind up with a polonaise, the "Danse Russe" from Stravinsky's "Petrouchka," or maybe Prokofiev's own arrangement of "Romeo and Juliet"—anything from the Slavic repertoire Olga adored. The librarian in Islesford, catching the excitement, cast a wide net for every book written on Chopin and Sand. An idea woke Maddy at four A.M. Why not do a multimedia "Evening at Nohant" with music, readings, and slides. She'd project Delacroix's painting of George Sand raptly listening, head partly dipped in shadow, as Chopin shook notes out of his sleeve.

Walking along the ocean in the sinking afternoon, she mentally worked over the devilish fingering of a barcarole; rehearsed her spiel out loud to a company of gulls, turned as one so the wind could slipstream around them. It was too warm for early December, as if the planet had overwound its clock. She wandered the broad beach into a haze of copper, tidal pools burnished by the dropping sun, winter-dark sea scrolling lazily up the shoreline. Her scheme to take out Nick lay rusting in the field like a downed *Spirit of St. Louis*. Far from giving satisfaction, her silent punishment of Laila had settled in her like a toxin. She worked "over" it, like when she'd torn a fingernail while performing the "Mephisto Waltz" and of course kept going, leaving blood between the keys. At other times she felt like a pianist she'd known who continued playing in a panicked hall after someone had yelled "Fire!" Let the whole mess wait. For now she'd taken asylum with the Great Bear and the Little Bear in their celestial park.

. . .

ANTON CAME DOWN on her run-through of Chopin-Sand as brutally as promised. Bloodied, furious, she remembered Sophie: *Humor me, please.* But after she'd remixed spiel with music, she grudgingly recognized he was right.

IN NEW YORK success translates into real estate and love: Anton acquired an apartment in the thick-walled "musicians' building" at 90th and West End Avenue; he was seen around with a Ms. Kim from Juilliard, sapling-thin in silvery dresses, jet hair plumb down her back. Clearly safe love had its limitations, Maddy reflected. Noting her own sourness. She stepped carefully along the icy sidewalk already lined with Christmas trees. Ahead loomed 1998 and with it pre-millennial hysteria about a coming computer meltdown—but closeted with the Great and Little Bear, she'd remained immune to the anxious season. She was on her way to see Anton's grand new spread and offer up for his bludgeoning her revised Chopin-Sand. He'd also promised to play her a new set of tangos by Astor Piazzolla.

When Anton opened the door, she squelched her surprise at the GQ fashion plate: burgundy plaid shirt, pleated pants, cordovan shoes, combed-back hair spiked with mousse. Moving in a cloud of aftershave, he showed her the living room housing two gleaming Steinways like a pair of whales; a climate-control gizmo designed to zap any rogue draft; the den hung with photos of Anton in '70s sideburns recording the Tchaikovsky Second with Ormandy and the Philadelphia on CD 283, Anton's favorite, now defunct piano.

He poured them some chardonnay (rotgut; there remained that nicety to master), and they sat in the den on the puce sectional sofa, where it formed an L. She raised her glass. "To all the new good things in your life, Ton. I'm truly happy for you." He looked unaccountably grim. "You've become quite the peacock," she added. When she touched his sleeve, his skin jumped like a cat's hide.

"Listen, I can't listen to your run-through."

"All right, another time, then," she said lightly, mystified; perhaps relieved.

His right-hand fingers drummed the sofa.

"So . . . what about those new tangos?"

"What? Oh, the Piazzolla . . . No, no." He shook his head once too many times.

"O-kaaay . . ." What in hell . . . ? Where was safe love? Maybe it wasn't any safer than the other kind. She wondered why he'd invited her.

"Listen, I thought I should tell you this in person," Anton blurted, addressing an invisible third party. "I think we should call it quits." She too stung to react. "I was full of shit, I can't do this buddy charade, it's just a head trip. You're the person I talk to in my head, damnit, and basically I've always wanted to fuck you. It's better I don't see you," he added for clarity. Looked at her, finally.

She focused on his hands lying tensed on his twill pants, darkly dimpled at the first joints. "I thought your Juilliard student—"

"You thought wrong."

She nodded, head down, as if humbled by this failure of perception, while wonder crept through her. Jesus, what underwear was she wearing?

"I didn't want to say this on the phone," Anton said, eyes mulish.

"No, of course not. Instead, you brought me all the way here through icy roads and traffic—"

"I apologize, okay? I thought you'd be *relieved.*"

"Maybe *you* thought wrong." A long moment, let 'im chew on *that*— and then she went shimmy-shimmy toward him on the sofa, till they sat noses touching, hearing each other breathe—except Anton had ceased to breathe, he remained motionless, rigid with suspicion, unyielding, unbreathing. She planted soft butterfly kisses over his face, over and over, then noisy smacking ones, till finally she heard him gasp—for air?—and felt his mouth smile, and he roughly reeled her in at the curve of the sofa. They grabbed at each other, his brushy hair, the taste of him, *This is what I wanted,* banked desire revved up in a roar. Her hands roamed him like the blind's, learning and liking this new heft. She squeezed the hard root through his pants, he groaned, she felt him go stone-hard. She kissed his beautiful hands. Their mouths drew nectar, they feasted, then they turned busy, frantic, unfastening, she an unholy mix of old lust, rage, she hardly knew. He nosed up her silk sweater, his hair against her neck, he drew her nipple into his mouth, his hand found her and she leapt against him.

"Oh, God, can we make it to the bedroom?"

"Mmff, don't think so."

A clunk as a shoe hit the floor, then a metallic shower of change. He moved over her and they went at each other, maddened, heaving about, and then a chasm opened and they pitched onto the parquet floor.

They lay sprawled like Brueghel's revelers. On either side rose the separated sections of sofa. "I'll sue the asshole decorator!" He helped her up; checked their fingers and wrists. His navy designer socks like in a porn flick, cock reduced to workaday size; her bra like a necktie, forgetting too late to suck in her gut.

"Guess the earth moved," she laughed.

THE GRIND AND RATTLE of garbage trucks. She struggled to sit. She'd hovered over sleep till dawn, unable to drop. Her right shoulder ached—a souvenir from their joint descent from the sofa. She felt well-used in the crotch and for a while was unable to pee. She found what she hoped was a spare toothbrush, before braving the mirror. At forty-nine you paid heavily for a night of impromptu passion.

"I wish I didn't have to leave," Anton said, busy in his antiseptic kitchen. "When I could be here with you."

He was flying out of Kennedy that evening for a concert date with the Cleveland Orchestra later in the week. She's hijacked by an image: low on her elbows, ass aloft. *I love this, I've wanted this with you,* he says. Hand on the small of her back. Her arms stretching out further and further, till her chest is flat on the couch, going flatter still, butt aloft, both drugged. "I should come to Cleveland with you," she said abruptly.

"Oh, can you? Would you?"

"You know I can't. And once I get my little show in gear, I'll be able to even less."

"It's all gonna be doable."

Nothing seemed doable in her sleep-deprived state. "You should've stuck with plan A. The groupie wife. Ms. Kim would fit herself to your life."

He awkwardly poured water into the filter of the Melitta coffee maker. "She wouldn't fit *me.*"

"The loneliness of the road, the stale hotel rooms, the stage for chrissake—oh, I *know.* And you need someone to take you down from the high after the concert."

He turned to face her. The pale stubble on his jaw made her heart ache. "Two percent milk okay?" he said.

"An international virtuoso spends two-thirds of the year on tour. You think I don't know the life?"

"Sugar?"

"Listen, I can't promise you anything."

"Too late," he sang out, stirring her coffee. "Just think: you were my first love—and now you'll be my last."

"Look, we spent one night together, and it was lovely, but—"

"Hey, you're gonna make me burn my finger. I can't afford an injury."

"You're right, you've had enough damage done. The level you're playing now, you belong to your public. I can actually remember your first reviews: 'Volcanic.' 'Despite the speed, the notes always legible.' You need someone to shield you from the trivia, the time-eaters. A secretary, handmaiden, smoother. And I'm not made to be the little woman behind the genius."

"Are you sorry about last night?"

"No, I'm happy," she said simply.

"Then why are you inventing obstacles?"

A sip of her coffee. "It's that—maybe I don't want a sophisticated bi-continental life, the stolen rendezvous every third month in Turin. I've had enough sophistication to last me."

"Only one thing matters: Do you love me?"

She walked to the counter, marbled black and puce, and inspected a flyer for the Cleveland concert. Braving his eyes: "It's not what matters most to me right now."

"Yes, it is. Do you?"

"Maybe you were right the first time round. If we could just stay allies, each other's ear—remember? I'd never lose you."

"You're saying, 'I can't be with you because I don't want to lose you'? You're saying something so moronic? When we belong together?" He snapped a dish towel against the counter.

"You see? It's happening already! The anger, the asshole things you do when—"

"*You're* being the asshole"

"Just . . . chill out. You're way ahead of me, Anton."

"I've been waiting for you since—forever."

"But we're not in lockstep, Anton. We have two separate lives. I've got all this shit to settle. Can't we have a decent interval here?"

"There's no time for a decent interval."

"How can I think clearly right now."

"*Don't* think." He filled his mug with coffee.

"There's something else. A long time ago, I walked out on myself when—I coulda been a contenduh." At his black look: "Now I have another shot. . . . Oh, I know, my little concerts are minor league compared to the Cleveland and Turin, but this time, whatever it is, I've gotta run with it. What time is it? I have to be somewhere. We'll talk when you get back."

"It's Nick, isn't it."

"Have you heard anything I said?'

"It's Nick. He fucks your kid and you still want him. Admit it."

She tried to remember where she'd left her bag. "I'll call you."

"We can't leave it like this."

"Anton, there's nothing we can fix right now."

"Don't use my name like that."

"I'll call. When you get back."

He seized the mug he'd just filled and in one motion dashed the coffee into the stainless-steel sink so it splashed up against the white wall and traveled down in three dark rivulets.

SHE RETURNED TO Jane Street with a single pressing desire: dive under her duvet and pull it over her head. Then she played Jed's message on the machine. A quick change of clothes, and she spun right back into a cab.

Sophie sat, head in hands, in a canvas bucket chair left over from the '50s. Maddy sank onto the futon in Jed's walk-up home-office in Hell's Kitchen, her heart still boogying from scaling four flights.

"Soph, I just got the news. Any new developments?"

"Nothing," Sophie said dully. "All we know is the military police 'detained' Global Watch and they've been 'disappeared.'"

"Your daughter's group has not been 'disappeared,'" Jed snapped from the desk where he was manning phones. "For the moment we've lost contact, is all." They couldn't learn why, he told Maddy, the military police had stopped Tara's delegation on December 10 south of Guatemala City. For once Sophie had good reason to panic, Maddy thought. The *Times* had just run a front-page story about a notorious military checkpoint in Guatemala, where soldiers routinely collared anyone whose face displeased them, and dispatched them to the bottom of a two-hundred-foot well.

"D'you know the special treatment reserved for political prisoners in Latin America?" Sophie said. "In Peru they put them in a living 'tomb' in the Andes, a dark concrete box measuring six and a half feet along each wall."

Jed rolled his eyes and picked up the ringing phone.

"Sophie, dear, it doesn't help to think about that," Maddy said. Guiltily savoring the return of her body. After a forced sabbatical, it was back on the job, tingling like after an autumn dip at the Point. Yet she'd done right to sidestep Anton's demands, hadn't she? *It's not what matters most to me right now.* She had work again. She had a house to put in order—though for now the most she could put in order, it seemed, was the music room. The rest she pictured like an extravagant ruin open to the elements, shat upon, overrun by jungle growth and wild-eyed creatures.

"In Guatemala they raped and tortured that nun," Sophie was saying. "And they just kidnapped a bird watcher in Colombia. He was searching for the *Cundinamarca antpitta*," she added, versed in bird lore from blear-eyed evenings hunting *Homo eligibilis* at the Explorers' Shelter for Border-line Men.

Jed hung up and fixed Sophie with molten blue eyes. "Let's not go there, okay? We may need to get on a plane for Guatemala at any time."

Sophie lit a cigarette off another. "I mean, anyone with half a brain can see what's going on in the world. But why would Tara want to set herself up for death, dismemberment—and dysentery? When she could have had a place at the party? And married a private asset manager?"

"Just chill," Jed said.

She turned to Maddy, who was impressed by Jed in this take-charge mode. "I mean, were we this dumb? Our most daring act was refusing to shave our legs. Thank God Laila never got to Guatemala." She snorted. "Too busy playing homebreaker—in her own home."

Maddy felt Jed's eyes burn into her. "What the hell does that mean," he muttered.

"What you think," Sophie said.

"Oh, shit . . ."

Maddy inspected a once-white flokati rug, now a catchall for debris.

"Maddy, I owe you another apology. I've been a righteous asshole. I never guessed—"

"Thank you, Jed, who would have? And while we're doing this, I'm sorry, too. I've never given you the credit you deserve." The hiss of the radiator. "We wanted the best for our girls," she said half to herself. "We raised them, we loved them, we did our fucking best. Why are we being punished?"

"It's for *us* we have babies, the joy is all on one side—they only grow up to hate us," Sophie said.

The phone rang. They anxiously listened to Jed's curt replies—but it was just a columnist for the *New Republic* wanting to interview Sophie to understand what kind of home had produced a Tara Gerson.

"Tell that writer to go fuck herself." Sophie windmilled her way up from her canvas bucket and joined Maddy on the futon. "I knew it could come to this. We don't do real altruism. I boycott the sale of foie gras at Les Delices. Or I get pissed at Nike's sweatshops, then rush off to the white sales. But Tara's *serious* about this stuff, she was always hot to play La Pasionaria. At Riverdale, when the other girls were getting the pill

from Dr. Mitnick-Gazinsky, she was collecting Christmas gifts for homeless kids. When she could have been a JAP like the others . . ." Her eyes
welled and she collapsed over her knees.

Searching the pocket of her corduroys, Maddy was stabbed by a sharp
object: the squirrel couple with parasol she'd copped unawares from Laila's bureau. She moved toward Sophie and circled an arm around her
shoulders.

Sophie shrank back, as if from a reeking street person, and fixed her
with bloodshot eyes. "When I think how you've wished harm on that
child. You're like the Nile perch—they eat their own babies. I mean, the
kid's down the tubes, wrecking her life—and you hole up with your piano,
doing nothing? I don't give a shit who Laila's fucking, she needs your
help. She's practically a child still. *Your* child."

Maddy stared at the flokati rug, squeezing the sharp metal squirrels in
her palm.

"You owe her," Sophie went on. "We owe them endlessly and can expect
nothing back, except grief, and that's the way it is and always will be."

She squeezed the squirrels harder, a giant yawp rising up from her
knees, through her chest, blasting like Chinese mustard through her schnoz
and out her head, so she barely registered the moisture in her palm until
Jed said, "Jesus, Maddy, what have you done to your hand?"

CHAPTER 16

Act Three

The Third Act. You might as well try turning the *USS Nimitz* around mid-Atlantic.

She located Nick through his secretary—ever her ally—at a hotel in New Orleans. Waiting to be put through, she remembered Nick had sailing buddies in State who could massage the network to help rescue Tara.

"That daughter of Sophie's always been spoiling for trouble," Nick said in his woolly precaffeine voice, sounding relieved. "Stevens in State—he's our man. Old Latin America hand, knows everyone. We'll get him on the case."

"Thanks." A beat. "Do you know where I could find Laila?" She heard him come fully awake.

"Have you tried, uh, Jed Oliver's?"

Oof, sloppy; everyone knew that was "over." Deep breath. "Nick, we need to talk." Universal code for *kick in the groin coming*. Nick's silence sluiced through the long-distance wires, an admission.

"How's Wednesday the 10th?" Voice clipped, conceding nothing.

"Fine." That left her time to get to Laila first.

"I'll phone you from the airport." Then, faux hearty: "Well, I better get on the horn to Stevens."

Only after they hung up did she wonder if Laila had been lying beside him.

. . .

WEDNESDAY THE 10TH the temperature spiked; by evening the thermometer outside the library window was flirting, in December, with 65. Global warming, polar ice cap melting—the planet's thermal disorder matched her inner weather. The little Sony TV in the kitchen showed blue-and-green graphics of a storm system traveling to the Northeast . . . record downpour expected . . . coastal damage . . . flooding—Nick's plane would surely be delayed. She'd finally flushed out Laila at Georgia Kidd's loft; at work in the darkroom, Laila had grumpily refused to come out till later tonight. An ominous stillness settled like a mantle over the grounds, broken by curls of thunder and carping crows.

She'd made up as she did for a concert, and chosen a claret cut-velvet top that enhanced her Mittel-European look. The occasion demanded ceremony. Sophie's assault had slammed her, like electroshock, into a new dimension. Hiding out in music, she'd prolonged the cycle of badness set in motion, like a perpetuum mobile, by Nick and Laila. But guess what: it was for *her* to halt the cycle. Sophie was right: your kid could lay waste to your life and break your heart several times over; begrudge you the moments—which filled you with gratitude—spent at your deathbed. But surprise: report for duty, Mom, no questions asked. Perhaps there lay the true human contract, what separated them from giraffes and emus. . . . She'd fill Laila in on the real story. Then she'd lower the boom on Nick, and walk without looking back.

At ten, nerved from waiting, she slipped on a slicker and biked toward the Point. The evening moonless, hung with swags of mist, the hardtop coated with slick like snail ooze. Eggleston Bridge uncrossable, covered in liquid fog. Enfolded in darkness, she was gripped by a primal horror at deprivation of light. A scratchy voice blended with the chorus of tree frogs. *I'm believed dead but I live on here. . . . This place was meant for artists. . . . One*

day we'll go to the far side of the island. . . . Jagged lightning lit the bay—
something ghastly stood preening on the island—faded on the instant. Get a
grip! A prickly sense of a presence breathing behind her. She thought of
Laila's suspicion that Fernande roamed the property at night. Fernande
would have seen her and Nick glide through burnished rooms in a ballet of
domestic contentment; come together, heads touching like horses; extin-
guish the ground-floor lights—then reappear upstairs in the bedroom with
the blue star-spangled ceiling, lit by the rosy glow of an antique lamp,
Nick's arms about her ass, like a diva cradling lilies. . . .

She wheeled around to see *two red eyes*—For godssake, just sensors
marking the drive to the boathouse. A branch snapped in the bayberry.
Suppose Nick had already arrived. And spotted the news clips tied with a
shoelace on his desk. He might kill her. Not likely. He'd picture the company he'd be forced to keep: lawyers with accents from the wrong schools
and suits from Syms.

She arrived back at the house just as the rain let down.

"Airport's closed in Atlanta," came Nick's nasal honk on the machine.
"I'll get there when I get there."

Eugene phoned. "They expectin' Eggleston Bridge to flood out by daybreak," he said in his ancient wheeze. "You won't want to be takin' Point
Road anytime soon." *The way they always drove in.* She phoned Georgia's
loft, but Laila had already left. Surely the cab driver from the station would
know to take Peniston in wet weather. She kept vigil in a spine-reforming
Gothic chair with a view of the driveway, till a white cone of light fanned
through the copper beech.

MADDY MIXED HERSELF a Dewar's and soda from the sideboard and
settled in Nick's green tasseled chair. Laila stood in the middle of the room,
watching her with shuttered eyes. Her breasts made rises through her ther-

mal shirt; in her ears diamond studs, damp reddish hair gathered in an elastic. She had the luxuriant look of . . . Could it be?

"Have a seat, I want to tell you a story."

"What kind of story."

"Siddown, why don't you."

"What kind of story."

"I first met Nick thirty-one years ago," Maddy began in the singsong of "once upon a time."

"What fucking story?"

Maddy shot to her feet and looked hard into Laila's eyes.

"I don't know what you're talking—"

She sprang forward, her hand caught Laila's cheek and she slapped at her openhanded, useless, blindly pummeled, blows landing helter-skelter, her hand with a life of its own, Laila cowering and shielding her face and chest, yet not moving away. And then, just as suddenly, she stopped. Hearing her own chain-saw breath. Her arms circled her ribs, as if she herself had been battered. She went vacant, her spirit seemed to have departed her body. Laila stood before her trembling, fingertip to her raw cheek, eyes fired with a fine impersonal hatred.

Then Laila folded onto the rug, mouth downturned in a clown grimace. A tear descended her cheek; she ground a fist into one eye.

"Why wouldn't you talk to me."

Laila's jade eyes turned incredulous. "You know why," she said in a childish singsong. "You're who I *couldn't* talk to. Anyway, what could I say. You would have been right—only there is no 'right.' The feelings between me and him"—she eyed the ceiling—"I can't justify it, and I won't apologize. I didn't want it. It came from nowhere."

Maddy felt the tear of some vital tissue inside.

"I tried to run away, I did."

"Guatemala," Maddy said half to herself.

"It would have violated something *not* to act on those feelings. Love makes its own laws." Nick's devil voice talking through Laila.

"A new one in the annals of chutzpah: daughter fucks mother's guy and then lectures her on the laws of love." Did she detect a ghost of a smile on Laila's mouth? For a wild moment Maddy teetered between laughter and the mother of all howls.

"Okay, you want me to apologize? Okay, I'm fucking sorry you ever took me into your life."

"Who started?"

"None of your damn business." Laila scrambled to her feet and moved to a chair. Her skinny outstretched legs ending in yellow construction boots made her look like Minnie Mouse. Casting her eyes about the room: "It started in Aspen—no, maybe before, the *Cherubino,* Block Island races."

She'd write the manual, How to engineer your own downfall.

"I can't explain," Laila answered to no question in a tranced voice. "'I' became like someone else. . . . We tried. . . . Until we couldn't not anymore."

They sat in silence for a while and Maddy suddenly realized she wasn't hearing what she wanted to hear. She wasn't hearing it was over. Their eyes met then, full of comprehension, Laila's flecked with sympathy, almost, yet diamond hard: *That's not on the table*—and Maddy felt she'd understood little about the world till this moment.

Laila cut her eyes away. Several moments, and then she leaned forward, hands on knees, regarding Maddy with curiosity and dread. "Why did you ask me to come tonight? Not just to beat me up, I don't think. You wanted to tell me—that story."

Maddy rose for a refill and her leg buckled. "You all right?" Laila murmured from old habit. Maddy switched to plain club soda. "Look, why don't we declare a temporary truce," she said. "Just for tonight, in this room. I'm going to tell you a story I think you should hear."

She focused on the rainbow prism in her cut-glass goblet. "I first met Nick in the spring of 1966 when I came to Conscience Point with his sister, Violet."

"Sister?" Laila gazed past Maddy, mouth loose like a child's. "Oh, the one we don't talk about. Lived in Paris, Amsterdam . . ."

"That one."

"It weirds me out." She gazed up at the triangular vaulting with gold cornices. "I once found a pastel of the Point. In that humongous cupboard, y'know, behind the stairs? A beautiful picture of green eelgrass and misty islands."

"Violet's," said Maddy, with a little shiver. "She was a gifted painter."

"So you knew Violet first. Before Nick."

"I knew Violet first. She was my classmate at Barnard, a campus beauty," she began, slipping into a storytelling cadence, like when they'd read aloud *Myths and Enchantment Tales* on the bunk bed on Barrow. "That Ashcroft beauty—they're made of a different clay." Laila's eyes slid away. "Violet was like a young Russian prince, the one from Eisenstein's *Ivan the Terrible*." Shining ecstatic eyes, color of rain; white-blond hair and dark brows and lashes, raw pink cheeks. "She cut a swathe through the Barnard campus; no one had seen anything quite like her. We met while I was doing a run-through of a concert at McMillan Theater."

An enchanted afternoon in May, only scholars and fools indoors. Maddy is seated at the piano in a Barnard studio, with its odor of chalk, glue, and crotches peculiar to schoolrooms. Sunk in the rapture of Chopin's *Aeolian Harp* Étude. She strikes the final note. Hears someone sigh. Startling, she sees a girl seated at the back of the room.

"I was walking by your window on Broadway and heard this divine music—"

"*No* one hears me practice!"

"Your fault, it *l-lured* me in here, like Orpheus playing his lute." The girl approaches. Gauzy Hungarian blouse embroidered with flowers, faded terra-cotta skirt of some burlap material. "Ever since your last concert I've been *scheming* to meet you." Voice cigarette-husky. In a fluid catlike motion, she stretches one arm along the piano and drops her cheek on it, pale hair flopping over, one grey eye visible. "Would you play that piece again? No, wait, I'm going to lie on the floor at your feet!" The girl arranges herself under the piano, arms crossed over her chest and ankle bones touching, like the mortuary statue on an infanta's tomb.

"Violet ended up inviting me home for the weekend. She warned me about her family. 'Mother hates Jews worse than RC's—that's Roman Catholics to you'—somehow she guessed I was half-Jewish. 'And you'll fall for bro Nick, everyone does, even though he's insufferable.' Violet spoke in the style of whatever novel she was reading—Evelyn Waugh that summer. 'And Nick will likely have his discount contessa in tow'—Vi's title for Fernande. 'And Christian, my soi-disant fiancé, has a way of c-c-crashing the party.' She also affected an English upper-class stutter—more Waugh."

"She sounds pretty intense. I'd be psyched to meet her."

A moment. "This family did not sound wildly appealing, and I couldn't take off just like that—"

"And of course you went."

Going home with Violet that Friday in May was like breaching a secret wall that opened on an enchanted country, that *elsewhere* she'd divined from the watery golden Eden on the biscuit tin; the place the *Harp* was reaching for; the far side of the little island—and launched her on the serpentine journey that had brought her with terrible logic to this moment in this house.

CHAPTER 17

Arcadia

W e drove out to Conscience Point that May afternoon in Violet's fawn Mercedes, dashboard a lacquered burled wood, upholstery a buttery blond." Violet of a piece with her car, smelling of buttery leather and Winstons, and, always, jasmine. "On the way out we bought baskets of the season's first strawberries. Picnicked and swam at the Point. Came back here for dinner. Imagine my reaction at seeing this place."

"Was Nick there?"

"And Serena and Fernande."

"Were you into Nick right away?"

"I knew nothing but music and Elmhurst, Queens; Nick was . . . the exotic Other, arrogant as hell, about to leave for Paris. You can imagine.

"That spring we started hanging out, Violet and I," Maddy went on in Laila's lingo. "We spent weekends at Conscience Point—by then Nick had left for France. Me in the music room, preparing for the Queen Elizabeth of Belgium competition—if I placed, I'd spend a year at the Paris Conservatory; Violet painting in the upstairs gallery, preparing for a group show at the Dintenfass on 57th Street. There were also the 'fiancés.' "

"Your husband, 'Dr. Leonard,' " Laila interjected.

Maddy checked an impulse to reach over and grasp Laila's arm. "In July Violet went off to art school in Skowhegan, Maine, and I back to Queens and a practice room in Juilliard. Then one afternoon, a bit gaga from the heat, I'm playing a Scott Joplin rag when in walks Violet—she had uncanny radar for finding me—*Don't they believe in air conditioning in this dump?*—and invited me to spend the summer at the Point."

Violet's scratchy voice: *You can take the train in once a week for your sessions with Ma-dahm. Serena's holed up with her bird-children in the aviary. We'll have the whole place to ourselves. Do say you'll come.*

"I barely hesitated. Though I might have. Turns out Vi had gotten booted from Skowhegan for driving drunk down a boat ramp into the lake—with another passenger—nearly drowning them both." The works in the hall clock geared up to strike. "It was an idyllic summer, me sequestered in the music room, Violet upstairs. . . ."

The sun wheeling over the sky in long days of discipline and pleasure. Afternoons at four, they bike to the beach—*Careful not to skid on the clamshells,* Violet calls over her shoulder. They swim naked; no one about but Eugene, the Point's all-purpose servant. Egrets stand like tipped white vases in the shallows. Twice they sight a great blue heron, its jive head and violet underfeathers, watch it lift heavily off from the eelgrass, trailing skinny legs like a Disney bird. They bike home wearing only shorts, breasts jouncing over the rutted roads. Wander the allée and walled garden seminaked, "wolf children," they joke. They linger luxuriously over dinner, just the two of them, in the vast dining room with the faux mahogany columns and trompe l'oeil pine ceilings, Vi tilted back in her chair, bare feet propped on the table, cigarillo in hand, cheeks burnished by the sun and 'toonies and Meursault. A nightcap of Kahlúa, Vi igniting one high off the next . . .

"Eugene was a fine cook. We ate just-caught striped bass, blues, when they were running; littleneck clams dug up with our toes from the shallows inside the Point; arugula from the local farms, yellow teardrop tomatoes, Cranshaw melons still warm from the sun. We raided the wine cellar. Violet made a serious dent in the Buffalo Grass Polish vodka. When it came to 'the sauce' I was a piker compared to Violet. I never understood how she got up the next day."

"And the fiancés?" Laila said.

"Leonard worked grueling shifts as an intern at Einstein. Periodically he'd come up for air and propose marriage—I was more 'refined' than the nurses, or the daughters of his mother's friends from Grossinger's. Vi was engaged to Christian Estabrook, fresh out of Princeton, working at Brown Brothers Harriman. That summer he gave her an heirloom engagement ring: a sapphire circled by diamonds in an antique setting. Christian was hopelessly smitten, though Vi treated her horse, Jasmeen, with more affection; she privately referred to Christian as 'the booby' and claimed to be mad for Dr.—I forget his name, her psychiatrist at McLean. Hard to imagine a marriage with less promise."

"But how did they—the men—fit into the idyll?"

"We began to consider them, well, trespassers in the world we'd created. And the future we'd conjured. I'd play with the world's major orchestras. Vi would study at the Atelier Hayter in Paris—though she badly underrated her 'little pictures,' as she called them, a female reflex of the period." Outside the French doors a spray of rain dimpled the silence. "We also planned to open this place to all kinds of artists—"

"So that's where that idea came from!"

"We began to envision this community as something we'd build together, the two of us."

She heard Violet sounding off over dinner: What has my family ever done but drink and pursue its swinish pleasures? Conscience Point should be an artists' retreat! I'm going to write that into my will. I can hear it already, the fiddlers tuning up through the oaks. . . .

"Soon the fiancés came to feel like impediments keeping us from our work." Violet's cracked voice: After we're married Christian will want to live in Bedminster near his family's alkie friends and ride to the hounds and brag about the little wife's artistic streak.

Leonard imagines me knocking off "Blue Moon" for guests after dinner. He keeps forgetting that a concert pianist is on the road two-thirds of the year.

Of course there's one advantage to marrying the generic groom: freedom! Even now Christian would rather terrify foxes or sell bonds than hang about me and screw.

So Violet has broken that rule, too. . . . Leonard always holds back out of "respect." She and Leonard go in for marathons of petting. Excruciating, hateful, and hot. Confusingly, Leonard is also a portal to the social universe.

Getting married is the happy ending, Violet says one afternoon on the beach. But what comes after the happy ending? Mother is dying for me to marry Christian because she wants Conscience Point for herself and the birds.

My aunt wants me to forget competitions, and marry a good provider. . . .

"So the fiancés became the opposition. And the more we trashed them, the harder they pursued. Christian would roar up uninvited in his silver Porsche and saddle shoes and there would be long drunken tiffs; from the lawn below I'd hear them shouting upstairs in Violet's room—he was no slouch as a boozehound either. Leonard phoned every third night from the hospital, trying to entice me to his parents' apartment in Riverdale while they were away on vacation.

"Violet and I began to feel we were fighting for our survival. In those days the pressure to marry came down on you like water over the Hoover Dam. Marrying meant capitulation, giving up everything we most valued: our lives as artists, our sense of purpose."

From outside came a rustle of rain. "And giving up each other. I think I know what you're going to say." Laila's green eyes gazed through her in an eerie echo of Violet.

"I suppose you do."

The house sighed through its innards.

"You loved the sister first." Laila's green eyes shining.

It dawns on her imperceptibly; her affinity for Vi is without boundaries. Is it the caress of fingers kneading orange Bain de Soleil into sun-warmed skin, Violet's elbows childishly dimpled, a scent of fresh-baked bread rising off her arms. Is it Violet standing behind her on the weedy tennis court, grasshoppers thrumming, apple-breast brushing her back, guiding her arm again and again through the backhand swing. Sitting beside her on the piano bench as they play four-hands, Vi atrociously, the kiss of bare thighs, the sun through stained glass bejeweling their fingers. The dusk murmurous with mourning doves and scented with honeysuckle and eau de Violet: turpentine, sweat, jasmine.

One evening Vi in jodhpurs and riding boots comes to her bedroom in the annex to show her the pastel of Eggleston Bridge she's done that morning. Above her upper lip a down like the silk from milkweed pods. They sit side by side on the white chenille spread, sit poised at the lip of a dizzying crevasse. From the hall comes Serena's muffled voice giving instructions to Eugene. At the brush of lips she almost falls from consciousness. From the hall, footfalls, voices growing louder. Violet barely shifts away. Serena opens the door. "Eugene will be coming by tomorrow to take up the rugs for cleaning," she says in her mild, absent way. "Perhaps you could"—she glances round—"clear the clutter, deah?" Serena sightless as the winged marble Psyche in the music room. Satisfied she's dispensed her duty as chatelaine of the manor, Serena looks at the grey cockatiel in her hand, with its yellow hieratic crest and blood-orange medallion above the eye, the bird's fit perfect to the hand. She brings its beak to her mouth.

Something about the eruption of *another* into their space sounds an alarm.

They've been sealed off in their own biosphere; with that blast of oxygen from outside, everything within twists and warps like fatigued metal.

The next morning she phones Leonard to tell him she's taking the train to Riverdale.

SHE ARRIVES IN the incinerated air of a heat wave. Leonard has a steeplechase smile and generous thighs and a bedside manner. They make up a pillow-bed on the floor beside the window high above the Hudson River. First a tight soreness and awkwardness, Leonard fiddling with a Trojan that keeps dribbling off. Later, he must have touched her in a particular way, she comes. They make love again, with some success. Leonard murmurs, *My wife, my life,* her arm trapped under his weight, his breath tickling her ear. Beyond his sleeping profile she sees a boat slipping up the river, its mast a triangle of colored lights. She could not have imagined such pleasure—and wonders, *Is that all?*

Back at the Point, Violet is nowhere to be found. Later, from the front lawn, Maddy sees lights on in her room. Maddy knocks, pounds the door, but it's locked. Alarmed, Maddy asks Eugene to pick the lock. Violet lies passed out, still in riding clothes, facedown on the carpet with one knee bent, like her own shadow flying through space—after being sick in the claw-footed tub, they discover. She and Eugene get black coffee into her, march her up and down the stairs. His proficiency suggests this isn't a first.

The next morning at breakfast, Violet, miraculously restored, announces she's taking Jasmeen to the Chatham Hunt for a week to work on dressage. "Did you know Chatham has the best dressage training?"

She didn't, no.

"Of course you'll stay on without me. As long as you like, it's become your place as much as mine—"

"You sleep with Christian."

"It's more amusing to ride Jasmeen."

Violet knows her well enough to read her silence.

After the overture with Leonard, a genie has removed the stopper from a bottle, abandoning her to bottomless, ravening hunger. At night she wanders the allée moist with dew, the walled garden with its white marble Cupid and Psyche. She crushes the silken petals of gardenia blossoms against her lips, her teeth. Aching all through her body, wanting to bellow like a wounded boar. She meets Leonard, who has forgotten respect, at the Hotel Earle on Washington Square, and pulls him onto her. The mercury's at 90, but he likes her in a white eyelet garter belt and black stockings. One night he brings poppers from the hospital pharmacy, and they blast off in a katzenjammer burst of colored stars that leaves a headache.

One evening she hears the crackle of Violet's Mercedes on the driveway gravel. The click-to of the door. She's agreed to move in with Leonard at summer's end, and must tell Violet flat out. She walks down the hall in her caramel shirtdress and Capezios, past the dark gallery, and into Violet's room. Violet is sitting on the bed smoking, wearing a blue Oxford shirt, jodhpurs, and boots, smelling vilely of horses and saddle soap. Not speaking, not thinking, she climbs under the sheets in her shirtdress and pulls the pillows over her head. They're both trembling, it's too much. Every place around the Point now an invitation. A giant tub with claw feet on balls, where they sit, smoking in the steamed water, at opposite ends. Violet a tawny peach, golden down glinting along the curve of her back. The fragrant cool of the gardenia grove. The other side of the far island, where someday they'll go and plant their flag, like travelers to Pluto. They claim a room in the west annex with a canopied bed, and windowed alcove edged in blue and red Bohemian glass, and a cloying Bougereau Virgin who extends her hand in blessing.

.   .   .

A RUSH OF rain drilled the glossy leaves of the rhododendron outside. Maddy sensed Nick struggling toward them through the streaming blackness. "Loving Violet was a girls' folie à deux. I'd led such a strict, blindered life. I was in love with Violet's . . . incaution. Nick was something else. I wanted Nick, I think, before I ever met him." It never started—it was a *continuation*.

"And Violet preferred women?

"For Violet the usual boundaries didn't apply. She was . . . omnivorous. There was the shrink at McLean's. And she claimed she was romantically involved with Linton, the older brother who died. The Ashcrofts may loathe each other, but they seem to need family to feel sexual." The words hung in the air like acrid smoke.

Toward summer's end, a torpid August night drives them outdoors barefoot, she in her dotted swiss gown, Violet in navy satin tap-dancing pants with stars, one of those garments from her fantastical attic. They walk the allée, dew kissing their feet, to the walled garden with the statue of Cupid and Psyche. A black lozenge of cloud fingers the moon. Violet sits on the base of the statue, looking up at the sky, pale chopped hair tucked behind her ears, throat an arch of white. *You'll love other people and forget.* A weariness she's not heard in Violet's voice. *You're just playing,* Violet says; *I'm not.* She squeezes Violet's tortured, nicotine-stained hand with the antique rings, squeezes till the rings hurt their fingers, to hold off the future beating down on them.

She'd watched Fernande and Nick at this very spot—was it only three months ago?—Nick's eyes fixed on her, as if it were her mouth holding him captive. Brother and sister commingle in her dreams like shifting features on a decal, melting one into the other, differing by a hair. Was Violet, she'd wonder years later, the prelude?

•   •   •

"DID THE FIANCÉS have a clue what was going down?"

Maddy startled, borne back up to the present.

"Only Eugene, and he protected us. Leonard, mercifully, was taken up at the hospital. Christian was too blockheaded to notice. One evening he cornered Violet in the greenhouse and 'raped' her." Fucked her in the ass, Violet would later confess, an experience she pronounced "heavenly."

"Fall was upon us, demanding decisions. Serena moved back to the townhouse in Murray Hill; I put in punishing hours on my competition program, while Leonard pressured me to 'make it official' and get engaged; Christian hassled Vi about wedding plans. . . .

"One Thursday we drove into town, I to a run-through with Madame O; Vi for a mysterious 'money conference' with the Ashcroft family lawyer. Vi suggested we meet for afternoon tea at the Palm Court at the Plaza Hotel—she'd surprise me by reverting to the old patrician rituals. We sat in the Palm Court, a little formal and awkward, painfully aware we'd reached the term of something."

A strange pair we make, I in the mustard shirtdress, bangs, and ponytail. Violet wearing red heart-shaped Lolita sunglasses, antique diamond earrings, a flapper-era lace shift—a parody of Palm Court elegance. Her raw cheeks give off a fever glow, like the sex-haunted women of Gustav Klimt.

A man in pinstripes peers at Violet from behind the potted palms. He sends over a waiter with two flutes of champagne. Next he sends his card with a scribbled invitation, to us both, for a performance of *La Traviata* that evening.

Violet ignores it all and quaffs the champagne. She has asked me to meet her at the Palm Court, it turns out, for a reason. "Let's dump our little boyfriends and go off to Paris. We'll sail on the *Flandres*. Rent an atelier

with a piano in the Quatorzième. No reason you can't prepare for the competition in Paris. And if you place, you'll be right there. I've already en-
rolled at Hayter in Montparnasse."

Is she serious?

Vi takes off her sunglasses and sets them down next to our watercress
sandwiches. I see she's as serious as a person gets. My stomach flutter-
kicks. "Paid for how? To live in Paris—to get there at all—I need the
competition money first."

"Why must you always obsess about money! I've just made arrange-
ments with our family lawyer to sell—oh, never mind. It's all taken
care of."

My eye falls on the engagement ring from Christian, the sapphire circled by diamonds. "Isn't there a wedding planned for after Christmas?"

"Oh, men are mainly in love with the chase; the woman yields, and
pffit! he disappears—into squash, eight-meter boats, secretaries. Teen-
aged handymen, in Father's case. I'll do Christian a favor by unloading
him now, instead of at the altar—he'd make a crummy Miss Havisham."
Violet works the ring off her finger. "I hereby break my engagement to
Christian!" She drops the ring into my half-full goblet.

I look, horrified, at the ring in the champagne; tiny bubbles rise streaming off it. How long could you live in Paris on the money from that ring?

Violet fishes in her bag and places a thick envelope on the table. I stare
at the envelope. "Well, aren't you going to open it?"

I gingerly slide out—two tickets? For the *Flandres*. "What's this."

I knew it, Violet's eyes say, *you're just playing.* Yet don't I mean it, too?
We've sworn to go to heaven together, we're fighting for our lives. Why
must it feel like leaping into an abyss?

The waiter hands Violet another envelope from pinstripes. I lean across
the table. "Let's promise that whatever happens, wherever our lives take
us, if one calls, the other will come, no questions asked."

Is *that all?*

No, not all; the words tumble out ahead of me. We clink glasses and I drink, feeling the cold metal of Christian's ring against my lips. Talking fast: "I've never been on an ocean liner, do you get seasick?"

"Certainly not, I've sailed in the Bay of Fundy." I think, *She's already bought the tickets. Don't look round, don't look back.*

Violet's eyes sparkle with mischief. Seizing my empty goblet, she empties Christian's ring onto her palm and places it in the envelope from her admirer. Then she instructs the waiter to deliver the envelope to the gentleman *over there.*

This frightens me more than anything.

Pinstripes, who hasn't yet received the envelope, is studying us with a knowing leer.

Again that blast of air from outside, deforming the world within.

Laila said, "Did you go to Paris?"

"Not exactly as planned."

CHAPTER 18

Belleville

About two weeks before we were to sail for France, a little indiscretion surfaced from Violet's past. The previous year, a girl had accosted Violet in a bar near Barnard with an ultimatum, *Love me or kill me*—then turned a butcher knife on herself. The tabloids went ape over the story of 'the love-crazed fabric heiress.'

"Suddenly this Paula, Violet's nemesis, reappears on the lawn of Conscience Point that September after our perfect summer. None the worse for self-mutilation. Serena was in the main house, along with three lady cousins with mustaches, all barking mad. Paula makes an appalling scene, standing on the lawn outside and shouting up threats, obscenities, professions of love. Then one of the cousins starts shooting moles in the lawn with an air rifle—from a window, if you can believe it. . . . Eugene finally managed to hustle Paula off the grounds.

"Paula's appearance called up rumors of Vi's expulsion from Radcliffe for another incident involving a girl, or several girls—but I threw myself into my competition pieces. And Violet and I were deep in plans, poring over ads for apartments to rent in Paris in the *Harvard Magazine* addressed to Nick. Dodging the fiancés. Smelling a plot, perhaps, they'd drive out to the Point at odd hours to stake their claim. Christian walked Violet about the grounds; should they wed in St. Thomas on 5th Avenue or the vicarage in Bedminster . . . I forget what tale she'd invented about the disappearance of his ring.

"The next evening Leonard, still in hospital scrubs, arrived with 'important news.' He was getting transferred to an army hospital in Fort Bragg, North Carolina—this was during 'Nam, remember. He wanted to get married. He'd even gone and bought a wire-thin gold band from Tiffany's. I tried to stall. . . ."

I can't leave New York right now, it's the center of the music world.

But you wanted to study in Paris.

A year at the Conservatory would open all sorts of doors. Anyway, I need to concentrate on the competition.

Look, they're offering me a great chance to work in neurology at the base hospital. This could be a big step up in my career. I want you to be a part of it.

It *is* a great chance—

We'll find you a piano, your career can shift into lower gear for a while. We won't be in North Carolina forever.

It's the wrong moment for lower gear.

Maddy, I'm talking about our lives.

So am I.

Once we have a child you'll have a whole different view.

Would she? She'd walked them unawares into the walled garden with the statue of Cupid and Psyche, now mottled with black lichen. Crimson leaves from the Japanese maple blew, rustling dryly, across its base.

You need to choose, Maddy. I would have waited as long as I had to— but events have overtaken us. There's a war on, screwed up as it is. I *can't* wait. Cast your lot with me, Maddy.

She stared at Cupid's reproachful smile, touched by the archaic *cast your lot*, like John Alden or something, touched that this near-stranger could so want her.

I'm truly sorry, Leonard, I can't wait either. I've been preparing for this career ever since I can remember.

You may regret this.

Oh, I know!

They'd come to the end of what there was to say. They walked back to the porte cochere, an autumn chill falling from the trees, and Leonard got in his car and drove back to the city.

"ONE EVENING LATER that week Serena cornered Violet in the library, brandishing a letter. I hung back in the hall, eavesdropping. The letter was from a lawyer retained by Paula Barnes's parents. It accused Violet of 'disrupting Paula's academic studies at Radcliffe'; 'spearheading a lesbian ring'—in all, painted Violet as some jackbooted seducer. The lawyer advised Serena that if she didn't 'call off' her daughter, the Barnes family would have recourse to further legal action. I think the word 'invert' was used. Some of the letter did in fact echo the rumors I'd heard at Barnard.

"Violet went ballistic: 'It's all a fabrication, it's Paula who's harassed *me* ever since Miss Porter's—'

"For the first time since I'd met her, Serena snapped out of her trance—though she showed zero interest in Violet's side of the story. Violet had 'disgraced the family,' Violet was 'ill' and needed 'treatment.' She'd cut off the flow of money if Violet didn't cooperate with this plan for her own 'reform.'

"I fled upstairs and sat in the barrel-ceilinged gallery hung with Violet's paintings. *Lesbian ring*. The term a blast of air from 'outside' that punctured the bubble again, turning everything frightening and ugly.

"I spent that night in the room with the starry ceiling, where I'd slept the first night at Conscience Point just a few months back—a lifetime ago, it seemed. I told Violet I had the flu. I lay awake most of the night, seeing her flayed expression; wishing I could revoke my power to disappoint her. My dreams haunted by leering horned creatures with wings.

"At daybreak I sneaked out of the house and located Eugene in the greenhouse and asked him to drive me to the 6:05 train to New York. I rode the subway up to Einstein, walked past receptionists, patients, a blur of dismayed faces, where does she think she's going, marched right into Leonard's office. He was sitting behind a desk with a grey couple, a doom-dealing X-ray illuminated on the back wall."

I want to marry you.

Leonard rose and ushered me out the door and stood looking down at me, shaking his head. You are a piece of work. Can we discuss this later?

I want to marry you *now*.

Somehow Leonard senses he'd better seize the moment. Fifteen minutes later we sit in the waiting room on a black Naugahyde couch with gill-slits in its middle, plotting our course. Suddenly, like a punch to the solar plexus, I picture a train dumping me and my piano on a barren strip. I'm stretched taut in warring directions. Music and the ruthless life of a concert pianist, which is somehow coupled with Violet. But I need to be safe. Shielded from the world's leers.

I move through the hours, a dazed moonwalker. Leonard rushes the Wasserman's through the lab and we take the IRT down to City Hall and speak the vows, giggling uncontrollably while a metronome ticks off the minutes before the justice marries the pregnant Puerto Rican couple up next.

I sit in the dim apartment with the motel furniture and a Gauguin poster of topless beauties from Papeete that Leonard shares with two other interns. I rewrite the letter to Violet a dozen times. The day we were to sail, I dive into a sleepathon like a creature shut down for winter. I've crawled back to safety from a limb overhanging a chasm. I didn't yet know I was pregnant. And I didn't learn about Violet's accident—they helicoptered her from Conscience Point to New York Hospital—till three weeks later. Though Serena kept me out of the loop, I learned that Violet had shattered her hip in a fall from Jasmeen. But the locals, who went Gothic when it came to the Ashcrofts, put it about that she'd tried to hang herself from a rafter in the aviary.

"Nick flew in from Paris and they sent Violet to a rehab place—she'd suffered 'deficits' caused by prolonged lack of oxygen—then McLean, her worst nightmare." A moment. "She ended up marrying her shrink at McLean. Briefly, anyway. Resurfaced in the drug scene in Amsterdam."

"And you never saw her again?"

She looked at Laila with anguish. "I saw Violet once again."

TWELVE YEARS LATER, 1978. I was living in New York in the basement on Barrow Street, subbing for the super—our old place. I'd been divorced about seven years and cobbled together a living playing tin pianos at ballet studios, working nights on my Clara Schumann book. Not the splendor I'd envisioned that summer in Conscience Point . . . Late one night in June, at an hour that augurs trouble, the phone.

Je vous téléphone de la part de Violette Ashcroft. I snap awake. *Violette vous prie de venir a Paris.* She wish you to come to Paris.

When?

Muffled background consultation.

The most soon possible.

I scribble an address. What madness. I can barely conjure my earlier self, that absurd girl who'd made a storybook pledge. The memory drifts down like detritus from a lost city. And how will I pay for the goddamn flight.

Three days later, to complete the folly, I take a taxi from Charles de Gaulle to Père-Lachaise Cemetery to visit Chopin's grave. Later I locate

Belleville, an immigrant enclave climbing the city's far hills. I stand with my suitcase in the blue air, looking up at the fabled *toits* lining the Rue Vieille du Temple where the young Edith Piaf sang. I have gooseflesh, I'm drunk on this June morning, its perfume and glancing light, and stand rooted to the spot.

Idled North Africans, I notice, are watching me alertly from the zinc bar of a corner *café-tabac*. A squadron of green men wash down the gutters from green trucks with vacuum cleaners suspended from the top like elephant trunks. Vendors set out their wares in stalls along the pitched, narrow sidewalk. In a *boucherie Musulmane* a sheep's head bares its teeth in a smile. I duck into the *café-tabac* and order my first *double crème*.

At number 45 I walk through a dank passage to a cobblestone courtyard. Past some sort of printing press with multipaned windows to the ground. I locate the *minuterie* in the far stairwell and climb several pissy flights.

Soyez la bienvenue. The voice from the phone. A woman with kohl-ringed eyes, skin like polished papaya, muumuu of parrot orange and pink. North African or Caribbean. I enter a dining space with windows giving on the *toits*. Dangling wires, the entire left wall draped in black velvet. A smell of plaster dust spiked with a sweetish odor, hashish maybe. Violet's friend watches me like a prism she's holding to the light and turning every which way.

In the living room a woman in a white Nehru shirt over black harem pants half-reclines on a bank of sequined cushions.

Hello, Maddy, I'm so glad you've come. It's Violet's low, thrilling rasp—without Violet.

I knew you would. Excuse me if I don't get up. My legs are not very obliging. Won't you sit?

She motions at a leather ottoman and smiles, and I see a black gap where she's missing teeth, and she sees my dismay and shuts down her smile.

She's someone's puppet-version of Violet, cheeks painted geranium like a clown, lids puffed, hair a flaxen bob that might be a wig. Only the eyes, the gemlike fixity, are the same.

Yes, well, time comes at some of us with a wrecking ball, Violet says. But you, *chérie*—you've grown into your looks; you used to be "ahead" of yourself; now you're perfect. Would you like some jasmine tea? Sandrine, *chérie, tu nous apporte une infusion? Du jasmin.*

The mention of jasmine affects me strangely. Sandrine stops appraising me like the local *épicier* weighing plums and disappears. I notice a bong on a round tin table, and some "works" I recognize thanks to Leonard's hobbies.

Sandrine brings back two fragrant, steaming mugs.

I've asked you to come for a reason of great importance to us both, Violet says formally, adjusting a cushion behind her back. You see, I thought I could prevail on our, uh, late lamented friendship to make a very serious request. That you've come at all is—well, I'm encouraged. In fact, touched.

She shuts her eyes; beneath the clown paint she appears sunk in illness. Alarmed, I look around for Sandrine, but she's disappeared. I hear mewling sounds muffled by the velvet curtains. A kitten? Someone weeping? Perhaps Sandrine has a child.

Violet bestirs herself. Madeleine, I would like to make you a gift of a child. I'm asking you to raise my baby daughter.

I must have levitated. She says, No, no, please sit. I'd make an appalling mother, you see—my style of life is hardly conducive to child-rearing. And poor Sandrine, here, she's like a second daughter, *elle n'est pas très débrouillarde, la pauvre,* she doesn't manage well and I have all I can do to look after her. I can't expect much from the Ashcrofts, I need hardly tell you. Nick has zero interest in children. And anything of mine he would despise. Then I thought of you. You have no children—I've done my research! So I'm asking you to become this child's mother. The father has long since disappeared, no need to bore you with that s-s-sordid tale.

Throughout, I've been shaking my head no. Marveling at how the rich, immured in their own desires, need never bump into reality.

Wait, hear me out, Maddy, it somehow feels right to ask you. There's no one else I could ask, you see. Or *would*. I trust you. You're good. You're solid. You always were.

A huff of exasperation. Oh, yes, money, you do fret about money. It's all been arranged. My lawyer will send you a monthly amount that will more than cover expenses.

All *arranged?* I'm back in the Palm Court at the Plaza twelve years ago, staring at an envelope, *Well, aren't you going to open it?*

Violet is watching my expression and can't be encouraged.

There's one more detail, she says, waving one hand, second finger extended, in a papal gesture. You must swear never to tell this child the identity of her biological mother. Never tell *anyone*. You will be her true and only mother. I want her to grow up in the clear. It could only blight her to know of a mother like me somewhere at large in the world. If she knew of me, she would try to track me down. . . . No, no—*pas question de ça,* I'm sure you agree.

Violet, I agree to nothing and I don't think you ever seriously believed I'd accept your outrageous proposal. You and your family have always had a taste for extravagant gestures. You seem to think you're part of a Dickens novel—

Wait, don't say another word! She captures a cane propped against the sofa and semiwinches herself to standing. I recognize that glint in her eye that heralded tasting the season's first strawberries, or sighting the great blue heron. She walks in a weaving lurch, one hip hitched high, toward the black velvet curtains, and regally waves me to follow. She parts the curtains, and we pass through a cluttered bathroom. On to a bedroom with a low bed on slats, TV, a freestanding clothing rack. She opens a door onto an adjoining apartment that's also primed for the wrecking ball. Plaster hangs like gold dust in a yellow shaft of sunlight. I hear Sandrine's voice murmuring in French. I follow Violet in. Sandrine stands bent over a cardboard carton set on an oak bureau. I come closer. A baby lies in the carton clutching a silver rattle and staring raptly upward like a star child.

Maddy paused a long moment. A great gust of wind rattled the French doors.

"And when I saw that baby I loved her instantly."

SHE LOOKED LIKE something hurled back against the chair, then left to drip down. Terribly small, eyes darting nervously about . . . Abruptly, Maddy saw into herself: she'd thought to harm Laila with silence; maybe she'd also meant to shield her.

"Big fucking deal, so he *is* Uncle Nick, big fucking deal." She was up and plucking at her thermal shirt as if on fire, plucking and pacing and plucking. She went still. "Knowing wouldn't have changed a thing," she said, looking fascinated by this insight.

Maddy tried to work that down her gullet. The hall clock labored like a tired heart.

"Did *he* know?" Laila asked suddenly. She sat and leaned toward Maddy, fingers splayed on her knees. "Does he?"

"God's truth, I've never been sure what Nick knows."

"Un-fuckin'-believable. I mean, you never, like—*discussed* this shit? Like who I fuckin' *am?*"

"It's hard to imagine, but anything to do with Violet was not discussable. Nick is phobic about his sister." She paused, on the lip of the Milagros tale, but again a protective impulse silenced her. "Our lives worked so smoothly without dredging up the past, why trouble the noon's repose?"

"Yet you lived this lie, every day, every hour."

"I wouldn't lecture about lies."

"I tried to want Jed. To stop from wanting—what I wanted. Jed was only a lie to myself." Laila stared out the French doors. "How could you have given me that shit about an orphanage in Rabat?"

"To protect you. The lie made better sense than the truth. Are you certain you wouldn't have done the same?"

"She just . . . unloaded me, the bitch. I want to find her and tell her I hate her guts!"

"Violet will never permit you to find her," Maddy said quietly.

Laila stuck out her chin, but looked unconvinced. "Why did you wait till now to break that cheesy promise?"

"After I . . . figured things out, I could only strike back, like a reflex. My weapon was silence. Betrayal by a guy . . . well, that's a predictable part of the plot. But when it comes from your *own*—" She steepled her fingers over her nose, unable to finish. Laila squirmed. "Then certain things came together: Anton's wife dying. A new chance to work—we're given so little time. I needed to level with you, so I could move on, I guess." A moment. "Besides, where was the joy in harming you? Maybe I'm just selfish."

Laila ground her fist in her eye. "Something I don't get. We were pretty broke when I was growing up, living in the basement on Barrow. But you said Violet had arranged about money—"

"That was the deal. But then, quite early on, in fact, the checks stopped coming. I never learned why. And I couldn't locate Violet or the lawyer. I might have contacted Nick, of course, but chose not to. Anyway, we managed." A moment. "It was warm and snug in our cave." The snow like powdered sugar on the sidewalk, eye-level with their window. The mangy

Christmas tree they'd bought on Hudson Street for half-price, the ornament for the top like an albino pigeon . . . "When I think home, it's that dump I think of, not Jane Street—funny, isn't it? Maybe because it's there I brought you home."

Laila turned a glazed stare on Maddy. "I'm sorry I've been such a burden to you."

Maddy felt her heart might crack open.

"One thing: did Violet say anything about . . . my old man? Was he some North African dude she did when she was wasted? One of the illegal aliens from the cafe in Belleville? Oh shit, never mind, I'm outta here."

"Where you going at this hour?" Maddy trailed her through the hall and out to the porte cochere. Watched her wheel out her bike. The night air smelled rank, as if a giant marine mammal had sloughed its lining. "You can't bike in this rain."

"It's stopped. I'm going to sleep in the studio."

"The roads are flooded, way too slick." Maddy grasped the handlebars with both hands. "Don't go. You can sleep upstairs. At least you'll be safe and dry here."

"Here, *safe?*" She yanked the bike free—then stopped dead, hypnotized by the cone of light fanning behind the giant copper beech at the head of the drive.

CHAPTER 19

Gamelan

I see you've convened the summit without me." He stood in his fencer's slouch, testy as hell, as if she'd authored some unpleasantness.

The familiar chutzpah in a land without signposts felt almost reassuring. For a moment they batted around three-way looks. Then she caught the sweet, hot glance between him and Laila, not the charade of the picnic, and she got it, the slimy, clotted thing she'd never been able to conjure. She reached behind to the plaster Roman bust that had served Violet as coat rack and slid to the ground.

Next she knew, they were both upon her. She feebly batted them away. In the library now, Nick, his smell of *Times* and airport, handing her a shot glass; asking when had she last eaten. Laila sitting cross-legged and watchful at her feet in the old darling way . . . For an instant time swooned backward.

Nick molted his Burberry onto the rug with preppy languor. Snapping her back. He waved his hand before his eyes: "Okay, okay—don't you think I hated what was happening?"

"But 'the heart has its reasons.' When did Pascal become the patron saint for middle-aged men who want to fuck teenagers?"

"And why do women always resort to sarcasm?"

"I am not 'women.'"

"I am not 'middle-aged men.' "

"Uh, excuse me." Laila unfolded from the floor. They both looked at her, as at an intruder. "I am not *'teen-agers.'*"

"You keep out of this," Maddy snapped.

"*What?* I *am* 'this,' " Laila squeaked. She looked to Nick—for confirmation?—but his eyes skidded off her.

"Where is family therapy when we need it?" he declaimed, throwing his head back.

"*Now* look who's being sarcastic," Maddy said.

"Yo, since when do I have to be the fucking mature one here," Laila burst out.

Again, Maddy and Nick both eyed her as if noticing an intrusive third. "She's got a point," Maddy murmured reflexively.

"Y'know, there's got to be a civil way—" Nick began.

"*Civil?* What piece of this that I'm missing is civil?"

"If you knew how desperately I've wanted to talk to you," Nick said, voice dropping, suddenly private.

"Wait, lemme get this straight. You couldn't talk to me—because of what *you've* done—yet somehow *you're* the aggrieved one here? Is that the mother of all mind-fucks?' she asked an invisible audience. Nick stood at a loss, hands open at each side, as if receiving an ovation.

"Hey, y'know what?" Laila said in disgust. "Why don't you two just . . . do your thing without me? Okay?" Her adolescent eye roll triggered in Maddy a silent bat-squeak of laughter. "I'm outta here."

Nick reached out his hand to stop her, the gesture somehow intimate—but she executed a graceful *pasa doble* past him.

He flopped his hand in exasperation, and fixed himself a drink. Maddy watched him crouch, in a single lithe move, to inspect the water damage along the bottom of the French doors, and she saw the line of his thigh and wet corduroy cuff, the blueprint for baldness, the set of his ear. Where was the rage? She'd been carrying it around like a cargo of nitroglycerin, careful not to jostle—and now? Nothing. She'd gone missing on her big moment.

"Just tell me," she said. "Why not Nessa? Why not *any* other woman? The world's swarming with lovely women."

He looked through her and suddenly Maddy saw Serena, clasping the cockatiel like a castanet, beaming her Ashcroft gaze of a mortuary seraph. "Maddy, you understand *nothing*, if you ask that. I wasn't looking for *any* woman—not any woman at all, can't you see? But desire makes a mockery of our intentions, destroys judgment—"

"Your judgment."

"It could have happened to you."

"But it didn't."

"Damnit, it *could* have. Since when does this sort of . . . thunderclap make any sense? People forget the rest of that Pascal, his whole goddamn point: the heart has its reasons—*beyond the grasp of reason.* Jesus, I just got sent a memoir about a woman in love with a tranny—"

"You fouled your own nest," she interrupted. "It's monstrous. Any decent person would take a deep breath and count to ten. You were the adult. Laila's a child—"

"You're quite mistaken there, Maddy." A blistering silence. She wrapped one arm around her middle, the other shading her eyes. He approached her. "Maddy, please, could we stop being adversaries? We're all in a hellish situation, the three of us." At her silence: "Listen, this is just between us three. Let's try, as they say, to think outside the box. Maybe something good could even come of this."

She shot to her feet. "Get away from me. I'm afraid of you. Go. No, I'll leave."

"You'd have to swim out, Maddy, please . . ."

"I'll tell you what's hellish—you, Nick, *you*'re the hell. You and your family. You even warned me thirty years ago in your car at the Islesford station. Why don't we listen? Why? Because you were right. You think you're above common decency. You think you can get away with murder." The word resonated. "Literally."

His eyes locked onto hers.

" *'Yo la mate de un tiro.'* I know who fired the shot that killed Milagros, Nick."

He looked suddenly diminished. "Good, Maddy, you're a good little sleuth." Voice clipped and nasal. Outside a bolt of lightning, then the snarl of thunder, like in some B movie. "Your find couldn't have been much of a challenge though, Miss Marple. Since I kept nothing under lock."

"Why didn't you? Or at least . . . destroy those clips?"

"Maybe I was taking a gamble." He walked a bit unsteadily to the French doors—had he knocked back a few before arriving?

"I hope I'm not going to hear William Blake about forgiving for all eternity," she said to his back.

He pivoted to face her. "And maybe I won," he continued in a tranced voice. "You can't admit it, but you haven't written me off."

"Yes, I could have . . . absorbed Milagros." A beat. "It wasn't against *me*."

"But . . . what's happened with Laila wasn't against *you!* Dear mother of God, how can I make you understand?"

Waving that off: "Knowing about that poor maid explained so much. The bit about your 'ill-starred' family. Your work for Americas Watch— your penance, I suppose. And why you hate Violet, of course. Violet *knew*—and used it against you as emotional blackmail. Was Violet maybe . . . *right there in the room* when it happened? But tell me, Nick: Did you really think I'd stand by while you fucked my daughter? Your daughter, too, in a sense. Your sister's child."

"*What?*" He was upon her, breath skating over her face. "Did you tell *her* that? Did you say that to Laila?"

She backed away, but he trapped her against a glass-windowed bookcase. "Oh, I should have withheld that little detail? And your obsession with having a baby. Was that a ploy to get rid of me? Or do you actually want to make a child with your own niece. It makes my skin crawl. I couldn't let my daughter add one more defective being to the Ashcroft line."

He raised his hand and she recoiled, but he brought his fists to his temples. "You moron!" He shook his head, incredulous. "I never imagined you were dumb enough to swallow that rumor Violet put out."

"Whaddya mean, rumor?

"Violet never had a child. The story's a total fabrication."

Outside in the night a spigot opened, liquefying all in a soft whoosh. "Of course it suits you to believe that," she said. "You would want to believe that."

"Violet loathed men. Anyway, she was so wrecked by drugs and booze she couldn't distinguish fantasy from reality. She may have actually *believed* she had a child."

Maddy shook her head no. "Violet slept with men. You're forgetting, she was married. To that Dr. Semmel." She'd just remembered, strangely, the name of the shrink at McLean's.

"Maybe that was an extreme form of therapy."

"And in Europe she came on like Lady Brett."

"Oh, maybe when she was shitfaced. She was also a bigot, in case you never noticed. Her taste in lovers didn't run to what she called a 'dinge.' Well, with one exception." He studied her, the ghost of a smile upturning his lips. "But you, Maddy, of all people"—he folded his arms over his chest. "You must have known Violet's tastes."

She held his gaze.

"I think it's fair to say you haven't been very forthcoming, either." He sauntered to the bar; dropped ice into his glass with a clunk. "The gossip traveled to Paris when I was at *Transatlantic*. Hell, everyone knew about you and Violet. Christian, the former fiancé, yakked about it on three continents. Serena only pretended to be blind. It was just that she didn't want to be bothered—with any of us."

His eyes burned into her, the twin of Violet's rapt gaze. "Even after so many years I've caught myself half-envying the feelings between you and Violet. That crazy love that has nothing to do with 'decent' or 'sense' or anything but itself—that's what landed on me and Laila." The lights browned, then shuddered to full strength. "How strangely mixed up together we all are."

Rain drummed the French doors. Nick consulted his watch. "Where the hell was Laila going?"

"To your trysting place."

"But you can't bike to the studio"—twisting his mouth at getting caught out. "That part of Wildmoor, where the road dips, is a lake. I had to turn around and come in on Peniston."

"My God, where would she have gone?" She stumbled toward the hall.

Nick pushed ahead of her, shrugging on his Burberry. "Stay, you'll just crack up the car."

"You're the last person Laila needs to see."

"I've got to set her straight, after you've filled her with lies."

She flung her arms about him from behind, but Nick wheeled and grasped her shoulders and shoved her backward, so she landed against the hall clock, setting it angrily clanging.

THE LIGHTS FROM the porte cochere picked up a crosshatching of rain. Slowly she piloted the Saab up Wildmoor, pitched forward over the wheel, getting only seconds of vision, wipers outpaced by the downpour. After the night's dramas and lack of food, she was running on empty, but she was running. Even if Laila had gotten past the flood on Wildmoor, the dirt road to the studio would be a swamp.

Her brights brought up Peniston Way on the left. Crawling along Wildmoor, she remembered Eugene warning that Eggleston Bridge was flooded.

A faint reddish light winked ahead of her, then disappeared around a curve: the taillights of another car, heading along Wildmoor—toward the bridge? That would be Nick, with half a quart under his belt.

On impulse, she hooked a right onto Neck Path, an adjacent carriage road, marshy with rain. The carriage road, often biked by locals to go crabbing, abutted on Point Road before the causeway to Eggleston Bridge. She hit the accelerator. The wheels spun in mire, then the car lurched forward, and she saw through the trees, this time more clearly, the taillights from the second car moving in a parallel line toward the bridge.

She saw it unspool in slow motion: the Lexus aquaplaning on the flooded bridge, the green car floating into the black chop, Nick hampered by booze and fumbling to open the door, which *self-locked,* against the crushing weight of water; saw him entombed in his coffin of fawn leather, lungs flooded, hair streaming upward in the murk, eyes open and sightless like Linton's angel in Green Glen . . . *God tidying the ledger—*

She floored the pedal and raced the second car. Caught up, then shot ahead, putting its headlights behind her. She swerved sharply up an embankment, lost it to the sand, wheels grinding—spurted forward and bucked onto Point Road, skidding sideways to block the oncoming car.

Blinding headlights, a shriek of tires as the car careened to avoid her—it spun off the road into the bayberry. She sat forehead on the wheel, heart rhyming with the Saab's wipers.

A man emerged from the driver's side and threw up his hands in the streaming night like a madman on the heath. Then he recognized the red Saab and walked, instantly drenched, to the driver's side. "What the fuck—"

"Eggleston's flooded. A hundred feet more . . ." She motioned with her head toward the bridge, where her brights lit the angry crests of warring currents.

THE NEXT SHE would remember in flashbacks.

Nick's at the wheel of the Saab, nosing through the streaming dark as if lost at sea. They comb the back roads of Conscience Point. Turn back at the lake engulfing Wildmoor. Take Peniston out to the highway and town. Circle back in on Beldover, aquaplaning over its humps. Past Green Glen Cemetery, they round a blind curve and suddenly: Laila. Pedaling toward them on their side.

The dark behind Laila fans with light: another car approaching in the opposite lane.

Time collapses: Laila's bike skids and points her straight into their headlights. Nick brakes, the car fishtails. Swing left and they meet the car now rounding the bend, brights blinding, almost upon them, its brakes useless. Continue straight on, and they mow down Laila.

A flick of the wheel, a jungle screech, and a thunderous one-two SMACK of metal on metal, she's hurled one way, then *whomp* into the side window, leaving her neck behind. Beyond the fractured windshield a red hood fills the frame, buckled and smoking. Mist curls lazily across the beam of a headlight angled skyward as if for a premiere. An echo of glass, tinkly and dreamy as a gamelan.

Silence. Even the tree frogs are silent, and the wild wet night, holding its breath.

CHAPTER 20

The Last Romantic

Eugene—driver of the other car—was treated at Islesford General for a concussion. Laila walked away with a nasty case of "road rash"— bits of gravel in the wounds on her elbows, hands, and knees. I escaped with hairline fractures in my neck and wore a high white collar like a grandee—an injury that talks to me still on raw afternoons such as this. Nick? Not a scratch.

He massaged his sailing buddies in State, and Tara Gerson's group got sprung from the Guatemalan paramilitaries. Sophie flew to Washington to meet her; the *Times* carried a page 19 photo of a teary reunion, Jed Oliver gesticulating in the background like mad Dr. Coppelius. A letter to the editor chided young radicals for going off half-cocked and sparking international incidents.

Nick's role in rescuing Tara compelled gratitude all round—just like him to mix it up so you couldn't hate him full out. He now lived openly with Laila. During a slow news week, a gossip sheet carried the inevitable comparison with a certain celebrity. Another columnist paired Nick with his goatish great-uncle the U.S. senator, gunned down at the races in Saratoga by the brother of a nymphet *he* had seduced. Nick and Laila were photographed together at the Literary Guild shindig at the Waldorf.

Things took on a grotesque normalcy, as if people walked around with eyes on stalks.

The story got new legs when the unstoppable Juno Kwan officially replaced me on *Sunday Chronicle,* which spawned a tabloid column on ageism in work and love. Meanwhile, as if mocking my refusal to get back at him, Nick got his groove back as an editor. An obscure English writer sued Stark, author of the book Nick had overpaid for, claiming Stark had "appropriated" his life and grafted on homosexual hijinks. The brouhaha made the Stark a best seller. With Nick himself a scandal, books walked off the shelves and Hollywood came sniffing, the whole package screaming—all genuflect together—*synergy.*

SOPHIE FURNISHED THE usual merriment. Grubb had had quite enough of snippy editors, thank you very much. He acquired a vanity press, published *The Island* himself, bought out two printings, and got featured in an article in *New York Magazine* on moguls with dual careers. After banking the rest of her advance, Sophie launched Project Dog Lady by acquiring Milou, a Jack Russell dedicated to killing all creatures large and small; and from the Islesford Rescue Home, an abused yeller hound who walked in a permanent cringe. Then another windfall, demonstrating a Sophie scripture: *Thems that got shall get more.*

"It's the damndest thing, I didn't think it could happen again," she said. They were walking the dogs in a nippy Central Park, Milou terrorizing squirrels, Old Yeller hugging the pavement, tail between her legs.

"It" could mean only one thing. "So who is he?"

"Come, you better sit." They settled on a park bench, and Milou sprang vertically, like a mechanized toy, into Sophie's lap. "Think ponytail," she said—"actually, I've got him into a Renaissance pageboy, and had his toenails clipped." She held up a gloved palm: "I know—but Jed's family's was beyond dysfunctional. Statistically he should have turned out a Ralph Bundy."

It had taken only a lecture on the club-assed mannikin at the Explorers' Home for the Challenged. "We both staggered out to 70th Street at the same moment. I said, 'Which way are you going.' He said, 'Whichever way you're going.' We've scarcely been apart since. We connected without realizing it during those all-nighters to rescue Tara. Jed's a brilliant legal mind, you know. He's just never grasped the concept of billable hours. But now I have a little cash, I can afford him. Of course, nothing's perfect—"

She broke off to rein in Milou, who had leapt to the ground and was barking savagely at a pair of donkeys. *Donkeys?* In New York you hardly looked twice.

"Turns out he's on goddamn Zoloft or Elavil, or some mood-smoothie that zaps the old libido. He says without it he turns into Quasimodo on acid. I bet those health police who dispense Zoloft were the 'husky'-size boys in high school with mashed potatoes in their braces who could never get a date—and now look who's having the last laugh. Get laid while ye can!—that should be the message at commencement." She bent down to shush Milou, now growling at an Asian toddler in a fur-trimmed hood, his parents shooting them paranoid looks. "But what the hell," Sophie went on. "That last go-round with Howard and his 'needs' has turned me off sex anyway. Remember that scene with Burt Lancaster and Deborah Kerr in *From Here to Eternity?* Where they're fully dressed and kind of deep-massage each other and they come?"

"No."

"Well, maybe it's only in the book. Anyway, romantic passion belongs in the past. Today, how could you get away with something like 'We'll always have Paris'? Me and Jed, we're ironic, postmodern lovers. Forget the old in/out. We'll love like the angels."

. . .

PITCHING "CHOPIN IN the Sand Years," she got stonewalled by folks who a short season back had licked her up and down. New York lesson number one: *Foolish enough to lose your footing? Feel free to start over from Go.* Then her old buddy Tad Sieverson at the Arts Consortium said that much as he liked her project, it overlapped with a new, remarkably similar series already skedded for fall. New York lesson number two: *A great idea? Someone else had it, too.*

Then in a sweet piece of timing, a call from Tom Leahy, her former boss at CNB. Seems *Sunday Chronicle*'s core viewers missed the highbrow stuff; ratings had tanked, her old nemesis Bern Conant had moved to the Golf channel, and Leahy wanted to talk over lunch at the Four Seasons about her role in the revamped show.

Well, there was vindication of sorts, sneaking in the back door. But Leahy could wait, she decided. Even if he couldn't. She'd been cashiered out once before in that world; tomorrow a suit could look up from a spreadsheet and wonder why they were throwing money at that old bag. And like a child needing to be born, her piano series lay heavy against her heart.

A SUNDAY MORNING in May; lurches of warmth in the air. A chorus of sparrows cheeped *fortissimo* on the fire escape festooned with grapevines that had delighted Laila. Over her second mug of Colombian, Maddy devoured a profile in the *Times*'s Arts and Leisure: the hand wrecked by focal dystonia; the downward slide, the quest for a cure—how America loves a comeback kid. She hadn't seen Anton since their ill-fated tryst in December. This very night at the Grace Rainey Rogers he was playing the Brahms F Minor Sonata, a huge work that demands the piano take on the role of an orchestra.

Seated in row W in the expectant hum, she smiled to picture Anton's preconcert routine: pulling apart, leaf by leaf, a roll of toilet paper. He bounced onstage and headed for the piano as if to make a train; looked around at the audience with seeming indifference. Anton eased himself into the program with Beethoven's "Andante Favori," its light filigree passages great for limbering fingers. Next came the Schubert B-flat Major Sonata, Schubert's farewell to life and music, a work that resided in her cells. She'd practiced the sonata's heartbreaking Scherzo a lifetime ago in the music room of Conscience Point, that afternoon Nick had driven her to the station. The polite, classical sheen of Anton's reading left her cold. "Damnit, you could have been more brazen!" she itched to tell him, "more scintillating!" During the "Mephisto Waltz," though, she expected to see smoke curling from his fingers; Liszt was surely smiling from whichever place he was. After intermission, the Brahms F Minor. Maddy tensed as Anton attacked with ferocity the opening flourish, the leaps from thunderous low octaves up to clamorous chords—plenty of ops for wrong notes. He blitzed through the finger-busting passages with absurd ease, the brilliant cascades of notes in the Finale drawing audible gasps from Maddy's row. The shouted *Bravos* were partly for the player's stamina. Following the string of encores, Maddy stayed in her seat for a while, humbled. Then she joined the queue of well-wishers waiting to greet the artist backstage.

Which is how 'round midnight, Anton Bers came to be sipping Prosecco at her oak dining room table.

The windows were open on the sort of mild air that incites folly, urges you to sink your teeth into whatever comes to hand before the show moves on—and while you still have teeth. Mourning doves rou-cooed from the fire escape. Across the courtyard an opera singer skittered up the high registers like pearls dropped into the night.

"My Chopin-Sand is the wallflower at the orgy. Only to you would I admit that."

"Lemme tell you, in the Liszt—I almost fell off the ride."

"Oh," she shuddered, "the worst."

"Only to you would I admit . . ." He blew out and raised his goblet of Prosecco.

"Well! haven't we traded places," she said brightly. "I was playing hot-shot, you were playing East Palookaville."

"Yeah, I was big in Palookaville."

"Maybe I should pick up where you left off. In Palookaville." *Actually, why the hell not? Stonewalled by the heavies? She'd take her show on the road. Start in Greenboro, North Carolina, where she'd been marooned in marriage, and made a few contacts . . .* "I'll bring my series to granges, nursing homes, the projects. . . . Women's prisons! Oil rigs! These are the people who need me, not jaded New Yorkers. Jenny Lind went out on the road in America. If it was good enough for her . . . I could even lease a truck and schlep my Steinway."

"Are you serious?"

"Aren't we uppity. It's just an idea . . ." And not half-bad. Amazing how quickly you could adjust your sights. "Bet I could snag a grant for bringing kulchuh to the hinterlands. Tony, how come you always inspire me?"

Across the court, a trumpeter essayed a riff, then cut off.

"Maddy, that last time in my place—why the hell didn't you tell me what was going on?"

"Honestly, I hadn't yet figured out how to play it." From that last time there surfaced a scorching memory. She was not so pure that Anton's re-stored glamour didn't add a buzz. She quickly marshaled all the old deter-rents, plus a fresh one: the supple, silver-and-black, very proprietary Ms. Kim, whom she'd sighted backstage.

"Tony—this is strictly between us. In the spirit of our *bruderschafft*. But now I *will* tell you something. The fact is, Davidine and friends missed the real scandal."

. . .

EVEN WHILE SHE was speaking, his odd frown chilled her heart.

"Maddy, I had no idea you believed . . . I don't think so."

"You don't *think* so?"

"Maddy, it's unlikely Violet ever had a child."

Seizing up at this echo of Nick. "Shit, Tony, I was there. I went to Paris and brought her home, goddamnit." *The room in Belleville with the black velvet curtain and the sweet smell of hash and doors leading to rooms leading to more rooms.*

Anton rested his forearms on the table and leaned in. "Listen to me. I was in Amsterdam with the Concertgebouw. At the time Violet lived there. We had a mutual friend, a violin-maker."

"That's right—you'd met Violet, of course. You're not going to tell me—No . . ."

"Well, yes, actually. It was a one-night stand—uh, well, two."

"Jesus."

"My motives were a bit fuzzy. I think I slept with Violet to work off my childhood lust, whatever, for you. And me being a horny bastard . . ."

A breeze warped the candle flame, dancing fantastic shadows on the wall behind him. "Go on."

"About a year later, I heard about this supposed baby of Violet's."

Her eyes riveted by the shifting shadows. *"Go on."*

"The dates coincided uncomfortably with the last time I'd seen Violet, roughly twelve months before."

"Go on."

"I had a concert date in Berlin at the time, so I make a quick hop to Amsterdam. I rush over to Violet's apartment in the Haarlemmerstraat, near the Red Light District. She's vanished. Her friends gone, too—mostly druggies, people who pull up stakes without leaving a trace. I'm frantic at the thought of this baby, that I'll never locate Violet. I reach my friend the violin-maker, who's somehow stayed in touch with her. She told me that Violet had moved to Paris with a beautiful young woman from Martinique, who had family there. I forget her name. When Violet got involved with her, the woman was pregnant. "

THE ROSEATE LIGHT of a June dusk spilled over the keyboard. She'd follow the Chopin with an evening on three French composers—Ravel, Debussy, Fauré. After that, a program on the ballade form as musical storytelling. Another on the fantasy, from Bach to Schumann to John Corigliano and other contemporaries—she'd bounce around the timeline, make connections between past and present. . . . Her series was now "under consideration" by the Carolina Arts Council, and this scintilla of interest had unleashed waves of energy begetting more energy. She rose to rotate the tension from her shoulders; looked out the parlor window onto Jane Street. A frail ancient couple bearing a shopping bag between them inched over daunting cobblestones, making the return trip from Gristedes, their major undertaking of the day. Later she would phone Anton; she wanted his thinking on some pieces by Clara Schumann—which might have more sentimental than artistic value—for a future program. He was soon to leave for Verbier, Switzerland, the crème of summer music festivals, about as far from East Palookaville as you could get.

It was now a month since that night in May when Anton had demolished her known universe. During much of that time she'd kept at a cautious remove from her old self, whom she regarded as some village idiot not to be trusted around children. Clearly she'd been—and doubtless remained—so grotesquely gullible, she could scarcely be counted on to describe the weather, and should wear a warning to that effect, like epileptics with bracelets.

That night in May . . . She'd gone on a tear through the Village streets. Anton, powered by postconcert adrenaline, had barreled along with her. Somehow they'd circled back to Abingdon Square. . . .

They sit on a bench in the little park. The white blossoms that New York's trees mysteriously produce in spring shine ghostly and festive in the lamplight. The night air is tender, with top-notes of pollution. They make out beneath a carton shanty in the center of the square what appears to be a human bundle.

"How do you go on when—" Maddy begins. Switching gears: "I once saw this horror movie. A woman runs around frantically locking all the doors and windows of the house—only to find the killer is *in* the house, standing directly behind her. . . . How do you go on when the enemy is not out there, but"—knocking on her head—"in here?"

Wisely, Anton attempts no answer.

Knocking away: "Here, in your own *mind*."

"Would you stop doing that to your head?"

"Her name was Sandrine. Violet's friend. Sandrine."

"Yah," Anton nods, "that was it."

"They conned me, they set me up."

"Maddy, Violet was usually pretty wasted, hard to imagine her conning anyone."

"This once she got it together. Sandrine's family probably got deported . . . leaving her and Violet with a minor inconvenience—So bring on the Girl Scout! The Ashcrofts are a sewer. Nick actually warned me. Why don't we listen when people warn us about themselves?"

"Maybe we think it's false modesty. Or we'd rather be in love. Maybe you're the last romantic. And you wanna know what? I think you bought their story because you're better than they are, that's what."

Anton's concern over "malarial" spring drafts drives them into an all-night dive. A handful of grizzled regulars huddle at the bar. She and Anton sit over Irish coffee in a dim back room that exhales a New York bouquet of impacted soot, eau de garbage and broken dreams. She sketches the long-ago scene at the Plaza Hotel; how she'd gone to Paris to honor a promise.

"I seem to specialize in outdated notions. It seemed the least I could do. I abandoned Violet in a brutal way."

Anton's eyes glow. "I kind of sensed what was up between you two. Gotta admit, it turned me on. In Amsterdam, Violet would fish for news of you. Maybe she slept with me because I was a bridge to you. Those funky sheets in Amsterdam were pretty crowded. By the way, if Violet was gay, you sure woulda had me fooled."

"Maybe in her warped thinking, palming off her girlfriend's baby on me was payback. For my desertion, whatever. And maybe the money for Laila dried up because Sandrine had expensive habits."

"It gets more sordid, I'm afraid. I saw my friend the violin-maker a year or so later. She said she'd heard the baby had been adopted—by an American. So that was accurate. And soon after, according to my friend, Sandrine ran off with the baby's father—white, French, I think. A piece of work, this Sandrine. Fobs her baby off on Violet's old friend, then dumps Violet. So Violet was had, too. If that's any consolation."

"Doesn't give Laila a distinguished background, does it. Guess she did a fine job of surmounting her genes. Till Nick. Blood tells. When I think how Vi ended up. After all her big dreams, her desperation not to 'miss her life.'"

Head in her hands, she tries to summon up the bold, beautiful girl of that enchanted summer.

"Maddy, didn't Violet's scam turn out a blessing?"

"Or a curse in disguise."

. . .

SINCE THAT NIGHT in May she'd also discovered that running a loop 24-7 of one's deficiencies as a human being starts to lose its allure. So she'd hitched up her socks and made a date with Laila. She'd relayed birth story number two—this version washing away the incest taint—an act of generosity that would put her on the short list for canonization.

As a perverse joke on herself, she'd arranged to give Laila the news at a French Caribbean hideaway on 14th Street called Bambou.

"You know, I never didn't believe Nick." Laila glanced nervously about, Maddy struggling to retrofit this face with cunning kohl-rimmed eyes. Jade-colored, of course. "Who set *you* straight?"

"Anton Bers heard from a reliable source that Violet never had a child." *So why the same gaze? Why Vi's mannerisms, even?*

"Oh, the pianist dude." Laila cupped the bowl of her wine glass in one hand, a moist lushness to her features. "Well, looks like I still get a dyke for a mother. Or a switch-hitter. Next you'll tell me I'm the love child of the Queen of Rumania." *The tough talk belied by the stricken eyes.* "That ho in the apartment passed me off like a hot potato." A beat. "Do I, like, look like her? Did Sandrine unload me because she didn't have the bucks? Or just hated my face. Oh, fuck it. In Calcutta the whores in the brothels have babies they take care of together. . . . Georgia Kidd once saw a beautiful dark-eyed baby sucking on a used condom. Sandrine was just one more dark-skinned woman fucked over by whitey. I lucked out, I'm one of the lucky ones."

The waiter appeared to ask about a refill. He eyed them with the exquisite tact of waiters, observers of lives: the peach-haired woman with the cheekbones and the thin, honey-colored girl who might be on the verge of tears; perhaps wondering what business brought them together.

"What happened to her, this Sandrine," Laila said dully.

She disappeared with your French father—after ensuring your safekeeping. You could say Sandrine was responsible, in her fashion. "No one knows," Maddy said. "Only that somehow Violet ended up as your 'guardian.' " *Forking one more lie onto the compost of lies. There was some small comfort to be had in controlling the narrative.*

Laila extended the fingers of both hands. "Violet scammed you. You conned me. Everything about our lives is a fuckin' lie. . . ."

"Remember that cold winter Sunday we went to Conran's to buy the white bowls with blue trim and ate Hungarian pastries that tasted better than—" She broke off. She was all scar tissue, nerveless. She'd done what she needed to do. Time to ring down the curtain on Act III.

Laila was turning her head this way and that, like a horse avoiding a bit. She looked up at the corrugated ceiling, Adam's apple alarmingly discrete. "Listen, thank you. Maddy," she added hoarsely. "Thank you. I mean, you didn't, like, have to tell me." Then she blew out in exasperation in a manner entirely like Violet, so nothing seemed certain.

CHAPTER 21

Flight 128

S he picked her out instantly near Delta Gate 3, among a blur of indifferent faces. Staring straight ahead, the only head in her row of attached plastic seats not tilted up tropistically toward a TV monitor. She wore her blue Land's End Squall jacket, and hugged camera cases and a Lufthansa flight bag Maddy recognized as the one she'd been combing her closets for.

She had not thought to see Laila again. But comes the call from Kennedy, and she goes on autopilot, dropping everything, deadlines be damned. Next thing she's sitting in a cab stalled in traffic on the Van Wyck, getting acid reflux plus the latest from the driver's radio on *l'affaire* Monica Lewinsky; wondering why the hell she's here. . . .

They found two seats together and sat in silence. On the TV a soap-opera star in a red dress stalked around on stilettos and gestured at the new Infiniti Q45.

"I'm leaving Nick." Laila upturned her palms, a shade lighter, on her lap. "I thought you should know."

"What happened?" Speaking through the cotton wadding packing her head.

"Don' wanna talk about it. I'm going to Oakland. There's space for me in Tara Gerson's commune."

"Shouldn't you finish the term at Hunter?"

"Term's over. Is that all you have to say?"

"What happened."

Long silence. "He woulda blown me off, too. I don' wanna talk about it."

"What makes you think he wouldn't have . . . stuck with it?"

She gnawed her lip. "Why?"

Try exhaustion. "Maybe he'd finally found the right person."

"Is there such a person?" She looked at her hands in her lap. "I decided not to hang around and find out. So I walked first." Her mouth twisted down into a clown grimace. "The whole thing sucks." She sniffed and searched her jacket pocket for a tissue. Reflexively, Maddy drew a mini-pack from her bag and handed it over. Laila gave a noisy honk.

It occurred to her that something had been won, but it seemed as inviting as a building site on Three Mile Island. "What about Nick?" Not certain what she was asking.

"Oh, he always makes out okay, Nick." She bobbed her head up and down. "Listen. You're gonna hate this. On top of everything"—the huff—"I need money."

Maddy couldn't help but smile. The predictability! No matter the circumstances, the moment arrived when you shelled out. She wondered if Lizzie Borden had hit up old Ma Borden for a handout.

"How much?"

"Enough to carry me a couple months. I'll pay you back. Won't cost a whole lot to stay at Tara's place in Oakland. Then I'm going to hook up with a filmmaker friend of Georgia's, who's doing a documentary on this village in Chiapas. I got a gig shooting the stills. And then I can pay you back."

"Good God, Chiapas—"

"I know, a guerrilla behind every bush."

"And after what happened to Tara . . ."

"Look, the fight for economic justice is not like hitting the hot club of the moment," she said, not unkindly.

Maddy scrawled a check for a big number. On her CMA account checkbook, which she'd had the foresight to pop in her bag.

"Thanks." Laila folded the check in half and stuck it in a pocket of her backpack, Maddy watching the febrile motion, so like Violet's, of her gnawed fingers. Laila stared up at the TV monitor, downturned mouth twitching. The soap star in the red dress was performing the same ballet with the Infiniti. "Okay, I might as well tell you. What I told you before wasn't the exact truth. I'll need the money because I'm pregnant."

The news, which she'd already guessed at, lay there like a dead flounder. "How pregnant?"

"Almost five months."

"Isn't that all the more reason to . . . stay put?" she said carefully.

"You don't get it. I'm leaving Nick *because* I'm pregnant. Nick doesn't want a kid." The loudspeaker came on, paging a Dr. Henry Hatton in doleful tones.

A sad thing I never had a child, he'd said in Nohant. . . .

"At least he doesn't want our—*my* half-breed kid," Laila said.

Maddy kept very still, eyes semishut like a dozing lizard. Instant incineration would be too merciful to Nick. Barely audible: "What makes you think Nick doesn't want this child."

"Hello! I'm not a retard. He was back and forth, going, 'It wouldn't be fair to you, or the baby.'" Perfectly mimicking Nick's nasal honk. "'Don't know how I could raise a baby at this late stage . . . the responsibility . . . want to do it right' blah blah . . ."

"Did you consider the alternative?"

"I made an appointment at a clinic. But the night before all I could think of was that sleaze Sandrine, scamming off her own baby—Hell, maybe she *sold* me, or *traded* me. Maybe Violet *paid* her to dump me. And I'm thinking, fuck that! I've gotta do better—*animals* do better. To make up for what she did to me." She paused. "I want something of my own. Because nothing else is mine, not this guy who's dicking me over, having his male menopause. Everything in my life's been lies. I need one true thing that's mine." Laila twisted her neck around. "You must be satisfied."

"Satisfied?" She must have cried out. From down the row, two Korean schoolgirls in white blouses and navy jumpers turned polite stares on her.

"It's human nature." On the TV robots were now goose-stepping around another car to Beethoven's Ninth. "Funny, when I was totally bummed, I actually thought, *What would Mom do.*"

That did it, she popped, as if surfacing from anesthesia, into the rush and racket of the world. She swung full around toward Laila. "Listen, you're only nineteen, with everything still before you. You can still set things right. Does it really make sense to run off and have this baby?"

Gazing at Maddy: "You know it's too late. And I want this child. I'm going to have this child. I love him already. Augusto."

"Augusto?"

"Yeah." She nodded her head. "His name's Augusto."

She seized Laila's cold little hand. "But you can't go have the baby in some Third World village," she cried, attracting more stares. "Chiapas, it's insane. Suppose there're complications. It's unsanitary, local doctors don't have the expertise, it makes no sense." She pictured the dirty forceps, bloodied gauze and flies. . . . The enormity of it brought tears to her eyes.

Laila squeezed Maddy's hand. "I'm young and strong. It'll be all right, Ma. You're such a worrier. You gotta have more confidence in me. You'll see, it'll be all right."

But she couldn't, wouldn't see . . . The loudspeaker crackled on: *We are now boarding Delta Flight 128 to Oakland at Gate 3, rows thirty through twenty.* Somewhere else they were still paging Dr. Henry Hatton in the same mournful tone.

"Flight 128, that's my flight," Laila said. She seemed too listless to join the crowd shuffling toward Gate 3. Then she stood and hoisted her camera bags. Maddy rose with her. She looked into Maddy's eyes. "I love you. I'm sorry I fucked up your life."

Passengers for Flight 128 shuffled around them, trundling carry-ons on wheels.

"Listen, Lo, about you and me, it was all true. We were happy. Remember how we could look out the window on Barrow Street and see the snow at eye-level like powdered sugar?"

"We used to joke it was warm and snug, living against the boiler."

"That mangy Christmas tree we got on Hudson Street for half-price."

"The ornament for the top like an albino pigeon."

"The pervert with the goatee—"

"—who liked to 'window-shop' at Shirley's Lingerie."

"Those white bowls with blue trim we bought in Conran's."

"And the Hungarian pastries afterward . . ."

"Those bowls are all cracked now, but I can hardly think of anything that made me happier. . . . Laila, don't go. Come back home. Have the baby here, where there's decent care. We'll fix up the top floor on Jane Street for you and the baby. Maybe then, after you've had time to get yourself together and think it all through—"

"I have to leave. It will be all right, Ma." She moved close and touched her cool cheek to Maddy's. She still smelt of raw timber. "I know this is pretty lame but—thank you. For saving my life. In all the ways." Her voice low and melodious. "The accident that night at the Point. I *saw* what happened. Nick said weren't we lucky no one got hurt. But it wasn't luck, was it. That's also why I have to leave. Nick would have loved the baby once he saw him. But it scared me, knowing what I knew."

Maddy hugged Laila to her, the shocking thinness, the slightest swell starting through her middle. Nick's child; hers, too, somehow, hers and Laila's.

"You'll come back soon, won't you? Promise you'll come back."

"I want *you* to be happy again, Ma."

"When will you come back. When."

Laila shrugged, letting herself be carried with the herd trudging toward Gate 3. Maddy moved beside her.

"We can both be happy again, at Conscience Point. The way it used to be. Nick despises the place, he's practically begging me to use it and keep it up—I've a plan to lease it from him. *We*'ll live there, you and me. And Augusto, what a glorious place to raise him. It'll be ours. Yours, mine, and Augusto's. We'll bike to the beach. Teach Augusto to swim. We'll build you a real studio—"

Laila stood still, the flow of passengers parting around her. "I can't. Because of what I did."

"I'll forgive you more every day. Starting right now—every day a little more."

"But can I forgive myself? I've fucked it up with the one person—" Her voice trailed off; lashes shuttered her eyes. "I can't go back to Conscience Point. I need to start fresh. I don't belong there. That world has no more connection to me, or anyplace . . . here." She gestured with her free hand. "I'm leaving to make my own life, hang with the folks I belong with. The *mestizos* and half-breeds—"

"Lo, don't romanticize poverty. Use our privileges to change the world."

"Those privileges were never mine, just on loan. I need to figure out my own way and make something right. Please tell me you understand. It would be—to give me your blessing."

Passengers pulled their wheelies past them on both sides. Maddy opened her mouth. No words came.

Laila nudged her flight bag forward with her foot, then stopped and looked at Maddy. "The bitch is, I'm still in love with the creep. How can that be. Can you explain that to me?"

Maddy's eyes blurred and an ache rose through her throat that seemed to stretch on and on.

They were almost to the gate. From behind, a group of Asian schoolkids in navy jumpers with badges pressed them forward.

"Please have your tickets ready and out of the folder," the airport attendant was repeating.

Laila fumbled in her blue jacket pocket. The schoolkids behind them chattered excitedly, then streamed around them. The loudspeaker boomed, WILL ALL PASSENGERS FOR FLIGHT 128 PLEASE BOARD IMMEDIATELY. . . .

Laila embraced Maddy, pressed her tightly against her for a long moment, Maddy limp, cold as death, then quickly walked down the boarding ramp without looking back.

CHAPTER 22

Luxembourg

W hat had she left to do here?

As always, when she wanted someplace else, she wanted France.

On a July afternoon she sat on a green slatted chair in the Jardin des Tuileries, watching an unvarying ritual. A Hinode bus, emblazoned with orange rays that evoked kamikaze planes, would pull up near the arch before the Louvre; tourists would clamber out yoked with cameras, and no sooner on the asphalt, start snapping pictures.

Since her last visit a year ago, much had changed. Paris in 1998 was becoming a suburb of Asia, and the Left Bank a theme park of high-end chains. And she had traveled a wide circle: it was in France that began a story that had also ended there, on their lovely stolen holiday in the Berry, when the sight of a German nymphet had crystallized Nick's lust for Laila, like that fatal love chord in *Tristan and Isolde*. Yet here she sat, reassembled from the wreck; bit of calking around the heart and listing to windward, but gamely rigged out for a new journey. Back in the concert career—scaled down, for sure!—that she'd jettisoned when the siren song of the Ashcrofts lured her into the shoals, those years now fanning out behind her like a cotillion of shades.

She headed for a basin where children guided their sailboats with Gameboylike gizmos; the year before, she remembered, they'd used long poles. A girl with coltish legs gamboled around the basin's edge. Maddy quickly averted her eyes. *I love you. All is well.* The card, postmarked June 10, Tapachula, depicted a horse-drawn tram. On the next card—a tram from Puebla with the caption *Avenida de la Libertad*—Laila had declined her offer to ship a washing machine. *95% of the world lives this way; why should I live better?* Now, twenty-three days later, *nada*. Awake, she could police her thoughts. But in the predawn darkness . . . Images and words surfaced with tantalizing clarity. Laila's brisk hands, tidying their toadhole after the phone got turned off . . . Laila in a white snood as Third Pilgrim in the school play . . . I *saw* you . . . You saved my life in all the ways . . .

Research had solved one mystery. Augusto came from Augusto Cesar Sandino, the Nicaraguan revolutionary and symbol of resistance to U.S. domination. Assassinated by General Somoza . . . Maddy rapidly fanned the air with her folded *Tribune,* and concentrated on a daily ritual: moving Laila through cracks in the heedless universe to avoid such dangers as State-sponsored assassins, unsterile forceps, dengue-bearing mosquitoes, planes on slick runways, the Humberts of Latin America . . .

She turned her attention to local pleasures. The crunchy demibaguette of her *sandwich jambon* brought joy to the mouth. She chucked back the tasty nickel-y Badoit—they didn't call the water *minerale* for nothing.

A tabloid tale from the States had made it to the *Trib:* Jealous man throws lye in his girlfriend's face, and goes to jail for fourteen years. When he gets out, girlfriend, now blind, marries him. Then when he assaults his current mistress, the wife defends him. Maddy thought the wife's literally blind passion so degraded that, like minuses making a plus, it landed somewhere near sublime.

Across the basin, a pair of lovers nuzzled each other. She thought of Tony Bers, whose body had never known sunshine or personal trainers, but knew a riding-high position that he might just have invented. *Only to you,* they would sing out after revealing some blooper or confessing some ignoble jealousy; in public they had merely to say the word "only" to crack each other up. . . . Damn, with her talent for disastrous choices, had she made yet another? Yet hadn't she finished with male divas; finished laboring at love like a Con Ed crew on a buried gas line? Servicing Anton's born-again career would leach off the energy she owed her fledgling series—she was no Wanda Horowitz. That was later-life romance: you assembled the shape of catastrophe from just a speck in the distance; younger, you saw nothing till the steel of the locomotive bit your cheek.

Unless you were Sophie. She reread the e-mail:

7/15/98

Maddy dear, I thought you'd be interested in this excerpt from my new novel.

"Why not go off the supercocktail for a while," Sally says to Josh one night. "Just to see what happens." Sally is not motivated purely by an interest in mental health. The proximity of Josh's forty-something body—the sweet ass, curve from shoulder to bicep, sprinkle of brown hairs heading south of his belt—is disturbing the rest of the Sleeping Giant.

Not without trepidation, Josh decides to give it a shot. This is heroism for the coming millennium. Perseus slew a dragon; Kennedy piloted the U-boat; today a guy goes off his medication. Sally steels herself for Quasimodo on acid, the psycho ward at Lenox Hill.

Then comes social nirvana: an invite to Amos Grubb's black tie Fred Astaire–style dance party at the Rainbow Room. And it's engraved. Josh turns ecstatic, literally. He might have downed

Spanish Fly. That night, well—so much for loving like angels!
Ol' debbil sex is what turns the planet.

Maybe Pangloss was right, and all is for the best in the best of
all possible worlds. If I hadn't passed through Repo Man and No
Affect and Cap'n Tom and Interactive and Houdini and the Luft-
mensch and Quik-Draw Sam and the Strom and the cavalcade of
Internet con men and mixer desperadoes; and if Tara hadn't tried
to save a piece of the world, and I hadn't spent nights brainstorm-
ing with my lawyer—I might have missed what was right under
my nose. To have found this so late in the game, so un-hoped-for.

P.S. In news from the Pound, I've just adopted the dearest fellow.
He's a mix of Pug and Lab, looks like a bull and can sing.
Name's Barkis.

Now, I don't suppose this would interest you, but . . . I heard
Anton Bers had a very public fight with Dorothy Kim in the Air
France VIP lounge. But she's still trailing him on his tour, stay-
ing in separate hotels. Funny, I've heard it's the Gen Xers who are
"firing" guys who don't make the cut—isn't that the revised sce-
nario? Maybe feminism hasn't penetrated the Far East? Or is it
possible we've learned nothing.

She handed her key to the concierge, and sailed into the Paris morning.
The Saints-Pères had long been "their" hotel. They'd sat foreheads touching, hearts full, in the mossy central courtyard, sipping their morning *café*
crème. After burrowing in each other's groins and spritzing the entire bathroom with the handheld French shower . . . She'd thought, to hell with
that, and booked a res at the Saints-Pères anyway.

The rookery of Left Bank *toits* peeled upward, a radiant city in the sky.

Hugging her lane of the narrow sidewalk bordered by metal poles called *bites* (French for "cock"), she chose the long route. She was headed for the new Bibliothèque Nationale to plumb the Chopin archives for her first concert in the new series. She wore the pricey lace-up Mephistos she'd splurged on—and that Parisiennes considered a capital offense—and carried under her arm, like a baguette, a large rolled-up score. She might be any middle-aged woman traveling alone and propping up her spirits with girders of steel. She took a deep drag on the morning air. Paris was so much its smells: something maritime, plus a bouquet of *boulangeries*, hosed-down sidewalks, scooter exhaust, all finished off with a faint fecal odor. Narrow doorways exhaled the same dank chill that might have breathed on Balzac's parvenus.

A hand grasped her upper arm from behind, she spun round, New York attack mode. Stared at the apparition, eyes smarting in the light. She tucked in her chin and barreled on.

He came abreast.

"Excuse me, I'm late for an appointment. And this sidewalk"—swatting him aside with her scroll, like a herding dog—"is too narrow for two."

He wove around a *bite* into the *trottoir*. "I'm in Paris on business. Arcas Press is copublishing—"

His words swallowed by horns blasting over a Peugeot that blocked traffic. Out slid an expensive blond, no rush, with autobronzed legs, and the foxy features of ancient Gaul you'd see in the Bayeux tapestry. Then a second blond in a tiny navy pinstripe dress with matching sweater, a riff on corporate regalia—two women who wasted no time on careers like America's trophy wives.

Maddy turned left into the Rue de Grenelle. The Sixth Arrondissement now tarted up with Prada, Sonyia Rykiel, Armani . . . She crossed to the Rue du Vieux Colombier against the light and oncoming cars, unleashing a pocket-sized pandemonium. Nick reached out a protective hand; she curved away. On past the Théâtre du Vieux Colombier, where they'd been playing Ionesco since the '50s. Next a pink leather bustier in a shop window. Now a halved grapefruit studded with tiny rosy shrimp and parchment-thin cukes—deli art! Ahead loomed the twin grey towers of St. Sulpice. She'd forgotten which Metro she was bound for, but they all connected.

"You're wondering how I found you," he said, catching up. "I asked myself, *Where would she stay? She'd think, not the Saints-Pères—'our' hotel. Then she'd think, to hell with that.*"

She sped along on her winged Mephistos. Eyes caught on Nick: the longish weave of hair, arching brows, alert set of the ears—the mysterious proportions of beauty made him leap into focus. Nature had slung together other faces like so much pudding and unfairly lavished all its care on this one.

She stopped, finally. "Nick, we have no business together. I'll need to move my piano and the rest from Conscience Point, but we can arrange everything by phone, fax, carrier pigeon. I'll be reachable through my lawyer at an address in France. And now I've an appointment—"

"Congratulations! Amos Grubb told me about your grant for a concert series with a sexy new angle. I see a book and TV tie-in—in fact, Arcas could do the book. Audio, CD-ROM . . . We'd create a whole package."

She flashed him a pitying look. The light went green and a squadron of maniac French drivers spurted forward in perfect synchrony.

"Maddy, please, the truth is I came to Paris to talk to you."

A beaten-down voice, unfamiliar. The twin towers of St. Sulpice, she noticed, didn't match: the left had a triangular pediment, the right a smaller rounded one. She turned down the Rue Bonaparte. Ahead, trees lofted their green tops over a black fence. That would be the Jardin du Luxembourg, and beyond, the Metro St. Michel she remembered she was headed for.

"Just hear me out—we need to discuss some details *in person*—and then I promise you'll be on your way."

She stopped before the Maison d'Indochine; swiped her fingers across her sweaty forehead. He was trembling, damn him.

THEY ENTERED THE Jardin du Luxembourg through the gate off the Rue Vavin. They walked past a statue of Paul Verlaine surrounded by glossy green foliage with white spots; pigeons perched on Verlaine's big, square head. Next came a bust of Jules Massenet. Then José Mariá de Heredia. It was reassuring somehow, the way the French loved their own. *I can do better, I can protect my own:* Was that what Laila had said? A grizzled *chômeur* glanced dolefully up at them from his bench, beside him a shaving kit and radio.

They found two chairs half-shaded by the glossy leaves of a chestnut tree. Sat facing a crescent of yellow snapdragons and fuschia-colored spires cut into the lawn like a scar. What was the name of that fuschia flower? It began with an A . . . The sun through leaves spattered faun-like markings on Nick's twill pants that they'd bought together at the Sail Loft in Islesford. A few chairs down, a white guy with dreadlocks and other slacker types, gnawed and unclean, were eating pizza from paper bags and horsing around. Out of view toward the Rue Vavin, the velvet *thwock* of tennis balls.

"Maddy, I want you back."

She stared at him. "Oh, Nick, it's too late in the day. You've smashed too many things."

"It's never too late for the right thing."

"You and 'the right thing'? They don't—"

"It's taken me till now," he said over her, "to—get at my own core."

"—belong in the same breath," she finished.

"It's a piss-poor excuse, I know, I'm appallingly slow, but it's how I'm made." A moment. "Ingmar Bergman once said he'd left puberty at fifty-eight." His smile closed down on seeing her face. "Maddy, I've realized— my true life is with you."

"But mine is not with *you*. You've blown it Nick, blown it big time. I trusted you, like my own self. You've become . . . *incomprehensible*."

"It was an illness, Maddy. The thing with Laila. A long fever."

"Oh, that's pretty, Nick, but I don't buy it. You just wanted to have yourself some fun, at whatever cost, and the thing got played out, end of story. So don't give me 'fever.'"

"I accept full responsibility, I do. 'The accused showed remorse,'" he intoned in a stagy voice. Irritation roiling beneath, like sargasso under waves.

"The baby—"

"I did everything I could to dissuade Laila. Before it got too late. She's headed for big trouble. You've got to help me locate her. She refused to take any money."

Good girl; let the Ashcrofts not imagine they could buy everything. "As I recall, you wanted that baby. As I recall, you were all set to bust us up to make your fucking baby." He opened his mouth to speak, but she rose over him. *"Did you ever stop to think it's not just about your cock?"*

"If you'd let me—"

She smashed her hand against his mouth, feeling his teeth against her fingers, forcing his head back. "Stop talking, all you do is justify yourself. Words, more words, they make me dizzy. I'll tell you why you didn't want that baby. Poopy diapers, reality. A rival center of the universe. Seemed less amusing than cruising on the *Cherubino* with Eurotrash. And now it's, *Oh! found my core, reverse course.* You think you can blow one way, then another, mowing down lives. You should be removed from human circulation. With all your bloodlines, you're nothing but scum." His affrighted eyes above her hand stared up at her. She snatched her hand away. The slackers were watching, transfixed.

Nick slowly bent to retrieve the score that had slipped to the ground. "Your thingy," he offered. He'd cut himself shaving and had a cold sore near his lip, and his eyes looked up at her with a dullish cast, as if age had suddenly claimed him, and she thought, *How pathetic we all are.* At least she'd finally given him the what-for. Her heart was thumping unpleasantly, though. A girl cut across the grass wearing Adidas sneaks built up like wedgies.

"Something I never told you," Nick said in the flat murmur of confession. "I've already outlived Father—just. The Ashcroft men check out early. Then Serena died, and even though she hated us, I went into a sort of panic. I felt that to have a child was to cheat death a little. But I came to realize how desperately I needed to repair my life with you. Nothing can make a dent in my longing for you. To be with you is like—you're *home.* It's like coming home. I know I don't deserve it—but if you could find a way to forgive me . . ."

Astilbe! The name of that fuschia flower.

"I know you still have feelings for me, Maddy," he pressed on, in his voice a contrition she'd never heard. "In spite of . . . everything. Because you won't, you *can't* do me harm. I ran into that Davidine creature. She said you were set to 'nuke' me, her word, and then got cold feet. I believe it was because you didn't want to kill my shot at Americas Watch." She looked away from his welling eyes, refusing to be drawn in. "You were protecting our future."

"You've lied to me in so many ways I wonder if you even know the difference."

"Maddy, you—well, *you* haven't exactly been forthcoming. I never dreamt you believed Violet's—but none of that matters now! We're what we both want. Eight years of happiness—until I found you, I couldn't have imagined it. Before, I was just getting through the days. Then comes a single lapse. Atrocious, yes—*yes!*—but just one. Against all the good." She'd tasted him tasting of her. . . . "You know the worst of me, and I know you haven't cut me out of your heart."

Suddenly he was at her knees. Down on the pavement, dog-level. "You want real remorse? Here it is, really real, not just words, I'm down in the dirt here . . . groveling, eating dirt. . . ." She felt his arms around her calves—for a moment she wanted to kick him. "I've been so lost," came his choked voice from her lap.

And then she was folded over him, the smell of his hair, overcome with the sheer waste. "Why did you need to spoil it. . . ."

He raised his face to hers, arms around her waist; eyes, face fearfully naked. "Give me a chance to deserve—you—us—your trust—" Bumbling around, Nick the eloquent. "No, no words, I'll show you. I'll . . . slay the Minotaur." Trying to recoup some cover.

In her peripheral vision she'd become aware of Dreadlocks, miming a berserk Romeo, the other slackers a prancing chorus. It struck her that she and Nick resembled a nineteenth-century lithograph of a lover and his mistress in a novel sitting on her bookshelf. Shit. Trust Nick to pull out the Ashcroft melodrama.

She straightened her back and wiped at her eyes. "Uh, Nick?" she murmured. "Let's not entertain the locals, okay?"

He struggled to his feet, fussily dusting off his knees; rubbing the one he'd injured skiing off piste in Alta. "Damn gravel makes little pit-holes. What's to become of us. The heart stays young but the joints feel like Tin Man."

"Let's walk."

The slackers hooted and waved. Nick shot off something their way that displayed his superb command of the vernacular.

They wound along a peaceful, sun-spangled path. On a running track, a few scrawny Parisians jogged past, probably fresh off a pack of Gitanes. They entered shaded woods with a gazebo selling sandwiches and drinks. The tinny fanfare of a band struck up in the distance. They came to a long, grassy court, where a policeman's association was staging a display of acrobatics. Men in blue satin warm-up pants performed flips and somersaults on a giant trampoline, while others wheeled one-armed through the air on trapezes like avenging angels. *Don't you love them?* she'd say to Nick, even with Nick absent. Without him at her side, the world happened at the far end of a telescope.

He watched her watch the acrobats. "I love the way you look. It's absurd, isn't it? To be in love with an overbite?"

Where was the overbite when he was fucking Laila? "The question is, Who would be next?" she said, eyes fixed on a tumbler. "After you had your realization of the month."

"I can't imagine starting with someone new. Trotting out the vital statistics—"

"Not energy-efficient?"

"Would you rather be happy or right? Something else you said to me."

"Stop quoting me to myself. Besides, I see no reason not to be both."

"I'll wait for you. However long."

She watched a tumbler in red perform backflips. Before Nick she'd made a truce with solitude. The years with Marshall were like paired solitude.

"Remember you once said there's no more time to waste? Maddy, think, we can go home to Conscience Point. Ever since the Stark blowout, Arcas is booming—on a pile of manure. We're publishing *How to Work with Your Angels, Death by Chocolate,* offensive jokes from the head writer of *The Howard Stern Show.* What better moment to jump ship?" He grasped her arm. "If I get to head up Americas Watch, I'll shuttle between Washington and Islesford. Write my book . . . With Serena's estate settled, there's money to renovate the Point. We'll do everything we've dreamt of. Gather writers, musicians at the Point. Just the way you've always wanted."

Abruptly the past year seemed a nightmare scrolling up into oblivion. She could resume her waking life, she could choose that, couldn't she? Something in her yearned strangely to choose that, impervious to what was right, what *people would say*. The guy throws lye in his girlfriend's face and when he gets out of jail, she marries him. Is the girlfriend wrong? Where is it written? She thought of criminals loved by women, undoubtedly a sizable population. The girlfriend who stood by Alex Kelly, the clean-cut rapist from Darien. Julien Sorel, who shoots Madame de Rênal twice, and she adores him the more. Let's suppose Nick's . . . *lapse* with Laila was just that: an aberration, a *freak*. An incubus fastening its claws on . . . Like Phèdre hot for her son-in-law—the Greeks! They did it all! They became swans and bulls to do it. . . . The French! They'd say, *pas grand chose*, no big deal. Lolita . . . Maybe there existed a certified disease, *Lolita syndrome*, listed under "L" in the Merck Manual . . . Einstein— wasn't there some hanky-panky with . . . Or was it Freud . . .

Okay, set Nick's *lapse* against the princely Nick of eight years, the joy he'd added to the planet . . . subtracting points for foul moods . . . Extra points for the nights in the Saints-Pères! Plus this remorse, the real McCoy, practically *humming* at her side, El Penitente here, next he'd be on the road to Taos, self-flagellating with the Brothers of Padre Jesus, whipping his own back to a bloody froth . . . Do the math! Didn't the math work out in his favor? In *their* favor? They could hide out in Argentina, she and Nick, like Nazi war criminals. Safe from the right-thinkers (Y'mean she *took him back?*) Was it the finger-wagging *shouldn't* that stopped her? The old compulsion to play good Scout? Where was *shouldn't* when she was alone with her goodness at the end of the day? Maybe she'd blown it with Anton because she wasn't made for what was right. Maybe she was made for the absolute bad-ass fucked-up—*happy-making*—fucked-up—

A hand at her elbow steadied her. She must be yo-yoing. "Would you like to sit for a bit?" Nick said in a tender, worried voice. She stared up at him, unseeing. "Maddy," he said gently, "you will . . . consider everything? I'll wait as long as I need to."

Suddenly she heard Sophie scoffing: *Turn down two men in one season?* A shudder of laughter. *Get a grip,* deep breaths. "That appointment," she said. "I'd better be off, I'm now very late." Let the bastard sweat it.

The band had struck up again and a new team of men in red satin warm-ups ran up the steps to the trampoline. Casting her eyes about for the nearest exit, she noticed a marble statue at the far corner of the court. Cupid and Psyche. Perhaps the original of the statues at Conscience Point. Psyche's white marble arms curved in an arc of yearning toward the winged Cupid, who hovered above, features grave, gesturing hand signaling dismissal. *Love cannot dwell with suspicion.* She wondered if the Luxembourg version bore the same legend.

CHAPTER 23

Conscience Point

"You loved him, didn't you."
"Oh yes. He was the forerunner."
　　　　　—EVELYN WAUGH, *Brideshead Revisited*

T he work on the main house is almost finished. The starry bedroom has been halved, each with its portion of heaven; the vaulted gallery on the second floor regilded, paintings still wrapped in plastic; dining room restored to baronial splendor, awaiting a communal chowdown; tennis court reclaimed from grasshoppers and a vegetable invasion. The autumn garden mounts its last hurrah, a tangle of purple and white asters, orange cosmos, and the luscious deep magenta dahlias I put in this summer. Only the library remains unchanged.

Laila's Studio, as we've decided to name it, will house a composer/musician; its isolation makes ideal soundproofing. We thought at first just to put in a new roof and deck. But the contractor insisted the wood was wormy, so we razed it—along with the aviary, of course. When the workmen finished, dust from the old timber and a hint of birdshit hung in the air, mingling with scents of pine and wild roses. There never had been a foundation; the cabin was that insubstantial. Little by little the Point banishes any malign spirits still tempted to linger.

Everywhere hammering and the whine of buzz saws; taxis dropping off Viktor Vadim and fellow members of the Davos Quartet, arrived for some music-making before the official opening. Olga, our registrar, shows them to their rooms. Yet another delivery truck rounds the curve at the copper beech. Food and drink courtesy of Amos Grubb, so nothing but the best: Piper Heidsick, prawns, Scottish salmon, local tomatoes and fruit pies; we'll set out the spread on the oak table beside the autumn garden. Grubb, now a certified member of the literati (with some help from his ghostwriter), has endowed two writer's studios in the main house. We've had to restrain him from flying in banks of camellias—after all, with the place still a work in progress, this evening's just a dry run, by and for the musicians.

To escape the racket and plaster dust, I bike to the Point. After a warning cold snap, Indian summer has checked in for an encore, the weakened sun beaming its poignant finale like Verdi's fading Violetta. It's all happened so fast: the bequest; the buyout; Grubb's gift—"plumping the pillows," as he calls it. The grant from the Dodge Foundation. And I've only just caught my breath after touring the byways of North Carolina. "Keyboard Commentary" is carving its niche; the bookings are coming in. Next up, Missoula; then Naples—Florida, that is. While I was in Durham, the Point's contractor walked—could it be otherwise? Literally had a nervous breakdown because his girlfriend ran off with the Episcopalian minister's wife. Of course the new contractor wanted to undo half the work of the first—

God, wouldn't Laila hate my kvetching about the renovation, the rich man's stations of the cross. Her compass would turn toward the world of privation and struggle that keeps Islesford beautiful. She'd want to know about housing for the Latino workers out here, their legal status, education for their kids; she'd zero in on the scrawny, bespattered workmen no larger than boys lined up every morning, slave-mart-style, at the Islesford station; hoping to get hired for the day to barber the privets or scrub toilets on Midas Lane.

Damn, where was I . . . Considering that I'm wrapping up an official history of sorts, I'd better keep the troops in line; swing back and plot out the coda. Pick up after Paris.

So: early September and the Boathouse restaurant in Central Park, where Nick sits down by the lake beneath the awning, in the itchy green tweed jacket he ordered from Debenhams in Edinburgh. The glance at the watch, drumming fingers, stoppered irritation as familiar as I am to myself.

"YOU LOOK LOVELY, what have you done with your hair."

"This is my real color. I don't think you've ever seen it."

"You should have kept it that way all along. . . ."

The old Nick, exempting her from his uncharitable gaze. Ripples from the lake strobe-lit the underside of the awning, and she was back in the emerald isles of Virgin Gorda, skimming with Nick over a sun-dappled bottom toward the jeweled grotto. At the next table a smart couple hedged in by shopping bags. Tourists. The man smiled, exposing bad teeth. English.

"To us," Nick began, raising a rose-colored drink, grey eyes determined. "You know, I was out at the Point to collect some gear, and I got to thinking, why not start fresh in a new place on the property. Build ourselves a shingled cottage up on the bluff with a view of the Point. We'd renovate the main house to put up guests—maybe divide our old bedroom—though of course we'll keep the music room there, with plenty of dehumidifiers, wouldn't want the pianos too close to the sea. I thought we might sit down with the architect who designed Artspace on the Pond—an Italian, I forget his name."

"Hmm, Piero Sartogo. Pricey. But yeah, he'd be ideal."

"Turn the stables into music studios—they're set back and we don't want the pianos too close to the sea—did I already say that? What do you think?"

A regular armada up in the sky, fierce galleon clouds vying with the sun for control. She dared not look at him. Finally, resuming the dialogue looping through her head these many weeks since Paris: "Nick, you were right about certain things. I couldn't feed Davidine the story about Milagros—but it wasn't to protect you. I was protecting *myself.* To use that story for personal vengeance seemed a desecration of that poor girl's death. And I didn't want to be yet another vengeful Fury from the old playbook. It offends the artist and snob in me. "

Uncertainty washed over his face—where did this leave him? She was a cat toying with a stunned vole. Enough.

"Nick, I promised I'd consider what we discussed in Paris. You've made me a gift of happiness. What a ride it was. Just like you"—her voice faltered—"I couldn't have imagined it. And I can still honor that." She braved his eyes. "But I can't come back."

"Oh, Maddy, hasn't there been enough harm done?"

A figure hovered over them. The Englishman! "Would you mind taking a snap of us?" Smiling, teeth like crooked gravestones. He handed her a camera. He showed her how to focus. He showed her which button to press. The world tended its business. In Brueghel's painting of a prosperous town, you have to look hard to see, off in the distance, the tiny figure of Icarus plummeting to the sea. She pressed the button; the shutter snapped; the man thanked her in a snaggle of teeth; the couple left, rustling their shopping bags.

He curved toward her. "I've filed for divorce."

"So you could set me up as Fernande?"

"That's absurd, you in no way resemble Fernande."

"But I would *become* Fernande. Your escape clause. The woman who keeps you from ever wholly signing on with whoever would come next. Till you got too decrepit for 'next.'"

"Maddy, marry me."

"So I'd become the *official* Fernande? I think I'd rather be the mistress. Gets to have more fun," she added, attempting levity.

The waitress had arrived, pen poised, to ask if they were ready to order. They looked up at her. Oh, dear, did they need a little more time? She backed away, eyes widening, as if she might summon the police.

"Don't you see, in your game of threes, I'd become 'the wife,' while you set up camp outside the marriage, as you've done with Fernande all these years. Breaking camp when a new 'fever' hits."

He draped an arm over the chair, jacket askew, and glowered at the lake. Easier to address his profile, the longish space between nose and lips. "It wouldn't have worked with Laila as the wife," she went on. "She's too raw and uncompromising and full of hope. I'm a better bet. I'm insanely, mercifully busy. I'm married, in a sense, to music."

"So you'd have one foot out, too." His glance revealed he'd been caught. "You know, Maddy, you take the moral high ground, but I've often felt your work comes first, everyone and everything else be damned. You're a monster of ambition, and I love you for it, even in my saner moments." A pause. "You're taken up in some other way as well."

She listened hard, for once he wasn't dissembling.

"I've sometimes sensed a part of you is . . . *elsewhere*. In the past. That passion for Violet was—how to put this?—the forerunner, and got mixed up with me. She's a part of it. I've sometimes felt we're . . . three. You, me, her, bound together. I've even felt that for you I *am* Violet. The continuation. It's mysterious and rather thrilling."

Out on the rim of the world the waitress hovered, fearing to approach.

"Violet gave me something no one else ever had," she said in a low, melodious voice. "Violet believed in me. She helped me keep faith with myself. Kept me focused and ruthless—every artist, if that doesn't sound too grandiose, needs such a voice in her head. For a girl back then—hell, even now—how easy to fold your tent and end up always regretting it. Even after Leonard, during the years of sour pianos in ballet studios, it was always Violet's voice egging me on. Our dream that we could live in 'the divine dissatisfaction of the artist.' We loved that quote! She couldn't do it for herself—but Violet showed me the way."

Clouds had erased the sun; a chill breeze raked the khaki water.

"Your former idol's been living in Mexico with a drag queen with AIDS. A sewing-machine heir from a good family—Violet usually went for pedigrees. She's in and out of the hospital in San Miguel for 'lifestyle-related' illnesses. Violet's a pathetic ghost. Only *we* matter now, you and I."

The breeze riffled the lake into a surface like crepey skin. She'd be a tiny speck in a vast, heaving ocean. Laila with her baby in another hemisphere. Sophie on a walking trip in Sicily with Jed. Anton somewhat seeing Dorothy Kim—an excellent thing, Ms. Kim, every virtuoso needs a Ms. Kim.

A test! Pumped with hope, she decided on a final test.

"Remember in George Sand's château that lithograph of women killing their bastard babies?" He shook his head no. "Well, once, when I caught you together in the studio"—ignoring his startled look—"I was ready to kill Laila. And then, God help us, we almost did kill Laila. In the accident on Wildmoor."

She paused, waiting. Let him say, *We didn't, because at the last millisecond, you reached across and swung the wheel.* You *chose* her.

"We almost killed Laila," she repeated like a prompter in a high school play to the doofus playing the lead. "In that accident on Wildmoor. I learned something about myself."

Again she waited. Nick not producing. Okay, if he couldn't say it, let him raise a pinkie, sign with an X, ring a leper's bell! *Oh, Nick, just recognize this one true thing. Get your arms around this one true thing, and maybe we can tell the rest of the world to fuck off and move forward together. Tell me you know me, as I know you.*

Nick rotated his bum shoulder and scratched his head. "It's damn lucky we didn't hit Laila. That's all we needed."

Her head drooped. She'd rubbed up against something furry and foul in a dark cave, she sensed a host of eyes, heard a chorus of insect screeches. He nested comfortably among layers of lies and foulness, his native habitat.

And so we come to the end. She powered up her will, a climber scaling Everest, sucking oxygen, one foot forward, now drag the other, now the other, up up the last leg to east of nowhere.

"You've robbed me of my daughter, Nick. Her absence would always be present. But how you've harmed me is not really the issue—that maybe I could forgive." He shot her a hopeful look; her eyes checked him. "It's the harm you've done Laila. With your help, Laila took a terribly wrong turn, so early in her life. A bit like I did around her age—maybe the self-betrayals are the worst."

"She's an underground Weathergirl in the making, if it hadn't been me—"

"But it was you. And you set your damage and blight on her. Marked and corrupted her. That's surely not for me to forgive. And now Laila's gone and it's too late. You are unforgiven. I used to tease you for going on about taints and dark stars—but now you deserve to say you are well and truly cursed."

Nick's face ashen. They eyed each other across a blasted landscape.

"You were right about one other thing, Nick. I still love you, God help me. Maybe I always will, as long as I have an appetite to live."

She drank him in one last time. He'd been the consolation for every-thing. "Oh, Nick. We don't get what we want. We're shown it. But we can't have it."

TWO MONTHS LATER, a November afternoon of wind and lashing rain. She clomps down the hall of her brownstone to sign for a certified letter. Sighing . . . no doorman to field interruptions, and she up against the usual deadlines.

The letter was typed on heavy bond. She read the letter. Frowning, she held the paper up to the light to inspect the watermark. She read the letter several more times, scowling like an old-timer suspiciously viewing a new-fangled contraption. Unwilling to comprehend what the words appeared to convey.

Dear Ms. Shaye,

I write to tell you the good news. With a sad prelude. And I shall keep this in nonlawyer's English, as much as I can.

Violet Ashcroft died on September 22, 1998, in San Miguel de Allende, Mexico. She left a will that has been probated in New York State.

You are the recipient of a bequest of five million dollars.

Under the conditions of the will, that money must be used to create an art colony, such as MacDowell or Yaddo, at Conscience Point, the Ashcroft family estate.

Such a colony would provide living space for artists in the broadest sense, from musicians to painters to writers.

Although Ms. Ashcroft refers to the colony in her bequest as "The Republic of Art," it is nowhere stipulated that it must be named such. As Violet put it, "Call it anything, anything you love."

Violet Ashcroft owns slightly over half of the Conscience Point property. Nicholas Ashcroft, Ms. Ashcroft's brother, owns a bit less than half the property (as well as a sloop named the Cherubino*). Technically, he and Violet are tenants-in-common of Conscience Point.*

How Mr. Ashcroft figures in the creation of the artist's colony will have to be worked out by the two of you.

You can telephone me if you have a question that you want answered immediately, but I suggest you consult an attorney soon so that you can move ahead quickly.

To ease your mind: Yes, you can be the principal officer of the trust.

Sincerely,
Dayton Everard
Everard and Hunnewell, etc.

"No way, you're handed a fucking fortune, bingo, just like that? Jed, wait'll you hear *this*." Voices off: Milou yapping. Yeller baying at what sounded like a passing fire engine. A mezzo—Barkis?—hitting the mid-range, Jed shouting he can't think straight . . . A canine cantata with human soloist.

"Life don't happen that way," Sophie came back on. "Only Dickens would dare use it in a plot." A moment. "Hell, maybe I'll use it. I mean, it's getting pretty desperate for us fiction writers, if Bob Dole can get on the tube to hustle Viagra."

. . .

SHE SAT IN the flame-stitch chair, letting dusk wash over her, gripping the letter in one hand, the chair's arm with the other. Eyes focused on the scabby sycamore beyond the bay window. To think Violet had kept faith all these years, a lifetime really, with their girls' dream. Perhaps, sadly, the dream had been Violet's best moment, and in the adventures that followed, the new ports, new loves, new deceptions, she'd discovered no match to a summer in Arcadia.

She remembered Violet's last one-line postcard from Positano: "More money forthcoming, Yours, Violet." Then for seventeen years, nothing. There must have been another pot of gold, too, for Violet to have passed on this sum. Perhaps the trust-fund drag queen in San Miguel? When it came to honoring promises, she and Violet had the memories of elephants. Perhaps in Violet's private reckoning—*I'm making you a gift of my ch-ch-child*—she was making amends. Maddy laughed aloud in the empty room—the logic, the imperious gesture, vintage Violet!

She rose and roamed her dim, silent rooms, touching her fingertips to the backs of chairs. How to get an art colony up and running. She'd interview architects. No, first apply to foundations for a grant—but that would take time. What about dear old Amos? His plans for an arts center had just been zapped by the town board. Perhaps he'd make a matching gift to get them launched?

Of course, there remained Nick, tenant-in-common of Conscience Point. Since the Central Park Boathouse, he refused to set foot on the property; he now kept the *Cherubino* in dry dock in Stonington, Maine, where he'd bought a place. His imprint at Greenaway had disappeared into the maw of a conglomerate, despite the Stark bonanza (most of the profits had gone to legal fees). Nick might welcome an infusion of cash from selling his share of the Point. He'd want to keep the *Cherubino* stocked with Cristal and Fauchon, especially while cruising the world's beauty spots. His first mate, went the gossip, was his second cousin—whom he alternated with Fernande, finally stabilized by the excellent new meds.

Since Paris, she'd had time to ponder the reasons behind Nick's allergy to the family seat. Perhaps another body lay in Bluebeard's room at the end of the corridor. Nick's brother, Linton, witness to the Milagros shooting, might have disappeared a bit too conveniently in his car off Eggleston Bridge. Violet, sozzled, had once told her—how we forget!—that Nick had urged his equally smashed brother to drive to the Point during a hurricane to secure the *Cherubino* in its mooring off Weymouth Landing. But it turned out the sloop had been at Sparky's Marina all along. Of course, given Vi's infatuation with Linton—and her whimsical sense of reality— the truth had likely vanished into the murky currents beneath the bridge.

She sat in a semitrance in the gathering dark, and it felt as if Violet entered the room, Winston dangling off her lip. The sprung curve of her haunch, enigmatic smile, splotch of geranium on her cheek. A press of beringed fingers on her shoulder, scent of jasmine and sweat. *I live on here*—Why, she might turn up anywhere, the chatelaine of the Point and household goddess. Slinging her duster over a marble bust; shooting a backward glance as she sloshed into the spangled water . . . *Someday we'll go to the far side of the island.* Balancing a sketch pad on her knees in the walled garden where Cupid hovered with alabaster wings in eternal reproach.

How can we start *without you?*

No answer. Nor to her second e-mail. Perhaps the importance of being Anton had shot him beyond her orbit. She would have felt betrayed, had she kept any capacity for it. His silence, though, surprised her.

He phoned her, finally, from Ravinia. "Maddy, forgive me, I've been traveling and just found out about your e-mails. You know I'm technically challenged, give me the Pony Express and rotary phones anyday."

"I'll forgive you only if you come out to the Point. See what we're putting together here."

"Who's 'we'?"

"Oh, a motley crew. Sophie Gerson and Jed Oliver, both writing books. Sophie's dogs—*five* of them now. Our registrar, Olga. Vadim from the Davos Quartet. Amos Grubb, a benefactor. And in the fall, a bunch of kids from the East Harlem projects for a music-immersion week."

"You sure that's it?"

"Uh, what do you really want to know. Do I hear the sound of fishing?"

"Now, why would I do that. Hey, I'll come for the grand opening."

"Good. But that's a ways off. Why not come for our preopening, September 15th."

"The 15th . . . Shit, I think I'll still be in Ravinia."

"Anton, I've got a proposal for you. No need to answer right away. You'll think it over while you're in Ravinia, Milan, Turin . . . wherever."

"Turin, never—it would jinx my performance. Because you once said you hated rendezvous in Turin."

"Here's my idea. I was hoping you might be a musician-in-residence here. Dip in and out between engagements. You'd have perfect quiet and seclusion in the cabin in the woods—Laila's Studio—which now has electric baseboard heat. We'll ship your piano."

"I love your idea."

"So it's a deal."

"Uh, there's a complication. I've kind of, well, you could say I've . . . uh . . ."

"What, for chrissake."

"I may have gotten engaged to Dorothy Kim."

"You're not sure?"

Silence.

"Well, why couldn't she come to the Point, too. It ain't a Trappist monastery."

"Given the awesome odds, why in God's name do we keep trying?"

"Tony, you know you need Dorothy Kim."

"I want you to understand: this is mainly about survival and other practicalities."

"Does Dorothy know how you view this engagement?"

"She doesn't need to know and if she did, wouldn't care."

"You're that irresistible, huh?"

"Yeah. Is this all there is? What about my ear, my toughest critic, my—best buddy. I miss you."

"I miss *you.*"

"I need you."

"But Dorothy—"

"When—*if* that happens, I probably won't resist, too much effort. But *you,* Maddy."

"Yes."

"We have deep history, you and me. You take precedence."

"You won't be here when we start. You'll be in Ravinia."

"Not *won't. Can't.* And you won't be in Ravinia because you'll be fucking running Conscience Point."

"Now I remember: this is the way it would be. Bicontinental. Sooo sophisticated. The battle of the Titans. How quickly we forget the problems."

"Oh, I remember the good. I remember it very well. I want to be all around and under and over you."

"What are we talking here, Anton."

"I don't know, what do you think."

"You tell me."

"I think you'll always have it for Nick in some way. Me, any other guy would be who you settled for. And how can a tub like me compete with a . . . an Anglo Apollo."

"The world's badness falls on Nick. You and I only bring each other good."

"A well-known advantage of passionate friendship."

"Why not stop trying to define everything," she said.

"You're right, what a pair of schmucks we are. And not getting any smarter either."

"A pair of schmucks!"

"We'll leave things open. It's green and windy here, Maddy. We'll leave the doors wide open for the winds to blow through."

"Hard for me, a control freak."

"Let the future play itself. Take us where it will. Improvise."

"The future as impromptu."

"There you go again," he said, "trying to pigeonhole—"

"Tony, let's not be apart again."

"Not ever."

"Even when we are."

"Not then either. Especially not then."

SO THERE IT IS, a story begun at a manor house in deep France—and, farther back, on an enchanted afternoon in May—that has carried me with its wayward logic to this moment. I've been writing—is it over two years now?—since the crackup that wild, wet night on Wildmoor. Scribbling this faux memoir during downtime in my composition notebook, often at the oak table beside the autumn garden. *Faux* memoir, since I've slipped undercover with "Maddy Shaye." The better to close in on the real Maddy

Shaye. The better to lay it out, as promised, pretty much the way it happened. If I've struck a few wrong notes—hell, great pianists do it, there's nothing to fear.

I've tried, too, to set down for my grandson a record of sorts. I've tried here to draw him a family tree—not the inverted espalier designed for blood families. No, something more fantastical and airy, upward-curving, with a nightingale from Nohant perched on a branch. I've written, too, for myself, to make sense of the days piled high like this autumn's leaves against the verandah; to decipher the larger patterns, and unearth, if such a thing exists, the hidden lesson. And to give a wave from our passing caravan. All that I wanted to hold on to so dearly slipped through my fingers like fairy dust. But fresh joys have come knocking, unforeseen. The blank pages in my notebook await new chapters. And when Augusto's of an age to read this—if only he will!—I'll tell him more about the trip to Mexico. In person, I can hope. For now, just this:

Laila quickly got involved with a land-reform group in Chiapas. The work required her to be constantly on the move. After Augusto was born, I flew down to Mexico City. Laila seemed so much older and very strong. And the baby . . . He was honey-colored and grey-eyed, the riveting Ashcroft gaze startling in an infant. Hilarious, actually; I'd wake in the night laughing. It's fair to say I was enamored. We'd planned a short holiday at the Villa del Sol in Zihuatanejo. Predictably, Laila was outraged by the resort's "conscription" of locals forced to "fawn and scrape"; she became convinced they'd been trained not to look at the gringo guests a second too long. Before my arrival, we'd agreed, Laila and I, that given her unsettled circumstances, she could not possibly raise an infant the way she would have wanted. I was to take Augusto back to the States and, for legal reasons, adopt him. At the last moment, though, in a scene wrenching for us both, Laila couldn't let him go. If Augusto should ever read this, I think he'll understand why.

A year later, Laila met a Brazilian Indian lawyer working for indigenous rights in the Raposa Serra du Sol Reserve in Brazil's northernmost state. She lived there for a time with her son and this lawyer—perhaps now her husband. I was thrilled to read in last week's *Times* that Brazil's president will soon ratify the territory. My great sadness, though, is that Laila may have decided to sever all ties to her past—a decision I could not accept even after several lifetimes. My recent letters return marked "addressee unknown." Perhaps, I tell myself, the fight for indigenous rights takes them all over the country, and beyond. Perhaps Laila needs time. I sift every word we spoke at Delta Gate 3 for clues. And cling to one certainty: it's not possible that Laila won't, when she's ready—when she's finished sorting what needs sorting—give a sign, one that I'll sense coming the way an elephant picks up signals across the savanna floor. Meanwhile, I learn the meaning of patience. I work. And I dream. I picture Augusto here so clearly. We'll watch the great blue heron lift off the eelgrass. We'll bike to the Point and go jouncing over Eggleston Bridge—*Watch out for the clamshells! Race you to the little island!* Conscience Point will never be entirely complete without you—in some fashion, of course, it belongs to you more than anyone. We're bound together, you and I; Laila, Nick, Violet—my loves are tangled up in you, a child twice lost and found. As Nick once said, How strangely mixed up together we all are.

IT'S ALMOST EIGHT now, time for our first concert. Shall we finish in the music room at our run-through for the opening of Conscience Point?

IT WAS ALWAYS understood that the evening ritual would center on music. So after dinner at the great table under the oaks, everyone straggles through the fallen light into the music room. The assembled "republicans,"

Sophie mockingly calls them. She and Jed, the fiddlers, two composers, Amos Grubb, Olga take their seats. Milou springs vertically into Sophie's lap, Old Yeller scuttles under a highboy; the others are out roaming the Point on doggy errands.

An orange harvest moon hangs in the sky. I walk to the piano. Jed douses the lights, the same as Nick some thirty years ago, and I think, *How quickly—too quickly—it's all flown by*. Seated beside me is a small boy with grave grey eyes and chubby wrists, legs dangling from the piano bench; precociously attuned to music of course. Moonlight casts a spectral glow over the keyboard. There comes a scrunch of tires spraying gravel under the porte cochere. . . . Perhaps he meant to surprise us all along? A faint smell of jasmine, can it be? wafts through the air. I raise my hands over the keys and the room breathes in as one. The first notes of Chopin's *Harp* Étude ripple out over the autumn garden as if opening the gates of heaven.

ACKNOWLEDGMENT

I would like to thank Greg Michalson, Garry Morris, Joyce Engelson, Gail Hochman, Jerome Lowenthal, Simon Mulligan, Adam Neiman, John Herman, Marlene Sanders, Marion Meade, and Richard Adrian.